STUCK IN ORBIT

Stuck In Orbit

YASMEEN MUSA

Yasmeen Musa

To my younger self - if anyone or anything asks you to choose, between them and what gives you joy, pleasure and wholeness, choose yourself. If you can safely do so, please choose yourself because in the words of Maya Angelou:

"You are only free when you realize you belong no place — you belong every place — no place at all. The price is high. The reward is great."

We belong to ourselves.

February

Chapter One

Laylah: Only Allah Can Judge

i was   but a child when they preached modesty.
cover they said, for it seems that this
flesh is sin.

for it seems that vulnerability,
that the leering eyes
and hands of men is
born   of this, the allure of flesh.

but what if i told them that hands
and eyes come, regardless of this flesh's
naked(ness?)

blind eyes and smoke screens,
closed doors and a world that *insists*
boys will be boys.
what if i told them
that *this* is true
sin?

Laylah Mostafa loved the world of academics. That's not to say she wasn't sad to say goodbye to her family but Laylah's life at university was hers and she was eager to return to it. Laylah was excited to see her best friend and flatmate Ariana, resume her powerlifting and of course attend her classes. To immerse herself in words, in learning and people that loved this world as much as she did. But mostly Laylah couldn't wait to embrace the quietness of mind that came with being alone. The potential for her mind to breathe. To dream. Almost impossible in her large family.

Laylah had arrived home late last night, dumped her things on the bed and promptly fell asleep. Today she had woken early to finish unpacking and was just now putting away the last few things. Laylah carefully arranged one of her favourite books 'The Book Thief' into its shelf and then stood back to survey her room. It was small but cosy. A double bed at the centre was covered with an indigo duvet and pillows. A desk faced the large window with her laptop, an assortment of pens and books neatly laid out. Her white walls were covered with photos of family, friends and quotes. Laylah loved quotes. Home she sighed, content.

Laylah checked the time, it was 10:00 am, she wanted to get a lifting session in before heading to the store for some groceries and then she would probably give *Mama* a call. Even though she was twenty-one *Mama* still worried about her constantly.

Laylah mused whether she should watch a movie or write after dinner but quickly decided on a nostalgic film, she needed that in her first few days back while she settled into a routine. Probably a 90s comedy. Yes, that sounded like a plan.

Laylah threw on some tights and her favourite workout shirt, grabbing her gym bag, keys and phone before heading out the door.

Laylah jogged down three short steps, landed on her sidewalk and spotted a man in front of the daffodil yellow house across the road. He was standing with a backpack and two large suitcases, staring down a particularly steep flight of stairs that led up to the front door

Laylah crossed the road and called, 'Hey, do you need a hand?'

He turned, straightened fully and there was only one thing to be said, he was tall. Really tall, something that Laylah most certainly was not, he towered over her. Laylah's eyes continued to sweep over him, taking in oak coloured hair and golden skin, that shone in the sunlight. His shoulders were large enough to bear the weight of the world and then there were those eyes.

Sky blue.

He gave her a half grimace, half-smile, eyes crinkling his voice dripped with an American accent as he responded, 'I wasn't expecting so many stairs but I think I will manage. Thank you anyway,' and he turned to his suitcases once more.

But Laylah didn't leave and instead watched him. Brow furrowed he grimaced as he bent to pick up the larger of the two suitcases.

Laylah sighed. 'Stubborn male,' she muttered and without asking, she took one of the bags. The American looked at her in confusion.

Clouds appeared in sky blue.

'I will help,' Laylah responded to the unasked question.

'No it's fine, I just hurt my back a little so I am being careful that's all. Anyway, it's much too heavy...'

But she cut him off, 'Are you implying I cannot carry this because I am a woman?!' Laylah's voice was deadly serious but a small grin revealed her undertone of humour.

'No, of course not,' he corrected himself quickly, embarrassment tinging his voice.

'Well, what are we waiting for then? Let's go,' Laylah said picking up the suitcase again. Quickly she established two things, first that the bag was indeed very heavy and second that the stairs might as well have been the Southern Alps. They were incredibly steep. Of course, she let neither show, smiled and grit her teeth, making sure not a single complaint escaped her lips.

After what felt like an eternity but was really only a couple of seconds, they arrived at the deck, Laylah was sweating slightly, breathing fast and her face was beetroot, not the best look with her fiery hair, but she played it cool.

'Well thank you,' he said, looking genuinely surprised and grateful but also completely sweaty and out of breath Laylah noted with satisfaction.

'Oh, it's fine,' Laylah said, trying to play it off as she gasped for air.

'Sam by the way.'

'Laylah,' she responded, shaking his enormous hand.

Only then did she glance at her watch, 'Oh god, I am late, I have to go!'

'Won't you come in for a drink?' He asked earnestly.

'No sorry! But another time, I am just across the road,' Laylah responded, pointing to her house. 'Knock anytime,' she said, already halfway down the stairs, waving at those eyes.

Sky blue.

...

A few hours later, lifting and chores done Laylah walked home through the park. Taking her time she enjoyed the warmth and sunlight of a February afternoon. Laylah stopped for a moment and leaned her head back. She gently closed her eyes and felt the sun on her olive skin as a breeze passed by, rustling the leaves of the surrounding trees which seemed to whisper, a secret only she could hear.

'Laylah! *Marhaba!*' A voice called.

Reluctantly Laylah opened her eyes, recognising the voice immediately her stomach dropped. Shahid.

Shahid was tall, thin with coal-like eyes and olive skin only slightly darker than Laylah's. She was dressed in a long, loose, sand-coloured *jilbab* and a matching *hijab*.

'*Salam.*' Laylah responded, noticing how Shahid looked her up and down, eyes lingering over her tights, midriff shirt and exposed shoulders. Judgment and contempt quickly coloured Shahid's expression and Laylah immediately felt self-conscious knowing that her bare midriff would become the talk of Shahid's little group. But of course, Shahid was silent, for Arabs, social etiquette was key.

'How are you sister?' Shahid asked.

'I am good, how are you?'

'*Alhamdulillah*, Mohammed, I am sure you remember my husband... well we are organising a potluck next weekend if you want to join?' Shahid said sweetly, her haughty features poorly masking a look of superiority, despite her seemingly innocent words.

'I will check my schedule,' Laylah nodded although she already knew there was no way she would attend, she would rather carry that American's luggage up and down the stairs fifty times and she hated cardio.

'Well *inshallah,* you can come. You never know, you might meet someone. Although of course, the men and the women will be in different rooms.' Shahid smirked.

Laylah shook her head suppressing a sigh. 'That's very kind of you Shahid, but I am not interested in meeting anyone right now.'

Shahid pouted and placed a hand on her belly. 'Don't wait too long, I want my kids to have some Arab friends. Some Muslim friends. To keep them safe from all the drinking and *zina*...'

Laylah stood stunned, lost for words, *she was pregnant?*

Shahid had not noticed Laylah's silence and continued her mini-rant. 'Or even worse, imagine if my little boy fell in love with a man...' She shuddered.

Laylah was aghast. 'Shahid, stop. First I have no interest in getting married. Second, *Mabrook* on the child, but you cannot say that. People should be able to love whoever they want to love. There is no need for that kind of talk.'

Shahid furrowed her brow. 'But Laylah...'

Laylah cut her off. 'No buts. I can make excuses for our parents but not you. We grew up here, be more openminded. Anyway I have to go,' and leaving a slightly stunned look on Shahid's face Laylah spun around and stalked off.

'*Salaam* sister.' Shahid called.

Laylah's blood pounded. She rarely lost her temper but Shahid had gone too far. Laylah had known Shahid since they were both tiny, they were similar in so many ways. They had both gone to the same Primary school and High School in Christchurch. They were both Arab. They had both chosen the University of Otago. But their similarities ended there.

Laylah didn't mind Shahid's conservative life, didn't mind that she wore a *hijab*, was married or even that she preferred to keep to her own. Laylah was okay with people living their life the way they wished, even if it was different from her own. What Laylah did mind was the judgment. The gossip. Especially if someone contradicted the very conservative version of Islam that she practised. A version that in Shahid's mind was perfect, one which every single person must follow.

Shahid was quite simply one of the biggest reasons for Laylah's separation from the Muslim community, she could not stand the judgment about the way she chose to live her life. Laylah believed in God, in *Allah*, but she preferred a more spiritual approach to faith, one that started and ended with her relationship with this universe and its creator, not the interpretations of people. Rigid and unyielding. It seemed to Laylah that many of her people had forgotten to be like the very sands that their faith was founded on, soft, malleable, flowing with the wind.

Laylah shook her head, reminding herself that not all Arabs, not all Muslims, conservative or otherwise were like Shahid. Taking a deep breath she looked up to the sky, it was so blue. So large. She felt like it could consume her and in that moment, she allowed it, surrendering herself to the vastness of the universe. Only *Allah* can judge she reminded herself pushing Shahid out of her mind, determined to enjoy the day. Taking a deep breath Laylah continued down the gently winding path of the park.

...

The rest of the day was peaceful but full and only moments before she drifted off to sleep did Laylah remember the American across the road once more and wonder how he was settling in. Sam, Laylah thought and mused what his story was. Before she drifted off into the land of dreams all she saw were those eyes.

Sky blue.

Chapter Two

Sam: This is Home Now

Sunday, one day before the start of the semester and Sam had so much to do. Thankfully he had managed to find the supermarket and get some basics yesterday. He sighed, reminding himself that this was why people didn't move to a different country a week before the semester was about to start. But the USA was no longer a place he wanted to live, no longer a place he could call home. At least for now. Sam shook his head trying to shake the darkness from his mind, his family hadn't moved halfway across the world so he could mull over the past.

Sam shook his head and rose, stretching and twisting to wake his body as his eyes wandered over his little room which was mostly taken up by a queen sized bed. A bookshelf in the corner was filled with a few textbooks and his favourite novels. A single photo of himself, Mum, Dad, Charlotte and James hung on his wall. It was small, but cosy and very sunny which Sam was immensely grateful for, the sunshine had such a huge impact on his mood.

Carefully Sam picked out clothes for church, a purple button-down shirt, black chinos, Chelsea boots and a simple but smart, watch. If there was one thing his dad had taught him it was the importance of being well presented and a good watch was an essential finishing touch. He laid them out on his bed neatly before hopping into the shower, and under the hot water, almost instantly, a moth to a flame his mind drifted towards Laylah, the woman who had helped him with his bags yesterday. She was small, almost a foot shorter than he was with brilliant copper hair, soft cocoa eyes and skin the colour of sand. Golden.

Sam chuckled to himself as he remembered how stubborn she had been as she carried his suitcase. Laylah was definitely fiery and not just because of her hair. Fire was her essence. Sam also sheepishly admitted embarrassment to himself. He had definitely underestimated her with his bags.

As these thoughts whirred in his head Sam finished showering, shaved quickly and carefully before getting dressed and heading out the door.

Sam jogged down the steps, glancing at Laylah's door, mentally willing it to open, but of course it remained firmly shut, he hadn't mastered telekinesis just yet and it was only 8:00 am on a Sunday, much too early for most university students he reminded himself.

Sam strolled down the street humming to himself, it was a beautiful summer day and within moments, with the help of trusty Google, he found the church. Truth be told, you could hardly miss it. It had grey turrets that soared, threatening to brush the heavens and ancient stone walls that made it stand out against the glass of the surrounding buildings. A warm piece of history in the midst of the cold, glass of innovation.

Bible clutched in hand, Sam entered the already open doors and found himself inside one of the most beautiful churches he had ever entered, it certainly rivalled his local church in Brooklyn but even compared to some of the oldest churches in New York, it was magnificent. The *First Church* Sam read, an odd name, was it perhaps the first church in this city? That was likely he thought because even though the church was clearly well-taken care off, nothing could hide its age. For one thing, it was huge with high ceilings, magnificent stained glass windows, oak pews and one of the biggest and oldest looking organs Sam had ever seen. They didn't make churches like this anymore.

Early, Sam settled into a groaning seat towards the back of the church to avoid blocking people's view and opened his Bible as the few people surrounding him chatted happily. Almost immediately a sense of calm and peace that had eluded him since his frantic arrival to New Zealand enveloped him. A cotton wool blanket on a snowy night.

What felt like only moment's but was, in fact at least ten minutes Sam was interrupted as the bench groaned once more under the weight of another and he was pulled out of his reverie.

The man that sat next to him appeared to be around his age, tall, athletically built with eyes green and soft like the flesh of an avocado and skin brown like the pit at the centre of the fruit.

He met Sam's eyes and smiled. 'Hey.'

Sam smiled back and extended his hand to introduce himself. 'Sam.'

'Nikau,' came the response, accompanied by a firm handshake. 'I haven't seen you here before, I am going to assume you are American?'

Sam grinned. 'What gave me away?' He asked innocently and they both laughed again. 'My family just moved here, we landed a week ago.'

'Wow, how are you feeling man? What brought you guys all the way here from America?'

'Honestly I am exhausted. I was about to start my PhD in Astrophysics and New Zealand seemed like a great place to do that. My mum was also born here although she has lived in New York for most of her life.'

'Wow, well I have to warn you, Dunedin is no New York City.' Nikau smiled.

Sam grinned. 'I am gathering, are you at College?'

'College? Oh you mean University?' Nikau chuckled. 'Yup, I am in my last year of Surveying, thank god, honestly sometimes I don't know if I am going to finish the degree or if it's going to finish me.'

Sam laughed heartily, appreciative of the openness and warmth that he had found in Nikaus avocado eyes. It felt like home.

'Goodness I know what you mean,' he replied, wiping a stray tear from his eyes.

At that moment their conversation was interrupted by the pastor who introduced herself as Ailsa. Her hair was short, black, slightly dishevelled, but in a way that looked intentional. Her ears were lined with piercings, at least five or six per ear but her face was plain, kind and open. She wore simple black trousers and a white linen shirt, sleeves rolled up to reveal arms covered with intricate tattoos. She didn't look a day over thirty.

'Are we all ready to begin?' Ailsa asked.

...

An hour later, sermon complete, songs sung, they were finished and Sam was hungry, he turned to Nikau and asked. 'Do you want to grab something to eat?'

Nikau's face lit up and he grinned. 'You never have to ask if I want food, I know a great place, how do you feel about pancakes?'

'I love pancakes!' Sam grinned back.

Nikau and Sam walked out of the church into the brilliance of the day. The sun had warmed the air so much that immediately Sam started to sweat a little. Thankfully it was only a short walk to the café but in that time Sam learned plenty about Nikau who was the definition of an open book. Sam liked that.

Nikau was the oldest of three with two younger sisters that he adored. He was half Maori half Scottish or *Pakeha* (a word they used for Europeans in New Zealand) and was still connected quite strongly to both sides of heritage. Nikau loved his family, Rugby – apparently a very popular sport here - and lifting weights.

'If you don't mind me asking, why do you go to church?' Sam asked curiously.

Nikau shrugged. 'Routine? Growing up my parents would take us all to church and I have found it's a nice way to start my Sunday. Ailsa is also very cool, not preachy, not judgmental and she somehow has a way of saying exactly what I need to hear.' Nikau smiled.

Seconds later, Nikau stopped in from of a little corner café. 'This is it. Best pancakes in Dunedin.' He grinned and

with a flourish he held open the door to a tiny but very packed café. *The Good Earth Café.*
'I will grab some menus, why don't you nab that table next to the window.' Nikau gestured.

Nodding, Sam made his way over and took a seat. His eyes, overwhelmed, weren't sure what to focus on first in this bustling hive of activity. Wooden floors were covered with intricate rugs, yellows, blues and greens. Sturdy looking, wooden tables were dotted around, filled almost to bursting with families and students. Nikau had mentioned that people liked to brunch in New Zealand.

Sam was just taking it all in, the golden warmth of the sun on his face, the smell of fresh coffee, the chatter, when Nikau returned with menus. 'What do you think?' He asked

Sam grinned. 'This is great.'

'The menu is really just for show though, trust me. Blueberry pancakes.' Nikau said solemnly.

Without even glancing at the menu Sam handed it back to him with a laugh. 'Blueberry pancakes it is, and a Latte?'

Nikau's smile widened as he took the menu back from Sam and went to order. Fifteen minutes later, they each had an enormous servings of blueberry pancakes smothered in chocolate sauce sitting in front of them. The pancakes melted like clouds in Sam's mouth, heaven. As they each devoured their plates, the conversation turned to Nikaus degree, Surveying.

Sam grinned to himself, he had known from the start that they would be good friends but if there was one thing that cemented any friendship, it was lamenting about university over a heaping pile of sugar.

. . .

Once they had both eaten their full, then some, Nikau gave Sam a quick tour of what truly was a magnificent campus. Sprawled throughout the city, it was a mixture of buildings that had clearly been there from the start, and others that were less than a decade old. They ended at the physics department which would be Sam's second home for the foreseeable future.

They were just about to leave when a bright orange flyer caught Sam's eye. Subconsciously he moved closer and recognised the name, Sandra Bennett, his PhD supervisor. Moving closer still Sam read the flyer which turned out to be recruiting lab demonstrators for a stage one physics paper. Sam's mind strayed to his dwindling bank account and he pulled out his phone, to take a photo of the flyer so he could email in his resumé in when he got home. He had tutored back home in college, hopefully, this would not be that much different. Sam paused and shook his head. This was home now.

Chapter Three

Laylah: A Good Arab Boy

                we are born and they tell us tales, fantasy,
                princes, princesses, happy endings.
                unicorns, dragons, pixies.
                a world beyond our own.
                magic. so, they whisper
be   brave. fight for your dreams.

                but then a little boy wants to be a
                princess for halloween. a little girl wants
                to play with toy cars and suddenly being
yourself(?) is wrong.

                because little boys have to wear capes,
                girls have to groom dolls and oh
no   didn't you know that we love wrong too?
                the wrong gender, race, religion.

                so, when they tell us these tales,
                lies, i question,

are these stories, this hope,
is it for us?
or for them?
a hint of dreams, bravery,
of magic,
smothered to
conform.

7 am on a Sunday and as usual, Laylah was flying out of the door, coffee in hand and decked out in activewear. She wasn't late, in fact, she was early, but this was the pace of her life and that's just how she liked it. Laylah swooped down the stairs of her front porch, coffee in hand.

Sip, step, sip, step, sip, step.

Tackling even a couple of stairs and drinking coffee simultaneously required the utmost coordination.

On the sidewalk, Laylah paused for a moment to take in the day. The sun was warm, the sky clear and the world calm. As she strolled down the street she nodded at an elderly couple, Max and Elle who lived down the street and often walked hand in hand with their gorgeous golden retriever, Scout in tow. Sometimes Laylah would stop and chat, give Scout a good head scratch, but today a smile would have to suffice, she was on a schedule.

By the time she arrived at the gym – which was blissfully mostly empty this time of day - she had finished her coffee and was mentally preparing herself for a tough workout.

Headphones on, music *loud*, she jumped on the spot and swung her legs to warm her muscles. Quadriceps, Glutes and Hamstrings stretching and groaning. Laylah nodded at a guy in the squat rack next to hers, a regular, as she adjusted the height and loaded the bar with her warm-up weight, she didn't have a competition for months but she still needed to focus. Powerlifting was all about focus.

She warmed up with the bar. Then 40kg. Then 60kg. Before pulling on knee sleeves, wrist wraps and her belt. Then it was onto 80kg, then 90kg before she put 100kg on the bar for her main working set.

She snapped her belt shut and approached the bar like a warrior, unracked it thoughtfully, carefully, making small adjustments so that it sat perfectly on her back. Laylah took a deep breath, filling her belly with air so that it pushed against her belt then squatted down to just below ninety degrees before rising as quickly and smoothly as she could. Still holding her breath tight she counted three reps before re-wracking the bar and taking some time to refocus, readjust, rest. Then she did it again. Then again. By the end of her last set, her quadriceps were screaming.

After the main portion of her lifting was done she moved onto some light deadlifts and finished up with bench press. Just over an hour later, she was done. She felt *good* but her stomach was growling, demanding to be fed always her signal to head home. No use trying to hit a personal best on bench press when she was daydreaming of blueberry waffles. *Blueberries* – now her stomach really was rumbling.

As she packed her belt, knee sleeves and wrist wraps neatly back in her gym bag Laylah chuckled at herself for her love of blueberries. It seemed ridiculous, it kind of was but something about them brought her such complete and utter joy. Perhaps it was their colour, the deep blue flesh lighting up any dish. Or maybe it was the taste; the little ones were often sour but the larger ones were plump and oozed sweetness. Or perhaps it was their texture, smooth flesh with a scar at the top, like a broken attachment point, an umbilical cord that at one stage tethered them to home.

. . .

Back at her flat, Laylah took a quick shower, made her waffles and sat down on her adorable second-hand round-table to give *Mama* a call while she devoured breakfast. Dina her youngest sister, eight years old and full of life answered eagerly and almost immediately launched into what she had planned for the day, a playdate with her Best Friend In The Entire World. Charlie.

Laylah noticed *Mama in* the background listening on warily and immediately noted her discomfort, her apprehension with this friendship. Despite having lived in New Zealand for twenty years *Mama was* still a conservative Arab at heart and worried about her eight-year-olds friendship with a boy. A non-Muslim boy for that matter.

As soon as Dina had paused to catch her breath, 18-year-old Ayat swooped in and took the laptop to her room. Dina was not impressed and Laylah? Slightly dizzy from the sudden movement but also resigned. One of the drawbacks of belonging to a large family was that sometimes you felt like a parcel being handed from person to person.

'So, how is Uni? Met any cute guys yet?' Ayat asked as soon as they were out of earshot of *Mama.*

Laylah rolled her eyes but grinned, typical Ayat, her mind was always on the other sex. 'No, it's the long weekend so a lot of people haven't arrived yet,' she responded.

'So you haven't seen anyone at all?!' Ayat asked, not even trying to hide her frustration.

'Well actually I met the person who lives across the road from me, an American, I helped him with his bags actually.' Laylah remembered.

'Oh an American, is he cute? What does he look like?!' Ayat asked, her blue eyes lighting up as she demanded details.

Laylah shook her head and laughed. 'I didn't get a good look at him, he is tall though, *really* tall, dark hair, oh and blue eyes,' she described, furrowing her brow as she tried to remember.

'That's exactly your type! And he is new, ask him out for coffee!' Ayat insisted.

'Ayat sweetie calm down.' Laylah laughed. 'That's my dream *type* but this is the real world. You know he has to be a good Arab boy, otherwise, *Baba* will have a heart attack. I cannot do that, I am the *good* child remember.' Laylah finished with a sigh, no longer smiling.

Ayat's brow furrowed. 'But why does that matter so much, Yousef is with Emma and she is not Arab. *Mama and Baba* got over that eventually.'

Laylah sighed again as her thoughts drifted to her older brother who had initiated family turmoil when he introduced his now fiancé Emma. Emma was beautiful, kind, talented, honest and most importantly she made her brother happy, bringing calm to his fiery nature. But Emma was not Arab, not Muslim and her parents were only just beginning to accept the situation, three years on.

'Laylah?' Ayat's voice pulled her out of her reverie.

Laylah nodded. 'Okay, okay, I will.'

'When? Today?!' Ayat demanded.

Laylah chuckled at her enthusiasm, sometimes Ayat was like a hound on the hunt, you could not distract her. 'Maybe, otherwise, I am sure I will run into him. Dunedin is a small town.'

Chapter Four

Sam: Thirty-Two Degrees Fahrenheit

It was 8 a.m. in the morning and Sam stood huddled with a group of strangers. He watched the sun which had completed a third of its ascent up the sky, hands in his pockets, pulling his jacket tighter around himself. It was still summer here in Dunedin but the mornings could be brisk, nothing compared to the winters of New York City of course, but brisk nonetheless making Sam impatiently wonder, *how much longer.*

They stood, silent and awkward, a jumbled group of lost lambs when a voice broke through the morning air, loud and strong. Deep. Haunting. Yet beautiful. Mesmerising.

Haere Mai.
Haere Mai.
Haere Mai.
Welcome.

Her words echoed in Sam's soul and his bones tingled.

She approached dressed simply, all in black, a blouse tucked into an ankle-length skirt, her midnight hair swept back into a bun. But she was anything but simple. Skin caramel. Eyes wide, on fire. Her arms shook, whimpering, to a beat of their own as she moved closer and gestured for them to follow. All the while her voice continued to ring through the morning air, clear and strong.

Haere Mai.

Welcome.

They followed and soon they arrived at a house which like the woman at first glance looked simple. But taking a closer look Sam could see that it was the antithesis of simple. The wooden walls were chestnut and a triangle peaked roof was decorated with intricate carvings; protruding tongues, bulging eyes and flowing bodies.

The Ancestors.

And occasionally a glint pāua could be seen; pinks, blues, greens, shimmering.

Mystical. Mythical. Magical.

Shoes off they were led inside where a group of men and women some pale like him but most brown like their guide waited to greet them. They stood in a line and faced their hosts, one by one they pressed their noses and foreheads together.

A hongi.

They sat and an elderly man with caramel skin stood in front of them. He was dressed in a simple grey suit with a cloak made of feathers covering his shoulders but what caught Sam's eyes was his face. It was covered in tattoos, green like his necklace.

Pounamu.

Two giant swirls, a bird's eye view of a tornado, covered his cheeks and extended out on either side of his head towards his cheekbones. His chin also had swirls, but they were tiny and intricate. Sam was immediately filled with respect for this man, he only had one tattoo and he knew how painful they were, he could not imagine enduring one so large, especially on the face.

Despite the man's age, stories told by the folds on his face, he exuded strength, kindness and wisdom in but a flash of his paua eyes, neither blue nor green but somehow both all at once. He spoke in a foreign tongue, his voice strong.

Māori.

Sam couldn't understand a word he said but was nonetheless entranced, captivated by these foreign sounds. Then came the translation, the English sounding harsh and rough compared to the beautiful sounds he had just heard. But his words? Transformative. Transportive.

He spoke of the carvings. Our ancestors he explained, the Gods. He spoke of the *hongi,* noses touching, foreheads meeting, breathing in the essence of another soul. Intimate. Powerful. He spoke of *Maui* the demigod and how legend said he had fished the South Island from the great Pacific. He spoke of history, culture and family. Of the strength that is born only when people come together.

After some light food and casual conversation, Sam stepped out into the now brilliant, warmth of the day. This wasn't New York, there was not a single tower in sight. This wasn't America, no star-spangled flags rippled in the wind here. But it was beautiful. It was home.

...

'Okay, so today is going to be BUSY, it's their first lab and I emailed them all in advance to make sure they pre-read the instructions so naturally none of them will know what is happening.' Sandy explained. She had insisted that under absolutely no circumstances would he call her Sandra.

'*Egh*,' she had muttered.

Sandy had piercing pale blue eyes and iron-grey hair that hung limp and lifeless just above her shoulders, but Sandy was the antithesis of limp and lifeless. A lioness. Kind, yet firm, she did not tolerate lateness or sloppiness for Physics was her life and she wished to instil her passion for it within all her students.

Today was Sam's first lab and they were measuring the wavelength of lasers by shining them through difference sized graticules. Sam glanced down and read through the instructions one more time, it was a very straightforward experiment but his loss of appetite this morning had nothing to do with his physics skills, an introvert at heart he was always nervous about meeting new people. Something that exasperated him to no end about himself.

Sam glanced up and Alice who he had also met that morning gave him a broad grin and a reassuring thumbs-up. Alice was the other lab demonstrator, she was about his age and honestly could have passed for his sister with her blue eyes and auburn hair except she was tiny. Not in the same way Laylah was though, she was taller, yes, but she looked like an elf, a wraith, almost like she might float away. Sam quickly learned however she was *not* wraithlike in the slightest. Despite her small stature and pink lipstick, Alice was brilliant, also doing her PhD but in quantum mechanics. She was also undoubtedly feisty, sassy and very warm.

They had set up all the equipment and just finished their debrief when students slowly started to trickle in. There were always the eager ones with the highlighted notes and the four coloured pens. Then there were the ones that arrived late and forget their notes. Ahh, student life.

The class was promptly split into two groups, Sam took one and Alice took another while Sandy floated. Sam quickly fell into his groove as he broke down the basics of Lasers, *Light Amplification by Stimulated Emission of Radiation*, and the formulas they would need for their calculations. Say what you will about Physics Sam grinned, but everyone thought Lasers were cool, the excited murmurs as soon as he finished made that clear.

The students all split off into their groups and Sam smiles at Alice as they strolled among the class. Taking in the Grangers, the ones who immediately took control and knew exactly what they were doing and the Longbottoms who looked immediately lost.

...

Two hours later the students trickled out, with the reminder that their pre-lab and lab write up was due next week.

Alice strolled up to him. 'You are a natural,' she said with a playful nudge.

'Not too bad yourself,' he chuckled.

Sam began to pack the lasers and other equipment away when he heard Alice shriek. 'Laylah!' And saw a small blonde mass run past him to hug a red-headed woman. Only once they had pulled apart did Sam realise that this was the woman that had helped him with his bags the other day, his neighbour.

Sam wanted to walk over and say hello, desperately, but his stomach immediately knotted so he kept his head down and finished putting away the equipment.

'Sam, come over here and meet Laylah!' Alice called.

Sam's heart stopped for a millisecond before it restarted, clamouring against his ribs. He forced a smile and strolled over.

'Laylah this is Sam, Sam, Laylah.' Alice waved as she made the introductions.

Laylah extended her hand out to shake his and very formally said. 'Nice to meet you, Sam.'

She must have forgotten Sam thought immediately.

Sam extended his hand to meet her small, yet firm grip. Only then did he finally look down to meet her eyes finding playfulness laced through the cocoa and a grin plastered on her face. Sam automatically smiled back, he couldn't help himself, she was infectious.

'Nice to meet you too Laylah,' he responded, echoing her formality into his tone.

'How is your back? Have you needed any more heavy lifting?' Laylah asked, sweetly, her smile growing.

Oh, *she remembered* him.

'It's okay and thankfully no.' Sam grinned back.

Alice looked back and forth between them. 'Am I missing something?' She asked in confusion.

Laylah laughed and immediately Sam was transported. Home.

'Sorry Alice, Sam lives across the road from me. I helped him with his bags a few days ago, get this, he thought that I wouldn't be able to carry them.' Laylah teased.

Alice shook her head. 'Grave mistake, my dear, a grave mistake. Laylah could probably carry you.'

Sam blushed. 'All I meant was that there were going to be a lot of stairs...'

'Don't worry hun, we are just teasing.' Alice grinned, interrupting his stammer with a playful tap of the ribs.

Laylah glanced down at her watch. '*Oops,* I have class in ten minutes, I have to run. Here is that dress Alice, thank you so much for letting me borrow it,' she said and handed Alice a fairly large bag.

'No problem, is dinner tonight still happening?' Alice asked as she took the bag.

'Definitely.' Laylah said and then glanced at Sam. 'Hey if you aren't doing anything tonight why don't you come over for dinner?'

'Oh, I wouldn't want to be a bother...' Sam started.

Laylah interrupted him with a wave of her hand. 'Please, I insist, I like to cook and we are neighbours. So 7:00 pm at mine, bring a friend with you if you want.' Laylah added with a smile.

'You should come, Laylah is a great cook!' Alice nodded solemnly.

Laylah grinned. 'Thanks, Alice, I will see you both at 7:00 pm.'

With that she was gone, her spirit flitting out the door and leaving the room oddly dull in its absence. Sandy came out of the office moments later. 'Was that Laylah?' she asked.

'Yeah, you just missed her.' Alice nodded as she organised the students pre-labs into piles based on the alphabetical order of surname.

'That's okay, I just had a question about the gym.' Sandy said.

The look of confusion must have been clear on Sam's face, so Sandy explained. 'She does Powerlifting.'

'Oh!' Sam exclaimed, her strength (incredulous for her size) finally made sense, she was probably five foot, couldn't weigh more than 120 pounds, yet she carried his 66-pound bag up a rather steep flight of stairs almost like it was nothing.

He shook his head. 155 cm. 55 kgs. 30 kgs.

Sam continued to put away the equipment whilst Alice began marking the pre-labs, muttering about her lunch. 'Egh I bet Dee made me a peanut butter sandwich. She *always* slathers on way too much peanut butter.' Alice moaned.

Sam nodded amicably but didn't really understand, how could you have *too much* peanut butter? That was an oxymoron. 'Dee?' He asked.

'My partner, you will meet her tonight. I assume you are coming tonight?'

'I guess I have too. Laylah doesn't seem like someone that you can say no to and she knows where I live.' Sam said with a smile.

'Damn Sam was that a joke? Good, you are getting comfortable and this will also give you a chance to get to know Laylah better.' Alice winked.

Sam blushed for the millionth time that morning. 'I don't know what you mean.'

'Sure you don't.' Alice said, wiggling her eyebrows at me him and elbowing him playfully. 'That's why you have been blushing since she walked in right?'

Sam stayed quiet, there was no point trying to fight Alice he thought. But he also couldn't fight the small smile in his heart and for some reason, he didn't want to.

. . .

After work, Sam headed to the library to get started on his work. He had a meeting with Sandy tomorrow and he wanted to have some talking points lined up.

Three hours later Sam could barely think, his mind has turned to sludge and he was getting antsy, scientific journals were not exactly light reading material. He flicked Nikau a text to see if he was free to head over to the gym which thankfully he was.

The gym was two buildings down from the Physics labs so within five minutes Sam was slipping on a pair of shorts and a t-shirt. He had just finished tweaking his playlist, truly an essential, when Nikau walked in, looking slightly harassed.

'Hey, what's up?' Sam asked.

'Oh it's nothing, one of my lecturers just told us we were having an in-class quiz next week, on the basics,' groaned Nikau.

'The basics?'

'Well, that's what he called it. What he means is all the things we learned in our first year, mostly aerial optimisation and I remember *nothing* and when I say nothing I mean *nothing*. I barely remember what I ate for breakfast let alone what he droned on about three years ago!' Nikau moaned.

Sam grinned as they made their way to the weights room. 'Well it's your lucky day, isn't it? I did my honours project on aerial optimisation – I am sure I can give you a hand, especially if it's *the basics.*'

Nikau stopped and turned to him, putting his hand on Sam's shoulder. 'Would you, would you really?' He asked weakly as they walked into the main weights room.

'Of course.'

'Man, you are amazing, I owe you one.' Nikau said, slapping Sam on the back before grabbing a bar.

'Don't worry about it.' Sam smiled looking around the huge gym. It truly was incredible. Bars gleamed, neatly hanging from the wall whilst plates were stacked perfectly, colour coordinated based on their weight. He moved closer to examine a stack of red plates, 25kgs. Thankfully you didn't get through even one year of physics without learning the metric system. Still, this was going to take some getting used to. Ahead of them, five squat racks stood ready and waiting in front of a wall of mirrors. It was perfect Sam grinned.

'What are you doing for dinner tonight by the way?' He asked Nikau, his mind rapidly returning to the crevice Laylah already inhabited in his thoughts.

'No plans.' Nikau responded as he slid a 20kg plate onto the bar. 'Do you want to grab something?'

'Actually, my neighbour invited me over to dinner and said I could bring someone if you wanted to join?' Sam enquired.

'Sure, who is your neighbour?' Nikau asked. 'And why do you sound like this is a death sentence, are they annoying or something?' Nikau raised his brow questioningly.

'Definitely not, Laylah is...well certainly not annoying. She is...' Sam started but quickly became lost for words.

'Beautiful, passionate and one of the nicest people you will ever meet.' Nikau said, finishing Sam's sentence with a smile.

'You know her?' Sam asked.

'Sure, everyone knows Laylah.' Nikau responded with a cheerful shrug, as if this was a fact of life, like water becoming ice at 32 degrees Fahrenheit. 0 degrees *Celsius* he mentally corrected himself.

'I went to school with her in Christchurch before my family moved here.' Nikau explained. 'Do you like her?' He grinned.

'No, no, I barely know her. I mean sure she is nice, I like her…as a friend.' Sam fumbled and immediately kicked himself mentally for losing his nerve. *What was wrong with him?*

Thankfully, Nikau dropped it but his smile made it clear he didn't believe him.

Sam warmed up with 60kgs, nice and slow as his mind, without his permission wandered to what he should wear tonight. Immediately his stomach knotted and he felt ill. Sam didn't know why he couldn't seem to forget those eyes or why the thought of that hair made him feel like the gangly fourteen-year-old boy he had been so many years ago. Or why despite being half his size Laylah, someone who he had only talked to twice was managing to scare the living daylights out of him.

While all of this emotion raged inside of him, a storm, Sam breathed out and stood, bracing his core before he sunk into another squat, nice and slow, his face smooth, the epitome of calm.

Chapter Five

Laylah: Beneath the Stars

love	we the ice. how could we not?
	it is beautiful, enchanting,
	we are enticed to step on,
	so, we do. only to discover that fear,
is	the only constant here.
	for even those
	who appear to have mastered,
	the ice, who glide and twirl
skating	with apparent ease.
	even they fall.
	even they hurt.
	even they break.
	for the ice is unforgiving,
	hard.
	so hard, we question is it worth it?
	but of course, it must,

for the chance to glide,
to come as close to flying
as we can
on   this earth.
          for when everything lines up on the
ice   it is joy. it is ecstasy.
          it is to touch the heavens
          with our feet firmly planted on this earth.

Laylah arrived home, tired but satisfied, it had been a good first day back at university.

'Ariana!' She cried as she walked through the lounge and spotted her best friend on the couch. She rushed towards her, pulling her into a tight hug.

Even though she had lived with Ariana for two years now, Laylah was always slightly taken aback by her best friend, and she was not the only one, no one walked past Ariana without looking at her twice. A Spanish mother and Malaysian father had endowed her with green eyes and an olive complexion that turned to gold over the summer. She kept her hair long and often untied so it glinted like the night sky against her sharp cheekbones, although some days, like today, she chose to wrap her hair in a beautiful headscarf – midnight with large pink blossoms adorning it, blooming. Ariana was beautiful, unique.

Finally releasing her Laylah sat down on the couch for a much-needed catch-up.

'How are you? How was your day?' Ariana asked.

'Tiring but great. Three lectures and then I went to the library to get a head start on an assignment. Oh, and I went to the gym of course.' Laylah said.

'Of course.' Ariana grinned, rolling her eyes slightly in amusement.

Laylah grinned, Ariana had no interest in fitness but she still listened to her personal record boasts. That's why she was her best friend after all.

'What are your classes like?' Ariana asked.

'Awesome! I love my law papers, they are so interesting but I am nervous about the creative writing paper I am doing. It's based on poetry and 50% of our grade is a journal that we have to keep. She wants us to write in it every day and then present some of the poems to the class.' Laylah sighed, biting her lip.

'Laylah, you are a fantastic writer, this should be easy for you right?' Ariana asked raising her perfect brows quizzically.

'But not poetry, it's so personal, so emotional...' Laylah explained.

'Ahh.' Ariana said and understanding rolled over her face. 'Sweetie I know you don't like being vulnerable, I know you think it makes you seem weak but there is nothing wrong with it. Vulnerability is a strength and you never know this might be good for you.'

'I guess you are right...that's the paper I started the assignment for today. I know it's going to be hard.' Laylah sighed. 'Anyway, how was your day? Did you manage to unpack everything?'

Ariana raised her brow at Laylah again, well aware that she had just deflected the conversation off herself but decided to let it slide.

'It was okay, I didn't take much home so there wasn't much unpacking to do thankfully. I even managed to grab a coffee with some friends from class.' Ariana responded.

'That's good! I am glad it wasn't too much of a hassle, you need your rest before you start hospital placements tomorrow?' Laylah asked.

'Definitely, it's going to be a hard year. Speaking of catching up with people who else is coming tonight? What strays have you picked up this year?' Ariana teased.

'Just Alice and Dee...oh and I invited the new guy who lives across the road.' Laylah added a slight note of defensiveness entering her voice.

'Who is he?' Ariana asked, her interest piqued.

'His name is Sam, he is American, very tall and he tutors Physics with Alice, that's actually how I ended up inviting him, I was dropping off Alice's dress.' Laylah explained.

'Well, hopefully, we will get to know this mystery man tonight.' Ariana said. 'We should get started on the food though if we want to feed all of these people.'

Laylah nodded and stood.

Soon they were chopping, sautéing and mixing. There was something oddly soothing about cooking; therapeutic, the simplest ingredients becoming nourishment and sustenance bringing people together.

Twenty minutes later the Thai Red Curry was done, beautiful chunks of tofu and green beans hiding just beneath the surface of delicious coconut cream. Coconut cream made everything better. Ariana placed the perfectly steamed rice on the table and waved Laylah away to get ready, people would be arriving soon.

With ten minutes to go Laylah threw on a black A-line dress, pinned her curls back and had just finished fixing her eyeliner when the doorbell rang. 7:00 pm on the dot, this was not Alice who was notoriously late.

Laylah opened the door to find Sam, looking well put together in dark jeans and a purple button-down shirt that perfectly accentuated those eyes.

Sky blue.

He tidied up nicely Laylah thought to herself, her heart ever so slightly aflutter.

Behind him was Nikau in a much more casual but equally aesthetic pair of flowered shorts and a fitted black t-shirt, his hair tousled in a casual way that guaranteed he had spent at least twenty minutes in front of the mirror.

'Hey! I didn't expect you here!' Laylah exclaimed at Nikau, reaching for him.

'Just try to keep me away when food is involved.' Nikau chuckled and gave her a bear hug, lifting her slightly off her feet.

'Hey Sam,' she said, waving from a distance once Nikau had released her. Sam seemed shy, best to not go in for a hug yet she thought to herself.

He smiled back politely. 'Thank you so much for inviting us.'

'My pleasure.' Laylah said as she led them into the living room.

Five minutes later Alice and Dee had arrived. Dee was the complete opposite of Alice, a touch smaller than Laylah she had glossy straight black hair, coffee-coloured skin and dark eyes that shone with warmth like coals.

Soon all the introductions had been made and they were seated for dinner. Almost immediately Nikau and Alice became engrossed in a conversation about the All Blacks next test match while Ariana and Dee debated the Middle Eastern crisis and whether New Zealand should open their doors to more refugees. Laylah who was sitting next to Sam was content simply listening in on the conversations as she ate, ravenous from a long day.

Her stomach finally beginning to settle she glanced at Sam who she noticed was also keeping to himself, Laylah hadn't figured him out yet and if there was one thing she liked to do, it was to unlock people, coax them out of their shell. He was like a puzzle, with all the pieces out in the open but for some reason, they weren't quite fitting together. *Yet.*

'So tell me about yourself, where are you from? What are you studying? Is your family still back in the States? How long have you been in New Zealand? What is your favourite book?' Laylah said, firing off questions one after the other.

Sam's eyes crinkled in amusement.

Sky blue.

'I am from Brooklyn New York and I just started a PhD in astrophysics.'

'Ahh a man who studies the stars.' Laylah smiled. 'Where are your family?' She prompted.

'My family is here, they live in a small town. I think it's called Wa...wa...*Wanaka?*' Sam stuttered his brow furrowing as he tripped over the pronunciation of the word.

Laylah grinned but didn't say anything, his accent was adorable.

'We have been in New Zealand for about a week now, my mum is a New Zealander but she moved to the States when she was five.' Sam continued.

'And your favourite book?' Laylah prompted.

Sam's brow furrowed and he was silent long enough that Laylah thought he might not answer.

'I loved the Harry Potter series when I was younger like everyone else, it's a classic. Now? I guess I enjoy reading poetry if that counts.'

'Oh, of course, that counts.' Laylah responded, raising her eyebrow at him. There was clearly more to Sam than Physics, more than just those eyes.

Sky blue.

'Any writers or poets in particular?' Laylah persisted.

'Pretty much anything I can get my hands on, Rumi, Rupi Kaur, I love Shakespeare's plays too.'

Laylah nodded in agreement, they were all brilliant writers. 'Any of Shakespeare's plays in particular?'

'Othello is probably my favourite.'

'Oh, I love that play too! We studied it at school.' Laylah smiled. 'I think what amazes me the most about Shakespeare is how progressive he was for his time. In high school I accidentally wrote a 10,000 word paper about how he should be considered a feminist for his time...it was supposed to be 2,000 words.' Laylah admitted abashedly.

'*Accidently? How?*' Sam chuckled.

'Dunno, I am not a concise person I guess, especially when it comes to William Shakespeare and feminism it seems.' Laylah grinned with a shrug.

Their conversation was interrupted by Nikau and Ariana standing to clear plays. Laylah could not help but feel a sliver of disappointment but she was finished too so she rose. Grabbing her plate and as many others as she could carry she made her way to the kitchen. Sam followed with his own stack of plates and headed straight for the sink.

'Sit,' he insisted to Laylah. 'You cooked, we clean.'

Laylah was surprised by his insistence, pleasantly surprised she admitted to herself.

After everything was clean, coffee and tea were made and they split off into conversations once more. This time Laylah got caught by Alice and Dee who were excitedly discussing the joint birthday party they were planning, by some amazing coincidence they happened to be born on the same day. Alice and Dee were arguing about what colour napkins they should get, Alice wanted pink (of course) but Dee wanted a more classic black.

'Would a rainbow theme be too much?' Nikau interjected.

'That would be amazing!' Alice exclaimed, her face luminous. 'We could go all out, get glitter and stickers for everyone! Pictures of cute celebrities on the wall and...oh, but you would hate that right?' She said her face falling abruptly as she glanced at Dee.

But Dee's face was thoughtful. 'Actually, I think that would be perfect,' she nodded, a smile breaking out onto her face.

As they excitedly began to put the details in order Laylah tuned them out and found her gaze had wandered to Sam once more who was sitting in the middle of a conversation between Ariana and Nikau. Laylah noted that again Sam didn't seem to be doing much talking, he was mainly listening.

By 9:00 pm Alice and Dee had decided on almost everything, even though the party was not for months, Ariana had called it a night and Nikau was standing to excuse himself, he still had an hour drive to get home.

Laylah was surely mistaken but thought she saw Nikau wink at Sam before he left but Sam didn't react at all. Instead, he sat on the couch, not saying anything, but not leaving either and suddenly it was just the two of them. He confused Laylah, confused and intrigued her.

'Have you seen the city at night Sam?' She asked.

Sam shook his head. 'I haven't had the chance yet.'

Laylah stood up. 'It's beautiful, come on, let's go for a walk.'

'Sure.'

'How did you meet Nikau?' Laylah mused.

'At church.' Sam said as he adjusted his shoes.

'Oh, you are Christian?!' Laylah blurted and immediately winced at herself. She should know better than to blatantly ask someone about their faith, sometimes she hated that she had no filter.

Sam straightened and met her eyes shrugging. 'Semi-Christian, more agnostic.'

They walked down the stairs in silence, Laylah could sense that he wanted to say something and for once had the foresight to keep her mouth shut, despite her searing curiosity.

They reached the sidewalk and it was indeed a beautiful night. The brightness of the street lamps hid most of the stars but the moon was bright and full, casting a pale, ominous light onto everything it touched. Everything was more beautiful at night, more mysterious, more magical, more terrifying. But certainly more beautiful.

As they walked down the empty streets Laylah's eyes remained fixed on the moon when it struck her that she had only known this man for a few hours, yet here she was walking down a dark street with him. He was twice her size but she had never felt so safe, so comfortable in her entire life. Never felt so calm. Strange.

'I was raised a Christian, my family are not even slightly orthodox, but the values and community of church were an important part of my childhood. As a teenager, I strayed, I began to question everything, to detest the rules and restrictions...' Sam began.

Laylah desperately wanted to question him but forced herself to remain silent as she fixed her attention on his towering frame.

'When I was fifteen I had a huge argument with my mum, she wouldn't let me go to a party because there was going to be drinking. I was so stupid. I said I hated her, hated her God and that it was all fake.' Sam continued, shaking his head and although Laylah could not see his face, she could hear the pain in his voice.

'It broke my mother's heart. I know it did but from that day on she never talked to me about God, never asked me to come to church with her. Then last year something happened...' Sam paused, his voice cracking ever so slightly before he took a deep, shaky breath and continued, his voice steady.

'Something happened and I returned to God. Since that day church is one of the most important parts of my life.'

Just as Sam finished his sentence they arrived at Laylah's favourite part of the city, a garden which had previously been an old deserted park, before the council had transformed it into a magical haven of sorts, with lights, seats and beautiful roses that filled the air with a heady scent.

Laylah and Sam walked over to a bench and sat down. Glancing at Sam's face Laylah recognised his pain and yearned to hug him, to ask what had happened last year, but instinctively she held back, somehow knowing that he would tell her when he was ready.

Instead, Laylah worked to inject every ounce of compassion, of empathy she could muster into her face and voice. 'I am glad you have that in your life, spirituality is...important.'

Sam nodded in agreement and asked. 'Do you believe in God?'

Laylah nodded. 'Definitely, life is full of uncertainties but that at least has been one thing I have always been sure of. My family are Muslim, more culturally than anything but God is still important.'

Sam's brow furrowed in curiosity. 'So do you consider yourself Muslim?'

Laylah was taken aback by his directness but slowly, attempted to arrange her thoughts, trying to explain in a way that made sense, 'Yes...but also no.'

Sam remained quiet, giving her the time, the space to explain, to put her thoughts into words.

'What I mean is, I don't think it matters. We get so caught up in these titles, even within Islam, *Sunni, Shia, Sufi.* And then people get caught up in the rules, they become rigid, consumed by the small things and forget the important things, the big things. Love, honesty, patience. No, the East is too busy hating ourselves, too busy picking ourselves apart to remember something as simple as love,' she said not even trying to stop the bitterness that leached into her voice.

'I understand, but it's not only the East you know, not only Muslims, Christianity also has the same issues. Humans are stupid.' Sam shrugged, a playful smile on his face.

Laylah laughed up at him and felt that odd wave of comfort and calm sweep over her once more, warming her very soul, her very essence.

So they sat under the moon and talked about, well, everything.

Laylah told him about her family, her kind but crazy Arab mother and her quiet father. Her older brother that had broken the families expectations, her boy-crazy sister Ayat and her youngest sister Dina, whose joy and childhood innocence was always a bright spot in her life.

Sam told her about his family. His mother, father and childhood sweethearts. How he grew up in the jungle that was Brooklyn, spent his childhood riding the subway and hours upon hours at the library. How he escaped twice a year to visit his grandparents in Los Angeles who hated the cold of New York. He told her about his little sister, Charlotte who sounded a lot like Dina. Chuckling, he told her about how he was a terror of a child.

They talked and talked and talked and time seemed to stand still. But of course, it didn't.

Laylah felt like she was in a dream which was only interrupted when her phone vibrated, a text from Ariana wondering where she had got to. Only then did Laylah realise it was almost midnight. Only then did she realise how closely their bodies had drifted, their arms centimetres apart. Only then did she feel the outside of his thigh-grazing her knee. Electricity.

Laylah pulled herself out of her reverie. 'We should get going,' she said, showing him the time, perhaps it was her imagination but Sam also appeared disappointed. Or at least she hoped.

As they strolled back home the conversation continued to flow, movies, books, music but time caught up with them once more and before she knew it they were outside her door.

Sam smiled at her. 'Sweet dreams.'

'You too,' she blushed, smiling back at him. *Had she just blushed?!* Laylah shook her head, calming herself and dismissed the thought before she entered the dark, silent house. Ariana must have been awake in bed though because as soon as she entered her room Laylah's phone vibrated once more;

'What happened, did you kiss?! I want to know everything!'

Laylah shook her head and laughed to herself, Ariana was such a romantic. But as Laylah brushed her teeth and settled into bed she finally acknowledged the flame that had been lit inside of her.

It was small. But it was safe and strong.

Within moments Laylah drifted to sleep, her dreams filled with the streets of New York City she had so often seen on the silver screen. White Christmases, Washington Square Garden, The Statue of Liberty, her head held high as she welcomed immigrants to the land of the free. And at that moment Laylah's mind was transported, to a whole new world filled with blue.

Sky blue.

Chapter Six

Sam: Hummingbird's Wings

Sam sat at the kitchen table, eating his oatmeal and feeling a touch sleep deprived. Partially due to his late-night conversation with Laylah but also his roommate George who had stumbled in at 3 am, waking Sam who had only just managed to calm his whirring mind and drift to sleep.

But Sam could not be anything but happy. Not today. Not after last night.

Sam's mind wandered back as he willed himself to commit every single detail of Laylah to memory. She was the second oldest of four. She was doing a conjoint, Law and Political Science. She was Muslim. She loved to power lift. She loved the moon.

Sam felt a deep sigh of contentment wash over him. There had been moments in his life where he had been stuck in debilitating loneliness, he didn't know what he had done to deserve people like Laylah, Nikau, Alice and Ariana in his life.

Breakfast downed Sam prepared his books before leaving for his meeting with Sandy to go over some potential research topics. Locking his door he glanced hopefully at Laylah's but just as it had been last Sunday it remained firmly shut. Only this time Sam knew Laylah wasn't asleep at 7:45 am, she was either studying or at the gym.

Sam wandered down the street smiling, it was a beautiful summer's day, the sun climbing the brilliant blue of the sky, not a cloud in sight. Ten minutes later Sam arrived at campus and caught sight of Nikau who blearily nodded to him as he walked to his own class.

Not a morning person, *interesting*.

Sam fumbled with the map on his phone as he tried to find Sandy's office in the maze that was the campus. Finally, after walking down the wrong corridor twice Sam admitted defeat and asked for directions. Less than two minutes later he was walking through her open door. Thank god he had left early, he was right on time.

'Sam! Perfect timing!' Sandy said, turning her chair to face him. She gestured to a comfortable looking indigo couch that sat in front of her desk as she stood and took a seat on an equally quaint couch across from him, a notebook in her hand.

Sam's eyes wandered around the office and he could almost feel his photoreceptors spontaneously synapsing. Unlike most academics there was not a single certificate in sight, no fancy pieces of paper with embellished seals, instead, the walls were laden with pictures of loved ones, intricate images of galaxies and sketches of all matter of apparatuses from telescopes to lasers. These were all haphazardly arranged on a startling yellow background.

'Some people think it's a bit much.' Sandy grinned.

'Well, I think it's brilliant.'

Sandys grin grew even broader. 'Okay, so I have read over your proposal and I think it sounds great. I do have a few suggestions...'

...

Two hours later, finished with his meeting and in desperate need of a coffee, Sam met Nikau outside who had apparently woken up at this stage.

'So a little bird told me that you didn't get back till past midnight yesterday and considering how tired you look, I am inclined to believe that.' Nikau began in an annoying, all-knowing voice. Oh, he was definitely awake now.

'Laylah and I went for a walk and we kind of lost track of the time.' Sam nodded nonchalantly.

Nikau rolled his eyes at him and grinned. 'Come on man! Give me more details, what did you do for four hours?! Where did you go?!' He demanded, sputtering '...*Four hours!*'

'We went to the gardens and we...well we just talked.' Sam replied with a smile.

Nikau sat for a second silently looking at him, brow furrowed he seemed to be focusing intently like he was trying to understand a difficult concept. Suddenly his emerald eyes sparkled as understanding dawned on Nika's face and a smile blossomed. He leapt from his chair and began pummelling Sam's arm. 'You. Like. Her!' He exclaimed.

'What? I barely know her, no. No?' Sam began, his statement becoming a question.

'Of course, you do man! Look at you, all smiles and blushes when someone brings her up. Also, no one spends four hours *just talking* to anyone!' Nikau said.

Sam remained silent, slowly processing his emotions, how awkward and silent he got any time she walked in. How much he had thought about what he would wear yesterday. How flustered she made him feel but at the same time how comfortable he had been with her last night, how the conversation had flowed with such ease.

'Oh my god.' Sam said and shook his head.

Nikau leapt up again, barely able to contain his excitement. 'You have to ask her out!'

Sam shook his head abruptly. 'No, no. I cannot do that. I barely know her.'

'Yes, you can and you have to!' Nikau said.

'She probably doesn't even like me.'

Nikau raised his eyebrow. 'You don't know that she might! And more to the point, you won't know until you do!' He said, frustration bleeding into his voice.

'Okay, okay we will see.' Sam replied, needing time to process what was happening.

Nikau looked at him once more, brow furrowed, eyes crinkled, frustration painted all over his face, he opened his mouth to say something and then stopped, deciding to let it go, 'Okay man,' he nodded.

'Do you have time for a quick workout before lunch?' Sam asked, promptly changing the subject.

Nikau nodded suspiciously but by the time they had finished their coffees and were on their way to the gym he had launched an excited discussion of what his deadlift, bench and squat numbers were and what he wanted them to be by the end of the semester.

They walked into the main weights room, drink bottle and towel in hand still engrossed in their conversation. 'Honestly, man I know people don't stop talking about protein but to be honest, you only need about 20%, now carbohydrates....' Sam trailed off.

Nikau looked up and his face immediately transformed from one of intense concentration to the biggest grin Sam had ever seen as he also spotted Laylah at the squat rack.

Without a word, they set up the bench which unfortunately in Sam's mind and fortunately in Nikaus just happened to be behind Laylah. Mirrored walls meant that Sam could see Laylah's face screwed up in concentration, sweat dripping as she breathed in and went down.

Nikau lay down and warmed up with the bar as Sam tried to avoid staring, but he was transfixed. Laylah re-wracked the bar and glanced up. Catching Sam's eye she smiled but Sam immediately looked down.

Ugh why did he do that, she was going to think he was ignoring her now.

After Nikau warmed up they switched and as he lay down on the bench Sam tried to force himself to focus on his breathing, on engaging his triceps and lats, desperately trying to ignore the whirlwind of emotions erupting inside of him. Inhale. Exhale. He repeated fruitlessly, his heart a hummingbird's wings.

Having warmed up Sam and Nikau started to progressively increase the weights, 60 kg. 80 kg. 90 kg. 100 kg. Although Nikau was a head shorter than Sam they had a similar level of strength, always a good thing in a training partner.

'Okay let's throw on 105 kg.' Nikau said.

'105 kg?! I have never benched that much before, I am not sure I can.'

'Of course, you can! Anyway, worst case scenario you fail and I lift the bar off you.' Nikau shrugged and for a moment Sam's heart warmed as he thought about how long it had been since someone had just been there for him.

Just believed in him. Not since James really...Sam stopped immediately, his mind recoiling as though he had touched something hot that had burned him, burned his mind, heart and soul. Suddenly he was lead.

Thankfully Nikau didn't notice, having taken Sam's silence as a yes, he was already loading the bar.

Just as Sam sat down on the bench, having managed to pull himself out of a spiral, a familiar voice rang through the air. 'Sam, Nikau!'

'Hey, Laylah!' Nikau said and deftly walked around the bar to wrap his arm around her. 'Working hard I see. What are you doing these days?' he nodded to the squat rack.

Laylah laughed as she hugged him back. '100 kg but I think I have hit a plateau, I cannot seem to get 105kg!' She said, her brow furrowing in frustration.

Nikau nodded. 'Maybe try doing 90 kg for more reps and then try again next week?'

Laylah's brow furrowed but she nodded slowly. 'Actually, that sounds like exactly what I need to do.'

Laylah caught Sam's eye and grinned. 'Sorry Sam, lifting is very serious business, how are you?'

'No, I understand.' Sam nodded with a smile, heart racing.

Laylah glanced at the weights and did a low whistle. 'Wow, is this a personal record?'

Nikau looked at Sam expectantly. Sam's hands shook and a pregnant pause filled the air for what felt like an eternity before Nikau jumped in with a smile. 'Sam's going to give it a go.'

While Nikau chatted to Laylah, Sam's heart raced, beat against his ribs so hard that he was astounded they hadn't heard it. That it hadn't betrayed him. Sam wanted to say something, *desperately*. To comment on how strong she was or even just to ask her how her day had been but he couldn't, it was as if someone else had taken over his body and stuck his lips together.

Sam couldn't lie to himself, part of the reason he was so awestruck (he had never thought he would be awestruck in his life) was because of how Laylah was dressed, Sam had been able to tell from early on that Laylah was strong, that she was fit, but nothing accentuated it like her workout clothes. Her tights enveloped her muscular legs and showed off every contour, her midriff singlet and the high waist of her tights hugged her waist, her arms toned and muscular. She also had a great butt, that was undeniable. Sam was struggling not to stare.

A few minutes later Sam was jolted out of his fantasy as Laylah said. 'I will see you later, bye,' she smiled at them and walked back to the squat rack.

As soon as was out of earshot Sam could feel Nikau's laser eyes on him but he didn't say anything.

An hour later they had finished their workout, showered and found a spot outside to eat lunch.

Nikau looked at Sam intently. 'Listen, I know we haven't known each other for that long, maybe I am over-stepping, but I consider you my friend and because you are my friend I have to say, you cannot do that, you cannot shut down like that.'

Sam searched for words. 'I didn't mean to, I wanted to say something, I did, I just didn't know what to say...and I couldn't stop thinking about how I think I *do* like her and how weird that is because I never like people this quickly and then what if I said the wrong thing...?' He trailed off anxiously.

Nikau listened intently with empathy. 'Man, I know you are shy, anyone from a mile away can tell that, but honestly, even if she doesn't like you *that* way, she likes you and is making an effort to talk to you. Trust me you cannot say the *wrong thing* to her. But you need to open up a bit more, she isn't going to keep saying hi and waiting for you to respond forever.'

Sam sighed and nodded, Nikau was right.

A peaceful silence filled the air and Sam's eyes fell to the branches of a nearby tree, lost in thought he watched them sway in the breeze.

'Speaking of love.' Nikau interjected. 'Or...maybe lust, guess what I am doing this weekend?'

Sam chuckled at the rapid change in conversation. 'What?'

'I have a date,' he said proudly. 'Friday night. He is an old friend and we recently reconnected online,' he said with apparent nonchalance. But Sam noticed Nikau's green eyes on his face. Those eyes were anxious but defiant too.

Sam was unphased. 'Cool, what are you two doing?' He asked, grinning now it was his turn to do the grilling.

Chapter Seven

Laylah: Fairy tales

                when i was a little girl,
                my life was filled with
fairy tales.   evil was always defeated,
                good prospered,
                and love?
                love was simple,
                oh, so simple.

                but i am no longer a little girl,
                evil seems to have the trump card,
                good people
are   failing all the time,
                and love?
                love is anything but simple.

                so, in the dark hours of the night
                when only those who are haunted
lie(s)   awake;
                the artists, the poets, the heartbroken.
                struggling over puzzles we cannot solve,
                things that we know not,

           only one certainty exists
           this world
is   harsh but
love?   it is still the most
           beautiful thing on this earth.

Laylah should be tired, no she should be exhausted. A grandmother at heart midnight bedtimes did not serve her well, especially since she woke up at her usual 6:30 am anyway. But strangely enough, she wasn't exhausted, not even in the slightest.

Laylah started her morning, just as she always did with a cup of tea and an episode of FRIENDS one of her all-time favourite shows which at this stage she had watched more times than she could count. In this particular episode, Monica and Chandler were talking about moving in together, Laylah heavily identified with Monica although she secretly aspired to Phoebe's unique charming quirk.

Once the episode had finished, Laylah set herself up on their kitchen table to finish an assignment, a critical analysis of the power structure of the United Nations and the failures that in Laylah's opinion often resulted.

Laylah's fingers tapped away on the keyboard but half an hour passed and she had made little to no progress. Five minutes of furious typing would be quickly followed by fervent pressing of the delete button. Garbage, she was writing garbage. True garbage was a normal part of the writing process but this was nonsensical garbage and she wasn't getting anywhere. Exasperated Laylah shut her laptop and grabbed a pen and a spare notebook, sometimes going old school helped. But another half an hour passed and she had nothing to show for it but a page filled with fervent crosses.

Laylah sighed, she wasn't focusing and deep down she knew why, last night was strange...she wasn't quite sure how she felt about Sam, why he had entered her life and she certainly had no idea what he meant. All she knew was that he simultaneously brought her calm and storms. He made her heart tremble, made it quiver and ache but also made her feel safer than she ever had felt before. Sam mattered, she didn't know how, she didn't know why, but he did. So no wonder she couldn't focus on the United Nations, who cared about the United Nations? Okay, she cared, but not right this second, right this second, her heart trembled, it quivered, it ached.

She stared out the window, the sun had risen completely now and it looked like they were going to be blessed with another Dunedin summer day. Brilliant. Blue.

Sky blue.

Almost mindlessly, Laylah picked up her pen once more and began to write, not about the United Nations, the brilliant blue sky had driven that from her mind completely. Instead, she poured the complex potion of feelings stirring inside her onto the page. Her tangled web of emotions. At first, it was slow, but soon she couldn't write fast enough, unable to keep up with her whirring mind. She was bleeding words.

. . .

Laylah wasn't sure how much time had passed but eventually, her grumbling stomach demanded to be fed so almost reluctantly she set her pen down and headed to the kitchen.

She grabbed some Almond milk and spinach from the fridge, frozen bananas, berries and mango from the freezer for a smoothie. You couldn't beat a smoothie in summer. As she chopped and poured Laylah quickly became lost in thought once more. She loved preparing food, there was something about it, not mindless exactly, but busy. And busy hands allowed her mind to breathe. To ponder and right now she was still pondering Sam.

Once everything was ready in the blender, Laylah glanced at her phone, surely Ariana would be awake, but just in case she flicked her a text.

'Hey girl, are you up? Do you want a smoothie?'

Moments later her phone vibrated *'I am, and yes, please! I will be out in a second, I have MANY questions!'*

Laylah grimaced at her screen but was also amused, she really shouldn't be surprised with Ariana.

Laylah topped up the blender so that there would be enough for two and had just finished pouring the green contents into gigantic glasses when Ariana walked in. 'Heyyyy,' she grinned, her midnight hair loose and following in ringlets down her shoulders. Eyes a touch bleary.

Laylah turned and handed Ariana her smoothie. 'Hey yourself.'

Ariana, sat on the kitchen table, her orb-like eyes on Laylah as she took an appreciative sip. 'It's funny usually people in *your condition* get a bit distracted, but this is amazing, thank you,' she said slyly.

Laylah sat across from her. 'Okay, okay. What do you want to know?!'

'What happened?!' Ariana blurted immediately.

'Nothing.' Laylah said truthfully.

A look of complete disbelief was painted on Ariana's face.

'I promise, nothing happened. We went for a walk to the gardens and then we...well we talked.'

'For four hours?!'

'Yes. We had a really good talk actually, but honestly, we are just friends, although...' Laylah trailed off.

'ALTHOUGH?!' Ariana demanded almost jumping out of her chair.

'There might be *something* there...' Laylah admitted.

Ariana *did* jump out of her chair this time.

'*But* it's way too early to know. Anyway, you know what my family is like, he is white, even if I did have feelings for him, well that would be a mountain.' Laylah finished sadly.

Ariana looked like she desperately wanted to argue but seemed to think better of it and for a moment they both drank their smoothies in silence.

Ariana finished her smoothie, set down her cup carefully and began to speak, choosing her words carefully. 'Laylah, I understand your family situation, honestly, I do, heck my dad's family are still not completely okay with his marriage to my mum or how I turned out. But you cannot let that stop you from living, from choosing your happiness.'

'Ariana...'

'Wait, let me finish.' Ariana took another deep breath. 'I know you barely know him, I am not telling you to marry him. But if there is something there, don't fight it, just see where it goes. Be open to the possibility of...something, of life, happening.'

Laylah looked at her best friend's earnest face, she knew Laylah better than anyone, sometimes better than Laylah knew herself and unlike everyone else she *did* understand her family situation. Coming from a mixed family herself Ariana's father was Muslim and her mother was Christian and Ariana? She was a fascinating mixture of the two, refusing to define herself. Ariana wore a *hijab* when it suited her and left her hair untamed when it didn't. She would attend *Jummah* prayers at the Mosque *and* Church service once a month but would then go half a year without stepping into either. Ariana believed in God with all her heart, believed in community and people. For her, that was all that mattered.

Laylah knew her best friend spoke the truth, knew that sometimes she picked men apart because it was easy, because it was safe. Because a small part of her was scared, scared of being in love, scared of her family's reaction, scared of losing control. But when Ariana, Alice, Sam or any of her friends came to her for romantic advice (she had no idea why) she would always tell them to be open, to try. After all, if you didn't try to squat 100kg, how would you know if you could? True you might fail, but you also might succeed and wasn't failure part of it all? After all, there were two ways to live. You could remain huddled in your own little corner and be safe. But you would never taste the raw sweetness of life. And that was a half-life, not really an existence at all. To live, to *truly* live, you had to risk failure. You had to risk collapse.

After a long pause, Laylah looked up and nodded silently.

Ariana reached for her hand and squeezed it. 'Okay, important question, do you want some peanut butter on toast?'

'Oh yes please.' Laylah chuckled.

. . .

After breakfast, Laylah went back to her essay and this time the words flowed a little more easily, but by mid-morning, she *needed* to move. So she put her laptop away and headed to the gym.

It was leg day so Laylah nabbed the first empty squat rack she could find, she adjusted the height of the bar then she swung her legs and did some bodyweight squats to prepare her muscles for what would be a heavy session. Muscles warm she placed the empty bar on her shoulders and went down. She focused on her breathing, stabilising her core and activating her lats. Tiny things that made the world of difference...but also stopped her knees caving in. She added 10kg plates on either side and then 20kg, but kept her slow, steady pace, constantly checking her form.

Soon, Laylah's muscles burned, sweat dripped down her face and she was going red but she felt amazing. That is until she spotted Nikau and Sam who walked into the gym, naturally, straight to the bench right behind her. Laylah glanced at herself in the mirror and quickly realised that although she felt amazing, she looked anything but, blister red face, a forehead gleaming with sweat, baby hairs sticking out here there and everywhere. She shrugged, she was going to have to say hi anyway.

Ten minutes later, having finished with her half an hour sweat session on the squat rack Laylah walked over to say hello, giving Nikau a sweaty hug. She glanced at Sam shyly, but he was staring off into space, his face blank and he only vaguely nodded in her direction allowing Nikau to lead the conversation. He didn't even say goodbye when she left.

Laylah walked away feeling surprised, confused and if she was honest with herself slightly hurt at the silence. These feelings stayed in the pit of her stomach, mixing together to form a batter, a recipe that she recognised almost immediately of anxiety and well, shame. *Maybe last night had meant nothing to him? Maybe he was humouring her? Maybe he didn't want to be friends?* Laylah hated mixed messages.

She finished the rest of her workout but her heart wasn't in it, in fact, it felt heavy, a feeling that hung with her for the rest of the day no matter how hard she tried to shake it.

That night even an exhausted Ariana noticed and asked her if she was okay but Laylah dismissed it as tiredness. She couldn't tell her closest friend what had happened, it hurt too much and if Laylah admitted how much it hurt, well she would also be admitting how much she cared even though she wasn't sure why. Why he shut her out but more importantly why it mattered anyway. She barely knew him after all. 9:00 pm struck and Laylah decided to call it a night and promised herself that she would back off, clearly he didn't want her around.

Chapter Eight

Sam: Time Has No Boundaries

The first week of university had come and gone and now they were already halfway through the second, time seemed to follow no rules, to have no boundaries. It would creep along, as slow as could be in a library study session but during evenings and weekends, hours felt like minutes, seconds.

Now? It barely moved as Sam sat stuck in a mandatory two-hour-long presentation that was supposed to help PhD candidates formulate their research proposals and literature reviews. In reality, it was a series of researchers droning on about their work, it was mind-numbing. After all, brilliance certainly did not save you from being simply boring. A situation made even more difficult since every presenter had exceeded their ten-minute time limit – *they were boring and they liked the sound of their own voice, great*, Sam muttered to himself. That was certainly the case with the current speaker who had droned on for almost thirty slides about his carefully derived method section. Sure it was interesting, but not thirty slides worth of interesting.

Sam tried for the millionth time in just half an hour to force himself to stay focused but the presenter's voice could have put even the most overactive toddler to sleep and Sam's daydreams called to him. He wasn't alone, the student in front of him was on Instagram and another was attentively watching a basketball game. Sam's hometown team, the Brooklyn Nets were playing the Celtics and very narrowly winning. Sam knew that wouldn't last long though, they had played horrendously all season.

As the presenter moved onto the next slide, Sam gave up, he had paid attention for half of the lecture, surely that was enough he justified to himself. And so he allowed his mind to wander, and wonder it did.

First to his parents who seemed to be slowly settling in the tiny town of Wanaka with his little sister Charlotte. A world that sounded like the antithesis of the hustle and bustle of Brooklyn.

Second to his research, he was still doing his literature review which meant hours and hours staring at journal articles at the library to find a single sentence. It was exhausting, tedious work. Although he would be moving on to devising his methods section soon which should hopefully be much more stimulating.

Third to his flatmate George, who despite Sam's best efforts was difficult to live with due to his constant state of drunkenness and 3 am kitchen rackets. Sam was exhausted, yes. Frustrated, yes. But also? Concerned. He barely knew George but he knew what alcohol could do to a person and Sam could not fathom how on earth George was passing.

Fourth to his job which was oddly enough one of the highlights of his week, he loved working with Alice and Sandy. Loved the students both those who came eager to learn and the ones that were clearly bored out of their minds. But mostly, he loved the expression on a student's face when they finally grasped a difficult concept. When as it eventually did the difficult became easy. Neurons alight. Sam grimaced though, already anticipating the coffee-fuelled late nights when they would all be marking the student's midterm test papers on top of the minimum 40 hours he needed to put into his own research. *Sigh*.

Eventually, however, Sam's mind went where it always did, Laylah. Sam had seen her in passing a few times since their encounter at the gym the prior week but she always seemed to be flitting off in a hurry, or she was so engrossed in a conversation with someone else that she did not notice him. Initially, Sam was disappointed but had thought nothing of it until he saw her cross the street when she caught sight of him yesterday. Dread had sunk to the bottom of Sam's stomach, clearly, she was avoiding him and of course, he knew why. He had been kicking himself since their encounter last week. *What was wrong with him?!*

And suddenly he was captured by a whirlwind of memories.

Five-year-old Sam ran along the grass, giggling in glee. His best friend James ran behind him trying to catch him in their deadly serious game of tag. Suddenly Sam heard a cry behind him and turned to see James on the concrete, bawling, hands and knees grazed, bleeding. Sam bent down, put his arm around James and walked him to the nurse's office.

Thirteen-year-old Sam walked into high school on his first day, all nerves, a growth spurt over summer had made him look lanky and painfully awkward. His ears on the large side, he looked like Roald Dahl's BFG.

Sam opened his locker and nodded at James who walked past him, they weren't best friends anymore but they still hung out now and then.

The first period was English, his favourite. Naturally, when the teacher asked how they had managed with their summer reading list Sam eagerly explained how he had languished in Of Mice and Men, been moved by To Kill A Mockingbird but had found Oliver Twist to be painfully slow.

'Teacher's pet!' Peter, the most popular boy at school had shouted.

After school, Peter and his friends cornered Sam, threw his books into the dirt and shoved him to the ground with a couple of kicks for good measure. Sam began to cry but that only made them kick him harder.

'Wimp.' 'Sissy.' 'Little girl,' they said.

In that second Sam realised one thing, he could never cry at school again. The next day he signed up for every sport his school offered. He stayed after school, learned to lift weights, ate until he was almost sick and never lifted his hand in English again. Soon he made the Varsity Basketball team and his weekends were filled with an endless array of parties. Girls, even the seniors now smiled at him, stopped to talk to him in the hallway. Touched his arm. Crawled onto his lap at parties. Now everyone respected him, especially Peter.

Seventeen-year-old Sam loved his girlfriend, Sarah, not that he ever told her that. Every weekend Sam got drunk, not much, but enough, enough to be numb, enough to not have to feel the things, big and small that tore him apart slowly every day. Every damn day. Sometimes it would be something as simple as failing a test, other times it would be Charlotte calling him in tears because the girls at school had laughed at her in class. And then there was the news that James had ended *his life, he refused to leave his room for almost a week after that.*

'Just tell me what's wrong.' Sarah would ask, beg, her eyes filled with tears of frustration.

But Sam just shrugged. How could he begin to explain how he felt inside? How he wanted to collapse, to crumble so badly. How sometimes getting out of bed seemed a herculean task. He couldn't. He had to be strong. And so his life became an endless array of silences, of too loud Basketball and Football games, alcohol, more and more alcohol and a ringing phone that he never picked up. Eventually, his phone stopped ringing. Everyone stopped calling. Even Sarah.

Returning to the present Sam admitted to himself that he had never been great at talking about how he felt, and although he was getting better, he still wasn't great at it. But he knew he *had* to apologise to Laylah, he had to make things right.

. . .

What seemed like hours later the speaker finally wrapped up and they were free. Sam walked into the courtyard and spotted Nikau who waved at him. Sam walked over and pulled Nikau into a one-armed hug before they quickly found a shady table to have lunch.

Taking a bite from his 90% avocado, 10% chicken wrap Nikau asked. 'Do you have any plans for the long weekend?'

Sam shook his head.

'Well Dad doesn't need me, the weather is still amazing, how about we go camping?' Nikau asked. 'We could head to the Routeburn track, it's a few hours drive but if we leave on Friday afternoon we will have plenty of time.'

Sam smiled. 'I haven't seen much of the country so I am up for anything.'

'Awesome, we can take my car so that's easy.' said Nikau and then paused before adding with a grin. 'Do you want to see if Ariana and Laylah are free?'

Sam was silent for a moment as he thought this over, Laylah was avoiding him, he knew that much, perhaps he could apologise in some way during this trip? Perhaps he could make her see that he was not rude, just insufferably shy...that is if she agreed to come.

'Why not?' He finally responded.

'Great! I will give Ariana a call now, Laylah never picks up.' Nikau said rolling his eyes as he found Ariana in his list of contacts.

Five minutes later everything was confirmed, Laylah, Ariana, Nikau and himself were going camping this weekend. He still had a hellish week to get through, then a load of packing and then of course he would have to face Laylah. Sam was nervous but also excited, very, very excited. Hopefully, he wouldn't screw things up.

Chapter Nine

Laylah: Silver Linings

p   ain,
never ending. a throb in the face of screaming.
a   pathy.
oh, is there a worse shame? than to love and face the
t   error of not being loved in return?
easy to say that these emotions should stop,
h   ard to enact
for actions, actions are always harder for the
e   xception. you are the exception.
i wish to be at peace with decisions from
t   he almighty above.
but these emotions are hard, they are
i   ntricate.
love, so completely and utterly,
c   omplex.

The assignments were beginning to pile in, but Laylah's meticulous nature and passion for learning meant she was keeping on top of it all reasonably well.

Naturally, Laylah had finished her paper on the United Nations but she was also throwing herself into her poetry assignment. It was funny how Sam ignoring her had inspired so much emotion, frustration, anger and eventually she admitted to herself, hurt. She was hurt and that certainly wasn't fun, but it also inspired her to write, poems seeped out of her in a way they hadn't for years. *Silver linings.* Laylah though. Silver linings that she needed because although she was hurt for some reason she couldn't talk to Ariana about what had happened.

She just couldn't

Her ego could not acknowledge the rejection but she also had no idea why it hurt so much in the first place. So instead she wrote. So instead she avoided Sam like the plague. So instead she threw herself into work and university like never before. All the while Sam did not leave her thoughts for more than a few moments. Naturally.

Laylah shook her head, trying to dislodge him from her mind but he was like pixie dust, no matter where she went, no matter what she did, he was always there, catching the light in the most unexpected moments. In the most unexpected ways. She sighed and shook her head once more, glancing down at her watch she decided she had time to pop home for lunch before her afternoon classes. A good thing really because after the training session she had this afternoon the peanut butter and jam sandwich she had made for herself was just not going to cut it.

Laylah headed home, trying to enjoy the caress of the sun, the last few days of summer on her skin as Adele's soulful voice rose and fell, swelled and collapsed in her headphones, in a way that was not that different to Laylah's own emotions.

It didn't take long for Laylah to reach her house. Allowing herself only a glance across the road she unlocked her door as quickly as possible. With a sigh of relief, she closed the door, her heart lifting as she heard Ariana rummaging around the kitchen. It was so nice when their schedules accidentally overlapped like this.

'Hey, Laylah! How is your day going?' Ariana asked as she carefully chopped an tomato into equal pieces. Today her hair swept up in a sky blue headscarf turban speckled with sunflowers.

'Pretty good, I just finished from the gym. What have you been doing?'

'Honestly, sleeping. Thank god yesterday was the last of my night shifts, I feel like I haven't seen you or anyone else for that matter in so long!' Ariana exclaimed, now moving on to cucumbers.

Laylah nodded. 'I feel like I haven't talked to you properly in ages! But you are enjoying your ward placement?'

'Definitely, the paediatrics ward can be a bit tough emotionally, so many of those little ones are really unwell, but it's rewarding.' Ariana responded strips of capsicum now being produced. 'Like today, I had a little girl called Zara, and while I was prepping her for an injection she was telling me all about how her favourite colour is pink and how she loves penguins. When I had to finally do the injection, she was so brave, she squeezed her mum's hand and just breathed. Then she chose a fairy sticker!' Ariana exclaimed.

'That is adorable.' Laylah sighed.

'Oh before I forget, you aren't busy this weekend right?' Ariana enquired.

Laylah paused her brow furrowed in thought for a moment. 'Hmm, no I don't think I have plans, I was just going to relax around here but I am open to doing something.'

'Well, actually Nikau called and asked if we wanted to do the Routeburn Track this weekend?' Ariana asked.

'That sounds like fun!' Laylah responded before immediately realising that Sam would be there.

'Perfect, I will give him a call and confirm everything. I am so excited!' Ariana smiled, now adding rice to a bowl before she tossed everything together in delicious maple syrup and soy sauce concoction, making sure that not a grain of rice dropped onto the counter.

'Me too.' Laylah responded, trying to inject excitement into her voice and hide the dread that had filled her heart. There was no way she could avoid Sam in the five-hour car ride or the two days of tramping. Laylah sighed internally, why hadn't she been smart enough to make up an excuse, to go home? But it was too late now and Ariana was so excited, she needed a break, she had been working so hard.

'Good! And this will also give you a bit more one on one time with Sam.' Ariana winked, giving her a gentle hip bump as she wiped the non-existent crumbs off the counter and sat down at the table with her enormous bowl.

Laylah joined her after throwing together a similar but much messier bowl with lots of avocados. Laylah was caught in a love affair of sorts with avocados which thankfully Nikau's father was gracious enough to provide, basically for free. 'I guess...' Laylah trailed and luckily Ariana was so excited that she didn't notice the edge in her voice.

Lunch came and went as Ariana chatted about the hospital, the children, the stickers they chose and of course what she was going to pack for this weekend, for example, *would she need a jumper?* In the South Island? Yes. The answer was always yes to layers.

Laylah chuckled to herself, it was funny, people thought Ariana was the quiet one. She was an introvert true, but once you got to know her, quiet was not the word Laylah would use. Since Laylah could be a bit of a talker herself, this was one of her favourite things about Ariana. Conversations just flowed. But today Laylah held back, she was also thinking about the camping trip, specifically, she was trying to think about how to deal with Sam. By the end of lunch Laylah had made a decision, she would be nice, of course, but she would keep her distance, only talk to him when it was necessary. That probably wouldn't be too difficult Laylah mused, he didn't talk much anyway.

Lunch finished, they washed up and headed out, Laylah to her international politics lecture and Ariana to the library to revise the latest round of drugs that she hard to learn.

Memorising drug names Laylah shuddered. She didn't know how Ariana did it.

Chapter Ten

Sam: Strokes of a Paintbrush

The plan was set. Sam finished work at 1:00 pm, he would go home, shower and finish packing. Then at 3:00 pm on the dot Nikau was coming around to pick them all up. For now, Sam was trying and notably failing to restrain his excitement as he finished marking one last lab report.

Alice sat next to him, ticking and crossing fervently with her pink sharpie as she sang along to the eccentric playlist she had chosen. Ed Sheeran. Kendrick Lamar. Taylor Swift. 'So are you all packed for the weekend, Sam?' Alice asked as she circled a giant 20 out of 30.

'Almost, but I have plenty of time to finish up before Nikau comes to pick us up. You should come!' Sam exclaimed.

Alice laughed and waved her hand over her perfect foundation, angled cheekbones, perfectly sculpted eyebrows, flawless eyeliner and spotless red lipstick. '*This* doesn't do camping. Anyway, Dee and I are visiting her parents in Wellington.'

'That sounds nice.' Sam said, secretly in complete agreement about her camping potential. Sam had never seen Alice not perfectly made up, in fact, he was sure she would wear heels to the lab if it wasn't a health and safety hazard.

The morning sped by and soon they finished the last of the marking. It had taken Sam a bit longer than usual, his wandering mind meant that he had to recount more than one total. He was nervous he admitted to himself about the prospect of seeing Laylah who still hadn't talked to him since that day. If he was honest with himself he was surprised that she had agreed to come at all. Surprised but also over the moon.

Finally finished Sam sighed with relief, put the papers away safely, hugged Alice goodbye and sped home. He unlocked the door and stepped into the cave that was the living room, windows closed, curtains drawn, George lay sprawled on the couch, surrounded by beer bottles, blissfully asleep in the gloom. Sam frowned in concern and as quietly as possible collected the beer bottles to put them in the recycling bin before spreading a comforter over Georges sleeping body. Then and there he decided he needed to speak to George, needed to make sure he was okay.

Trying not to let his concern dampen his spirits too much Sam hopped into the shower and then finished packing, checking then rechecking his list meticulously. Once he was satisfied he hadn't missed anything essential like socks or underwear Sam stood in front of the mirror and assessed himself. His grey shorts sat just above his knees, his blue t-shirt fit snuggly, but not too snuggly and his hair seemed to be cooperating for the moment. Sam shook his head, bemused, he had never cared this much about his appearance but of course, he knew why it mattered so much today.

A gentle knock on the door pulled him out of his thoughts. 'Yes?'

George slowly opened the door, squinting as he entered Sam's sun-soaked room.

'Did you clean up and...' He gestured at the comforter that was still wrapped around his shoulders.

Sam nodded, zipping up his backpack.

'Thank you so much man,' he nodded, sincerity painted on his face.

Sam shrugged. 'Don't even mention it.'

'Where are you off to?' George asked his curiosity sparked by Sam's massive bag teetering on the bed.

Sam looked up. 'The Routeburn track with some friends.' Sam paused and at that moment made up his mind. 'You should come.'

Surprise flooded Georges pale face. 'Me? Oh, thanks, man, I totally would but one of my boys has his 21st this weekend and you know how it is,' he shrugged.

Sam frowned and gestured for George to take a seat next to him. 'George, I know we don't know each other that well yet and maybe I am overstepping, but are you doing okay?'

'Okay?'

'Yes, with school, I mean university, your family?'

George's eyes met his, and for a moment Sam saw a flash of something – pain? Felt as though George was on the brink of telling him something. But the moment passed as quickly as it came and George shrugged. 'Of course. Everything is fine.'

Sam nodded slowly. 'Tell me about your family.'

'Not much to tell, they live in Auckland, Mum is an environmental engineer, she works for the council and will bust my balls if I don't put things in the right recycling bin.

Dad is an ophthalmologist, he isn't around much and then there is me. A perfect family.' George said with a small smile but Sam hadn't missed the undertone of bitterness, barely concealed. 'Oh and Newt, my dog.' George added, his face breaking into a real smile now, eyes shining.

'Newt, as in Newt Scamander?' Sam chuckled.

George nodded. 'I am a Harry Potter fanatic, to be honest, a bit of a theatre fanatic too.'

'Why are you studying business then? Why not English? Why not Drama?'

'*Yeah, na.* I love movies but I don't have the patience to be a writer or the talent to be an actor. What I would really love to do nursing.'

'Nursing?' Sam raised his eyebrows in surprise.

George nodded. 'But dad...' He sighed heavily. 'Dad thinks that if you are a bloke and you become a nurse you are a bit of a wanker.'

Sam frowned. 'A wanker...what?'

'It means weakling...you know, not a man.' George explained.

'But your dad works with nurses all day, I am sure that includes male nurses!' Sam exclaimed in exasperation.

George shrugged. 'He is old fashioned.'

Sam sighed. 'Well, I think if you want to do nursing you should do nursing. I am sure you would be great at it.'

George looked at him seriously. 'Thanks, man.'

Sam nodded and glanced at his watch. 'I should head off, are you sure you don't want to come?'

'Next time.' George grinned and slapped his arm affectionately. 'Have a good weekend and we should grab a drink when you get back.'

Sam grinned and picked up his backpack. 'Definitely.'

Strolling across the road Sam's heart was warm, light. But all the warmth, all the light was quickly seeped out and was replaced with nerves as he stood outside the white door of the Laylah and Ariana's house. His eyes scanned the cracks of the wooden surface, taking in every detail as he attempted to articulate his thoughts, what he would say, how he would explain himself to Laylah. Questions that below the surface had plagued him for the last few days.

But his decision was made for him when the door opened and a small person walked straight into him. Laylah. Of course.

Sam automatically reached an arm out to steady her but she pulled away, quickly. Sam grimaced internally but fought through the pit of snakes in his stomach and forced himself to smile. 'Hey! Sorry I was just about to see if you two were ready.'

As her scent enveloped him, wisps of Jasmine wafting through the air Sam realised that this was as close as he had been to her in over a week. She was as beautiful as ever, her long red hair pinned so it flowed down her back like the ripples of a flame. She was dressed in a black singlet with high waisted shorts embellished in tiny flowers that showed off her legs. But as she looked up at him with those cocoa eyes of hers Sam noticed how tired she looked, wary. Those eyes didn't look anything like the eyes he had gotten to know. 'That's okay, I was just running out to grab a few last-minute things.' Laylah responded coolly.

'Oh, do you need a hand...' Sam started.

But Laylah had already walked away calling. 'No that's fine,' over her shoulder.

Luckily Ariana came to the door at that exact moment and invited Sam in. Ariana's midnight hair was unrestrained today, flowing down her back as she immediately ushered Sam to the couch, promising a cup of tea. Tea was the solution for everything in Ariana's book, it certainly helped when someone was distraught.

Moments later she returned with two steaming cups of chamomile tea and took a seat beside him.

'Are you okay? What's happening between you two?' Ariana asked.

'I am fine...we are fine, I think...' Sam started.

Ariana shook her head. 'Sam, I am Laylah's best friend and that wasn't a *fine* interaction, trust me. Laylah is never that cold without a reason. Never. Tell me, maybe I can help.'

Sam paused as he thought things over. 'Well...Laylah has been kind of avoiding me recently, she doesn't talk to me when she sees me and I even saw her cross the road when she saw me the other day, I don't think she realised that I noticed. But I did.' Sam explained. The hurt that he had been holding back for so long now colouring his voice.

'Why?'

'I think it's because Nikau and I saw her at the gym a couple of weeks ago and...I guess I kind of ignored her, it was the night after I had dinner at yours...' Sam trailed off.

'What? Why?' Ariana asked confused.

'Honestly, I didn't mean to...I am such an idiot!' Sam said. Placing his head in his hands he laced his long fingers in his hair and yanked in frustration.

Ariana placed a hand on his shoulder comfortingly but waited, her nursing instincts kicking in she knew he would speak when he was ready.

Finally, Sam lifted his head, his striking eyes crinkled in concern, his brow furrowed. 'I just didn't know what to say.

I am not the best at starting conversations, it takes me a while to talk to people sometimes and with Laylah it can be even harder because...' Sam stopped, unsure how to finish that sentence.

'You have feelings for her.' Ariana finished for him.

Sam looked incredulous.

'Trust me, it's obvious to everyone *but* her and honestly, I thought...' Ariana paused. 'I *think* she likes you too. But Laylah can be quite guarded with her feelings, it takes her time to like someone and unfortunately, that incident at the gym wouldn't have helped.' Ariana sighed.

Sam pushed aside the possibility that Laylah might like him, knowing he would over-analyse that later and tried to focus on what Ariana was saying, her openness allowing him to speak, to feel more freely. 'Have I ruined everything? Honestly, I wanted to say something...but she was so intimidating at the gym.'

'Ah Laylah in yoga pants next to a squat rack, yeah that would disarm anyone, to be honest.'

Sam felt his face colour, but didn't protest, she wasn't wrong.

'Okay listen, Laylah is kind, really kind and there is something between you two. You just need a chance to patch things up so that she understands that you didn't mean to be so aloof. How about this, I will sit up front and you two can sit in the back on the drive?' Ariana proposed.

'Perfect!' Sam responded hope re-entering his voice.

'Good, but you *have* to talk okay. None of this shy business, she doesn't bite I promise and if you get her started on food, the gym, politics, feminism...she won't stop, even if you want her to.' Ariana laughed and grabbed the now-empty mugs, which she promptly washed, dried and put away.

Five minutes later Sam and Ariana were engrossed in a conversation about religion as Sam learned of her surprising heritage, she was the definition of a melting pot.

They looked up as the door opened and Laylah walked in, with two reusable bags full to bursting.

Ariana grinned at her. 'What on earth is that?'

'Snacks!' Laylah protested defensively as she half walked, half waddled into the kitchen.

Sam stood and rushed to take the bags off her but she simply ignored him and placed them on the floor. Thrown off but determined Sam ploughed on. 'What did you get?'

Not meeting his eye Laylah dismissively answered. 'Apples, bananas, blueberries and some almonds. Chocolate too.'

'Laylah cannot live without her blueberries.' Ariana joked as she stood to join them.

'I love blueberries too!' Sam said.

They are amazing...' Laylah responded, her voice softening a fraction.

Okay, blueberries would help to win her over Sam thought and added that to his arsenal.

A moment later Nikau arrived and they all hoisted the luggage and food into the car. Laylah clearly wasn't pleased about being in the back seat with Sam but didn't refuse. A victory.

Soon they were off, but even the music blasting in the background and the spectacular scenery could not distract Sam from the way Laylah was sitting. Her, body language not encouraging in the slightest as she sat with her body angled away from him, arms crossed, staring intently out the window. Sam cursed himself again as his mind went to the night of the dinner party, her body language then compared to now was night and day. But Sam was determined. Food, Ariana had said, food was a good conversation.

'So Laylah, blueberries? Do you like them fresh, frozen?' He asked internally wincing at the awkwardness of the question. *Blueberries, seriously? This was the gouda conversation from She's The Man all over again.* But at least this seemed to catch her attention.

Laylah turned to him, raised her brow and although her arms remained crossed she responded. 'Both, they are good with pancakes.'

'Have you ever been blueberry picking?'

Laylah shook her head, her voice softening even more. 'No, but one day, I hear Canada is the place to be for that.'

'Definitely, one of my aunts lives in Canada, we have spent many Summers picking blueberries. Usually, I can barely move afterwards.' Sam confided with a smile.

'That sounds like bliss,' she chuckled.

Sam nodded before launching into follow-up questions. 'Any other fruit?'

So they talked about fruit, then chocolate, then ice cream. She liked anything that wasn't Hokey Pokey or Sorbet while Sam admitted he didn't know what Hockey Pokey was to the horror of Nikau in the front seat.

The plan was to ask questions so fast that he wouldn't have the time to become anxious and hopefully Laylah would respond. It seemed to be working. Although Laylah still sat in the corner of her car, she was softening and finally uncrossed her arms as laughing they are argued about raisins. Laylah thought they were a waste of space. Sam argued that they were pretty good in trail mix.

Sam caught Ariana's eye in the mirror at one stage and she nodded encouragement at him engrossed in her conversation with Nikau about what the best route was and which Ed Sheeran song they should play next.

As the sun began to set, darkness steadily blossoming, they decided to stop at an Indian restaurant for dinner. Their waiter, a young pimply teenager, showed them to their table which was covered in a emerald cloth, sparkling plates and cutlery. The waiter handed out four menus and ran them through the specials.

Laylah skimmed through her menu and within ten seconds set it aside. 'Dhal.'

Sam looked at her incredulously but she simply shrugged. 'I am a creature of habit.'

Not long after Ariana and Nikau had also decided on the spiciest Tikka Masala they had.

Finally after a full five minutes, of going through the menu, twice and asking the waiter several questions, Sam decided on a spicy Vegetable Korma. Everyone grinned at him and now it was his turn to shrug defensively. 'I need to evaluate my options!'

The food arrived quickly which was good because they were all famished. Sam inhaled the scent of the array of spices wafting towards him. Turmeric and Garam Masala, definitely. Coriander, probably. Maybe some Cayenne Pepper?

Swapping dishes and eating off each other's plates, they ate quickly, their conversation evolving and mutating, injected with the laughter and ease inherent in good friendships.

'So I hear there is quite a nightlife here.' Sam asked.

Nikau nodded. 'Definitely, the first years can go a bit crazy. I wouldn't say any of us here are hugely into that scene, but I am sure we can think of a few places to take you...Ariana?'

'Don't worry, I know all of the good spots for dancing, and not a single first year in sight.'

They all laughed.

Soon dinner was over, Sam nonchalantly commenting that it was *nice* but not as nice as Laylah's cooking. A look of surprise flooded her face and Sam was willing to bet his favourite sneakers on the fact that he saw a hint of a smile. Sam ticked that off in his head, *food compliments were good*.

They split the bill and wandered outside, Ariana and Nikau stood next to the car, inspecting the map on their phone, Ariana offering to take over if Nikau was tired. Meanwhile, Laylah had drifted away to the edge of the hill where they were parked. She leaned against the fence of a farm, looked out beyond the rolling green hills and watched the pink of the sunset as the breeze ruffled the grass.

Sam joined her, 'Beautiful,' he sighed.

Laylah's eyes never left the sun which was travelling down the sky at a surprisingly rapid rate, she nodded. 'I know its cliché, but I love the sunset, how the sky blushes. Ariana has explained the science behind it to me so many times but honestly, how can the sun moving make the sky look so beautiful?'

Sam could also think of a textbook answer to that question, but was too entranced by the beauty around him. The sky. Laylah. *That* was something science could not explain.

A moment passed and the sky changed again, purple hues now entering the canvas. Laylah sighed in appreciation, waving her hand at the horizon. 'All the colours, look at how they mix. And then there are the clouds, they are like the strokes of a paintbrush. And you know the best part? Every day it's different. A new painting. If this isn't proof of God I don't know what is,' she paused. 'Now you are going to think I am mad.'

'Not at all, remember you are talking to the person who has dedicated his life, and thousands of dollars he doesn't have to study the sky,' he grinned.

Laylah's laugh filled the dusky air around them.

'And you know that was pretty poetic for someone who claims they struggle with poetry.' Sam teased wanting to hear that laugh again.

Laylah turned to him, surprise lit her eyes. 'You remembered?'

'Of course.' Sam nodded, Laylah didn't realise that he remembered everything from that night.

They stood in silence for a few moments more, Laylah transfixed with the sunset, Sam transfixed with her, how the sun hit her face and lit up her hair, she looked like she was on fire.

She *was* fire.

His gut clenched but in that instant, he decided that he had to explain himself, he had to apologise. 'Laylah...can we talk? You know when Nikau and I saw you at the gym?' He started.

Laylah turned to him once more but this time her face had fallen.

Sam hurried on before he lost his nerve. 'I am sorry for being so reserved, I honestly don't mean too, it's just me, I am quiet by nature and terrible at initiating conversations, especially when the person is new.' Sam paused, forcing himself to meet her eye.

But Laylah stood, silent, her face expressionless, her warm cocoa eyes, coals.

'I am not always good at talking about how I feel, at showing people I care and I know we haven't known each other long, heck, we have had two conversations? But I know you are important.' Sam paused again. 'I know that's no excuse but it's the truth and I am so sorry...god I am just rambling now aren't I...' He finished.

Silence.

His eyes dropped to the ground. He had just bared his soul but it wasn't enough, it was too late. Or maybe Ariana was wrong and she didn't care at all. God now what would she think of him?

But then Sam felt the warmth of her hand on his arm and looked up to meet her eyes once more, this time they had melted, cocoa once more, yet they still pierced him, filled him with emotions, with warmth.

'Thank you for telling me Sam,' she paused and Sam remained silent, knowing she wanted to say more. 'I don't mind the fact that you are quiet, I like it actually,' she bit her lip. 'But if there is something wrong, you need to tell me, to talk to me, I cannot read minds and I am a *master* overthinker. I make assumptions, I get anxious. I know I should have given you the benefit of the doubt, not taken this so personally. I am sorry that's my fault,' she admitted, biting her lip. 'But sometimes, sometimes silence screams, especially...especially if you care about the person,' she finished, her eyes saying so much more.

Sam nodded, and as if by some magnetism, a language all of their own, he knew everything was okay. Better than okay in fact.

'Communication right?' Sam said, lightening the mood with a chuckle.

'It's a nightmare,' she smiled, rolling her eyes.

Without thinking he reached over and took her hand in his, tracing small circles gently while they stood for what seemed like an eternity just the two of them as the sun came down. Him squeezing Laylah's hand and her squeezing right back. Sam was enveloped in peace, calm and joy. Feelings that had been missing from his life for so long had returned. Settled. Dew on a spring day after a long winter of frost.

Eventually, they were interrupted by Ariana and Nikau, Sam dodged Nikau's teasing eyes as Ariana slid into the driver's seat, he and Laylah slid into the back again.

The rest of the drive was uneventful but perfect. The scenery was beautiful. The music was fantastic. And as he sang along, in a truly, horribly out of pitch voice, a sense excitement washed over Sam once more, this was going to be a good weekend.

Chapter Eleven

Laylah: Dulce Et Decorum Est

                you see, even though
                red and white,
                blue speckled with stars
                does not run through
                these veins,
this   still scars me.

                for when my insides ache
                with the moon
                as this body cries for a child,
                red. dripping. i see life,
                but i also see death.
                for good or evil,
is   there really a difference anymore?

                i should be numb to this,
                for doesn't
america(?) looks the other way
                as my own people die?

but i cannot,
for men, women and children,
are robbed of life,
while leaders preach liberty
white canes in hand, stuck in centrifuge.
are they too blind to see that these
innocents, whose faces are painted
on the news – they are you
they are me, they are humanity.

They arrived at the campsite and were met by darkness, the sun had already disappeared, the stars twinkling quietly in its place. They set up their tents, one for Nikau and Sam, the other for Laylah and Ariana before exhausted they settled in for the night.

'Laylah?' Ariana whispered once they were lying in their sleeping bags.

'Yes?'

'Are you and Sam okay?' Ariana asked.

Laylah paused thinking for a moment, she understood Sam a little more now, knew where he was coming from. Laylah's degree had forced her to examine the treatment of women, the social expectations placed on them and how it had shaped them. How it had led to thousands of years of abuse. *Thousands.*

Sometimes it was easy to hate men.

But she had also examined the social expectations placed on men and although the patriarchy dealt them a kinder hand it was still poor. That's the thing about the patriarchy, ultimately everyone lost. Laylah could always go to Ariana, Ayat or even *Mama* when things were hard. But if she was honest with herself she had never seen the men in her life be vulnerable.

Her older brother, Yousuf? People thought *she* was fiery until they met him, he was the definition of fire and although he had the kindest heart any emotion that was deemed weak and thus unacceptable? It became ablaze.

Then Laylah thought of *Baba* who had played the role of the strong silent type her whole life, never showing a moment's weakness or fear, never being sad. And although it balanced her mother nicely, even as a teenager Laylah remembered thinking that surely he felt these emotions, everyone did. But it was almost as if her brother and father weren't allowed to *feel*. Her brother didn't, he turned his emotions into anger. *Baba* turned them into silence. And Sam? He was like *Baba*.

True, it wasn't an excuse, he had no reason to be shy around her, she wasn't scary or unfriendly. Or at least she hoped she wasn't. But he had opened up, he had explained himself, his apologetic smile and brilliant eyes, an avalanche, crumbling every single one of her walls.

Sky blue.

Ultimately she respected him for having the guts, to be honest with her and had decided to start afresh. A new leaf. Laylah also meekly admitted to herself that she had no right to be mad at him, even if he was ignoring her, they barely knew each other and he didn't owe her anything.

'Laylah?' Ariana called pulling her out of wandering thoughts.

'Yes, yes we are.' Laylah replied with a smile.

'Good.' Ariana responded smugly, joyfully before promptly rolling over in exhaustion.

It took Laylah longer to fall asleep that night, her thoughts straying to Sam like a boomerang. And when she eventually did? He followed her to the land of dreams.

. . .

The next day Laylah woke to the first rays of the sun shining through the tent, casting a golden light on everything it touched. Ariana was still sound asleep beside her so Laylah lay in her sleeping bag for a few moments, lost in thought. Now that she and Sam were in a better place her excitement for the weekend had arrived with vigour and she couldn't wait to set out.

It didn't take long for her to become restless and hungry so as quietly as she could Laylah unzipped their tent, allowing the brisk fresh mountain air to caress her face. Just as carefully she exited the tent, zipped it back up, turned towards the sunrise and promptly walked into Sam.

'Yelp!'

Sam's hands caught her, his eyes crinkling in concern. 'Are you okay?' He mouthed.

Laylah nodded and they stood for a moment, making sure they hadn't woken Nikau or Ariana, but neither tent stirred. Ariana could sleep through a thunderstorm and it seemed like Nikau was no different.

Laylah gestured for Sam to follow her, and carefully they wandered away from the tents and began making breakfast in silence which Laylah was thankful for, it always took her at least half an hour to become human in the morning, chatting was definitely off the agenda.

Laylah glanced at the sky as they worked. The sun rose and rapidly warmed the air, painting the sky with vibrant purples and hints of soft pink, before eventually settling on blue. Laylah inhaled the crisp morning air once more, it was going to be a beautiful day.

Sam laid out empty bowls, a bag of muesli, a couple of punnets of blueberries as well as an unopened Oat Milk carton while Laylah with a grin of satisfaction lit their little gas oven. The tiny blue flames danced as she poured water into a little pot and by the time she added a few spoonfuls of heady smelling coffee the water was also beginning to dance, to writhe. Soon the smell of the coffee was intoxicating.

'SHIT!'

The sound filled the silence around them causing Laylah to turn her head so fast she cracked her neck. 'Are you okay?' She asked watching a sheet white Sam back away from a seemingly innocuous bag.

Laylah strode over, and at the cue of his shaky finger pulled up the flap of the bag to find...a spider. A large spider. But a spider.

Laylah looked up at Sam, trying to hide her amusement at this six-foot human being, so shaken by a creature that could do him no harm.

Laylah squatted down and gently laid her hand near the spider and waited. Slowly, ever so slowly, it scuttled onto her hand, its tiny legs, a whisper, the gentlest of caresses. Again, slowly, careful not to disturb it she rose. Out of the corner of her eye, she saw Sam immediately backing away from her, if possible, turning even paler than before. Laylah grinned to herself and walked a fair distance from their campsite before she found a suitable shrub. Squatting down once more, she rested her hand on the dirt and waited for the spider to scuttle off into the shade of the shrub which would provide some relief from what was going to be another very warm day.

By the time she returned Ariana and Nikau were up, roused by the commotion. 'What on earth happened, who was murdered?!' Nikau demanded, hair awry, lids still heavy with sleep.

'Oh, that was just me.' Laylah said nonchalantly. 'I thought I saw a mouse. Breakfast is ready by the way,' she nodded brightly at the spread.

Ariana and Nikau looked at her sceptically, but clearly, both were still half asleep, and the smell of the coffee was now too intoxicating to resist.

Sam sat next to Laylah, still looking slightly paler than usual, and in the clatter of bowls and spoons muttered. 'Thanks.'

'Spiders?!' Laylah smirked meeting his eyes.

Sky blue.

'Eight legs!' He protested causing Ariana and Nikau to glance up again.

Laylah simply laughed, handing him a cup of coffee. 'I am quite scared of mice, so next time you can rescue me,' she mumbled under her breath with a smile and finally, he smiled back, a little colour returning to his face.

'We better get cracking.' Nikau said once everyone was fed and awake. Standing he stretched his arms above his head and began packing efficiently, rapidly. They all followed suit and soon they were on the trail.

With seamless ease, they walked, at times consumed by conversation, in pairs or as a group, but mostly in silence, the beauty of the mountains and trees having stolen their breath away. Stolen their voice in the way that nature sometimes did. It demanded silence, demanded awe.

Religion came up, of course. 'So okay, Ariana has tried to explain this to me, but I still don't understand. If Jesus is the son of God, who do you pray to? Why Jesus and not God? Or why God and not Jesus? And how does the Holy Spirit fit into this?' Laylah asked Sam, hoping to gain some insight into the complexities of his religion.

Sam paused, taking his time to order and articulate his thoughts. 'Well, different groups of Christianity believe slightly different things but the church I grew up in described Jesus as God in human form and the Holy Spirit is like another dimension. Kind of like the soul of a human being.'

Laylah wrinkled her brow in concentration and looked up at Sam. 'Wait so you *do* believe in one God, so Jesus and God are not two different entities?'

'Yes...and no. I don't completely understand it myself.' Sam admitted.

'That is so interesting.' Laylah responded adding his answer to the myriad she had received from Christians.

Sam looked down, met her eyes and with a glimmer of shame in his voice asked. 'I realised the other day that I don't know anything about Islam, how do you view the whole Jesus-God paradigm? Wait do you even believe in Jesus?' Sam asked backtracking in confusion.

Laylah laughed, unsurprised. 'Don't worry, I don't think most people understand Islam, sometimes I am not sure how much Muslims themselves understand it.' Laylah shrugged. 'We believe in Jesus, I think our stories about the early parts of his life at least are almost identical to Christianity, but we believe that he was a prophet, like Adam, like Muhammad, like Moses. Jesus was sent down to spread the message of God. We also do believe that he was crucified, but that didn't die.' Laylah explained.

'What do you think happened?' Sam asked, his brow crinkling in thoughtfulness once more.

'We believe that the man that was crucified was a man that looked very similar to Jesus. A doppelganger if you will. But that Jesus himself was taken up into the heavens and that when we approach the day of judgment Jesus will return with Gods message one final time.' Laylah explained wincing internally, anytime she had explained this to her atheist friend's she had been met with confusion and disbelief as if she had just announced that she had received her Hogwarts letter or that Unicorns did in fact exist. She didn't blame them, it sounded like a children's fairy tale. But Sam? Sam nodded, his eyes lost in thought.

Sky blue.

'And how do you view God? What is God in Islam?'

'God? God is complicated.' Laylah said.

'What do you mean?' Sam asked.

'Well, for one thing, God or *Allah* as we call Him has 99 names.' Laylah said.

'99?'

'Yes, 99. God is fair, kind and loving. God is the one and only judge, He is patient. God is all of these things and so much more.' Laylah responded.

'That's incredible.' Sam said.

Laylah nodded. 'Actually, if you look at your palm...' Hesitantly she reached her hand out and once Sam realised what she wanted, he obliged, placing his hands in hers. Like a book, she turned them, enormous in her own, so that they faced the heavens. 'This is the number 18 in Arabic,' she traced on his right palm. 'And this is the number 81,' she traced on his left. 'Together...'

'Together they make 99, the 99 names of God.' Sam finished in awe.

'Exactly.' Laylah said. 'I like to think it's like we all have a little bit of *Allah* in us, that we all carry Him in our hands and our hearts.'

'That is amazing.' Sam said, his eyes shining.

Sky blue.

'Can I ask a personal question? You don't have to answer if you don't want to.' Sam asked, brow crinkled.

'Go for it.'

'Why don't you wear, um...goodness, is it called a headscarf?' He fumbled slightly. 'Like Ariana sometimes does.'

'Headscarf, yes, *hijab* is more correct though,' she paused, organising her thoughts. 'I cannot speak for Ariana. The *hijab* is complicated and every woman has a unique relationship to it. There is a lot of pressure for women to wear it. To be honest, there is a lot of pressure on women to do a lot of things, we are religiously and culturally very patriarchal, and group-oriented societies. When I was younger it was simply because I lived in New Zealand, it would have been harder for me at school if I had.'

'Kids can be cruel.'

Laylah nodded before continuing. 'It's hard because I am very liberal and even my parents, by the standards of a lot of more traditional people are quite liberal. My mother doesn't wear it, and only a couple of my aunts do. So I guess it also wasn't an expectation, but as I have become older, I have started to question it, to be honest, to question a lot of rules. Of course, I still support women that do wear it, but we mix culture and religion so freely sometimes that I think we forget they are different things. We read ancient texts with a lens that demands conforming, that demands constraint and naturally, we come to the conclusions we want to come to. A women's sexuality, for example, people just assume that doesn't exist in my culture, it's the biggest taboo.'

'It sounds intense.'

Laylah nodded once more. 'It is. I guess it's easier to view the world in black and white. In absolutes, which is what a lot of conservative Muslims choose to do. But if you don't fit into those moulds it makes life very hard. Would you say that things are quite black and white for you?'

'In the beginning, Christianity had views like this, certainly, some Churches still do, but I also think it has softened. People have realised that the world isn't black and white like you said, but a hundred shades of grey. That every situation, every person is multifaceted, complex.'

Laylah looked up, in awe, it felt like he had plucked the words from her very soul and in that moment, she felt home, in the same way, she felt with her family, in the same way, she felt with Ariana but at the same time, it was a different kind of home, nestled in those eyes.

Sky blue.

The conversation continued, back and forth although as always with religion, no real conclusion was achieved. No one was *right*. No one was *wrong*. But understanding and connection was blossoming and that was arguable more important. The world could do with more understanding, with more connection. As they fell into the peaceful lull of silence once more Laylah could not shake one nagging question, *why would someone as logical as Sam, a physicist, believe in God?*

They continued along, gravel crunching beneath their boots, surrounded by mountains. Ariana and Nikau were well ahead of them and Laylah couldn't help thinking that their speed walking was intentional. A tiny fantail swooping, from tree to tree, just ahead of them made Laylah chuckle. 'Oh, he is so excited.'

Sam's eyes followed her gaze, and he smiled softly and for a moment he looked like he was in a different universe. 'Let's name him, James.'

Laylah glanced up at him and mused. 'James, a bit of a serious name don't you think? What about something like Pip? Or Alice, that bird reminds me an awful lot of Alice,' she laughed.

Sam stayed silent, silent long enough she would have thought he had not heard her except she knew he had. 'It can be James,' she whispered, placing her hand gently on his arm.

He looked down at her, and for a moment, just for a moment, Laylah thought his eyes had become wet, oceans instead of the heavens she had grown accustomed to.

Sky blue.

But the moment passed and he laughed. 'No I agree, that's an Alice for sure.'

...

The day continued to march along and so did they, taking plenty of breaks and marvelling in the beauty all around them. As the sun began to descend once more they made their last stop to set up for the night and make dinner. Ariana and Nikau cooked today, while Laylah and Sam attempted a small fire; anything roasted tasted a million times better after all.

Laylah glanced at Sam as they worked and couldn't help thinking about how everything was so easy with him. How she was slowly, ever so slowly, beginning to understand the chasm that was beneath his silence.

They all stayed up late that night, as they roasted fruit, marshmallows, chocolate, anything they could get their hands on above the flicker, the dance of the orange flame as they talked about everything and anything.

Laylah sat around the fire with her best friend, one of her oldest friends and this new person that had entered her life and was very quickly becoming immensely important. At that moment she felt at peace. This peace filled her and followed her until she drifted to sleep.

BANG!

Startled by the noise, Laylah woke and immediately looked over to check that Ariana was safe. Thankfully she was blissfully unaware and had not even stirred. Ever so slowly Laylah got up, unzipped the tent and cautiously slipped outside.

'Hello, is anyone there?' She whispered out into the pitch-black night.

'Laylah?' A voice responded.

'Sam?' She called and finally saw his tall, broad silhouette as her eyes adapted to the dark.

'Yes it's me,' he said pulling out his phone he turned the torch on and without a word, as if by some silent agreement they walked away from the tents to not wake Nikau and Ariana, unnecessary considering what those two managed to sleep through. Once they were a fair distance from the tents, Sam turned to her and Laylah finally took in his paper-white face, his neat hair and wide eyes, it didn't look like he had been asleep.

'Was that noise you?' Laylah asked.

Sam nodded. 'Sorry, I think I walked into a pot we didn't put away after dinner.'

'Why are you awake? Are you okay?' Laylah furrowed her brow, her voice laced with concern.

'Everything is fine. I just...I, I am just restless and I wanted to go for a walk, stretch my legs.'

Laylah recognised the hesitation in his voice, the sadness that filled his eyes, there was something he wasn't telling her, but she also knew him well enough already to know that he would talk in his own time when he was ready.

'Let's walk then,' she said.

'But don't you want to get back to sleep?' Sam protested.

'No it's fine, I am awake now, and anyway it's a beautiful night.' Laylah responded looking up at a star-kissed night, they had stars in Dunedin but not like this. Nothing like this. Here you had to search for the blackness of the sky in amongst the dim glow of the stars, and now that her pupils had enlarged, adapted to this new environment, she didn't even need the torch to see the mountains in front of them, the rocks behind them, or Sam, most importantly Sam.

They walked in silence and absorbed the beauty, the calm that only night could bring and then as if through a language of energy, one all of their own, so powerful that it needed neither words nor touch, they sat on a boulder. A boulder smoothed by years of wind, rain and snow so perfectly that it had no sharp edges but sloped seamlessly. A chair, designed by a hand above just for the two of them.

A moment of silence passed. 'Laylah, what do you think happens when you die?' Sam asked and for a second he sounded almost haunted.

Laylah frowned at the question but answered. 'Islamically it is believed that as we go through life, we have angels on our shoulders. The angel on our right shoulder counts our good deeds, the angel on our left shoulder, our bad deeds. On the day of judgement depending on which side has greater points, we either go to heaven or hell.'

'I see, what is heaven like? Do you have to be Muslim to enter?' He asked, earnestly, shadows clinging to his face.

'Are you okay Sam?'

'I...I, yes, sorry, I am just curious.'

Laylah didn't know why, but she got a sense he was not telling her everything, but slowly, choosing her words thoughtfully she answered. 'Heaven is exactly as you would imagine it, a beautiful place, filled with the most beautiful things. There is no pain, no suffering there, no one ages and food is plentiful and amazing,' she paused, having conjured a beautiful forest scene, filled with lakes, streams and of course a blueberry bush around every corner.

'That sounds ideal,' he breathed.

Laylah nodded. 'And do you have to be Muslim to get in? I don't think it matters, I think what's in here,' she placed a gentle hand on his chest and felt a pounding heart. 'I think that's what matters. Conservatives and traditionalists will likely lean towards a yes, but no one will say for sure. The decision of what happens when we go on is *Allah's* and *Allah's* alone That at least we all agree is not our place.'

Sam nodded and clasped her hand in his, fingers entwined, she felt the rough parts, the callouses and sores, as well as the soft parts, the very tips of his hands and at that moment she felt safer yet simultaneously more alive than she ever had.

A moment of silence passed and Laylah witnessed it, respected it, knew she had to just hold it.

'I told you about my younger sister, Charlotte but I didn't tell you about my older brother, James.' Sam paused and Laylah let him, knowing that he was about to tell her something important, why he was awake in the middle of the night. 'James died...' Sam's voice broke as he looked out into the distance, up into the heavens.

Laylah enveloped their tangled fingers in her other hand and squeezed them. If she could give him her strength, in a heartbeat, she would.

Sam continued to look at the stars, but he squeezed her hand back and continued, voice shaking. 'James was a high school teacher, he was the bravest, kindest and stupidest person I knew...' Sam chuckled despite the tears that had begun to fall. With his free hand, he swiped them away impatiently. 'Ever since we were kids, he always thought he could save the world. So when a shooter entered his school and he noticed that one of his students was missing...naturally, hero complex alive and well he went looking for the kid. But then...but then he met the shooter and he tried to talk him out of it. It didn't work. Of course. He was shot.' Sam explained. 'James would have been 28 today,' he sobbed, tears now flowing with no restraint as he finally turned to face Laylah.

Laylah looked at him and for once she was lost for words, she knew nothing she could say would take away his pain. So instead she placed her free hand on his tear-sodden cheek and said the only words she knew. 'I cannot imagine what that must have been like for you.'

Sam sniffed, silent, but as he looked down at her in the darkness around them, his eyes said it all.

Midnight blue.

'The gun situation back home is bad, it's out of hand. So many people know someone that has been impacted. Or know someone that knows someone. It's infuriating because if it happens to be someone that is Muslim or a person of colour the uproar is huge, they are immediately labelled a terrorist, but why is that different if the person is white? And most of them are white.' Sam said, his voice filled with sadness and frustration.

'It's horrible, and if it's a Muslim or Arab, I feel so ashamed.' Laylah said, not knowing how she could ever explain.

Sam shook his head and squeezed her hand. 'Don't. This isn't your fault. Christianity is not the Crusades and Islam is not terrorism, I know that. Religions are what people make them.'

Laylah nodded in appreciation and they fell into silence once more. An owl hooted in the distance and their shadows danced under a star-kissed sky that was larger than all of them, larger than they could ever be.

'I think one of the reasons you have become so important to me so quickly, why I felt such a bond with you is because you remind me of James. It's like when I am with you, that hole that he left in my life is not quite so big, not quite so all-consuming.' Sam paused. 'I know I can be quiet sometimes, once James described me as ice...' Sam chuckled. 'And it's true, I know it but you? You are fire and he is...he was fire too. And the two of you thaw me out, you bring me to life.'

'I am glad.' Laylah whispered, holding his hand tightly in both of hers, trying to convey what her words alone would surely fail to. 'You mean a lot to me too.' Laylah said, leaning into him she placed her head on his arm.

Slowly, hesitantly, Sam lifted his arm and wrapped it around Laylah who rested her head on his chest directly over his heart which beat. Fast. Strong. Alive. Laylah could feel Sam's arms tightening around her, tentatively at first but then more firmly as if the world depended on it. As if his life depended on it. They sat under the stars like that for hours, as if the world was made for them. Only them.

Eventually, reluctantly, Sam loosened his grip. 'I don't want to leave, but if we don't go to sleep, we are going to be zombies tomorrow...well today.'

Laylah nodded, it was time to go.

They arrived back at the campground and outside of the tent they held each other one last time, his heartbeat as fast as ever, his arms strong. Laylah knew then that she never wanted to let him go.

'Have I told you that my favourite poem is *Dulce et Decorum Est?*' She said suddenly.

Sam pulled away and looked down, his blue eyes almost pitch black in the darkness, piercing the night. '*The old lie,*' he whispered and in a voice so quiet it was barely legible. A single star in the darkest of nights he recited;

'Bent double, like old beggars under sacks,
Knock-kneed, coughing like hags, we cursed through sludge,
Till on the haunting flares we turned our backs,
And towards our distant rest began to trudge.
Men marched asleep. Many had lost their boots,
But limped on, blood-shod. All went lame; all blind;
Drunk with fatigue; deaf even to the hoots
Of gas-shells dropping softly behind.
Gas! GAS! Quick, boys!—An ecstasy of fumbling
Fitting the clumsy helmets just in time,
But someone still was yelling out and stumbling
And flound'ring like a man in fire or lime.—
Dim through the misty panes and thick green light,
As under a green sea, I saw him drowning.
In all my dreams before my helpless sight,
He plunges at me, guttering, choking, drowning.
If in some smothering dreams, you too could pace
Behind the wagon that we flung him in,
And watch the white eyes writhing in his face,
His hanging face, like a devil's sick of sin;
If you could hear, at every jolt, the blood
Come gargling from the froth-corrupted lungs,

*Obscene as cancer, bitter as the cud
Of vile, incurable sores on innocent tongues,—
My friend, you would not tell with such high zest
To children ardent for some desperate glory,
The old Lie: Dulce et decorum est
Pro patria mori.'*

Laylah pulled Sam close again as a sob escaped his throat on the last passage. The old lie. She was well aware of the old lie.

Once his breathing became more even, more measured, reluctantly she pulled back, let him go. Laylah wished she could reach up to kiss him but she brushed his cheek one more time instead.

'Thank you for telling me, goodnight,' she whispered.

'Good night,' he whispered back as they parted for the night.

...

That night Laylah dreamt of home. The home that she had known only for a short period of time. A home that now felt more like a dream. Syria. A land that wept.

Her parents had left long before the Syrian revolution had begun but not all of their family had. Now their house, the house she had taken her first steps in, learned to say, *Mama, Baba, Teta* and *Sedoo* had crumbled back into the desert.

It had all been so simple at the beginning of the Arab spring. A corrupt dictator that needed to come down. People were tired of going hungry, tired of living paycheck to paycheck, tired of the power turning off. But mostly, they were tired of working themselves to death only to live this life, a half-life, whilst the elite jetted across the world. Their backs were breaking.

In the beginning? People were hopeful. Sons kissed their mother's goodbye as they went off to protest, to fight for the homeland. A *revolution*. A better life they promised. But they had underestimated Assad who came down with an iron fist, he showed no mercy. And those mothers, the mothers who had just kissed their son's goodbye? Now they wailed on the streets. Their tears, unstoppable as they asked for justice from the heavens. But perhaps no one was listening because things went from bad to worse.

Initially, the rebels had the world behind them, people were horrified by the actions of their leader and weapons were sent, support was everywhere. But then the terrorists came, they came and Assad began to look like the good guy.

Now, so many years later, so many years after they had begun, hope had been exterminated. The wails of mother's, a daily hymn. Rubble and dust the new norm as homes and people returned to the sandy desert of Arabia. Dust to dust.

They were going backwards. And death? It was constant.

All while little boys were born, little boys like her cousin, who was 12 years old at the beginning of the war, had the *old lie* whispered to them from fools. And this little boy, this little boy at the age of 15, well he thought he was a man. But he was a child? His beard nothing more than mottled patches of hair, his voice had only just broken and sometimes he still woke at night drenched in sweat, screaming for his mother when he dreamt of death. But this boy-man went to fight and became yet another victim of the old lie. Just another face. And now? Now his mother screamed too. As did the mothers of thousands of other boy-men. And so the old lie continued to be whispered from everyone, everywhere.

Join the rebels and die boy-men. Join Assad who has killed thousands of you boy-men. Join the terrorists and kill boy-men.

All lies, all death.

So the old lie lived. In a different tongue, yes, but it was still whispered, and whilst everything around it died, it would not. It had not died in the beaches of Gallipoli or the horror of Hiroshima all those years ago. It had not died in Palestine or Israel. And it had certainly not died in her home. Her sweet, sweet home. Syria. It would never die.

'Dulce et decorum est Pro patria mori. It is sweet and proper to die for the fatherland.'

The old lie.

Chapter Twelve

Sam: Falling

Sam felt like he had barely closed his eyes when he was woken by the twittering of birds and the rays of the sun warming the tent. Physically Sam was exhausted, his muscles ached and was not quite sure if he would be able to force them to move today. But mentally his mind was at peace, he had expected today, James's birthday to be hard. That was one of the reasons he had been happy to go on this trip he had hoped that it would distract him. But last night or this *morning* Sam corrected himself, talking to Laylah had helped, had taken a weight off his chest. It was only after he said goodnight to her that Sam realised he had not talked about James, had not wept for him, since the funeral. That's what was expected of him after all, he was expected to be strong for mum, dad and Charlotte, he was expected to get over it. Of course, no one ever said that but it was implied, after all, nothing brought people down like hearing that you had a dead brother. Nothing. But last night he couldn't keep it in and for once he hadn't wanted to. Laylah...she had understood, she had listened and brought him a sense of calm that had been missing from his life for months.

Sam closed his eyes and for a moment all he saw was the red of his lids as the sun streamed through them, warmed them. He thought of Laylah, hair and soul on fire. How seeing her made him smile, how her jokes made him laugh, even if they weren't particularly funny, and how her absence, her pain, made his heart clench. But mostly how if for the rest of his life, all he did was hold her, that would be enough. More than enough, it would be a blessing. This feeling felt different, it felt new, but also like something that he had been waiting for his entire life. Last night his heart had unfurled, bloomed and now, although he didn't even remember jumping, Sam knew that he was falling. Falling fast. Falling hard. He was terrified, but he didn't regret it, didn't want it to stop. Even if he was going to crash, break, into a million pieces, it would be worth it, for her.

...

The last day of the long weekend came and went much too quickly as they continued to be surrounded by the rugged beauty of the landscape.

During this last stretch, the group flowed just as it had the prior day, splitting into pairs, merging into a group and then splitting once more. Sam talked to Nikau, who complained thoroughly about the number of assignments he had due in the coming weeks, he chatted with Ariana who was fascinated with the unfortunate politics of the USA and of course, Sam talked to Laylah. They didn't broach anything serious, aware that Ariana and Nikau were always in earshot, neither of them knew about James yet. So they kept their conversations light, happy, hopeful.

Sam knew that sometimes he frustrated Laylah, they were so different in so many ways that it was almost inevitable. Fire and ice. But after last night? There was an understanding, a calm, a gentleness between them that hadn't existed before. So for now, Sam immersed himself in this beautiful land and let himself be happy. For the first time in a long time, he let himself be truly happy.

...

Laylah and Sam shared the drive home while Ariana and Nikau dozed off in the backseat. It was a peaceful, mostly quiet drive. The difference in atmosphere was tangible, as their excitement and energy was replaced with quiet contentment. They were all very tired.

By 2:00 pm they were home, Nikau was staying with Sam for the night to avoid a long drive to the farm. After saying their goodbyes, Nikau and Sam lumbered up the stairs and promptly collapsed onto Sam's bed.

...

Sam's ravenous stomach grumbled and demanded that he wake. Still only semi-conscious Sam reached for his laptop and through half-opened eyes he ordered pizza for himself and Nikau who was still fast asleep next to him.

Sam stood and let out an almighty yawn, stretching his long arms to the ceiling before he grabbed a towel and hopped into the shower. As soon as the hot water hit his muscles he felt them relax, become softer and more limber while simultaneously his mind awakened.

The pizza arrived just as Sam hopped out of the shower.

'Is that pizza?' Nikau called from his bedroom.

'Yup.'

Nikau emerged, bleary-eyed and ravenous. 'Man you are the best,' he grinned, grabbing one of the boxes and making his way to the dining room table. For almost ten minutes they were both silent, devouring the meal.

'So when are you going to ask Laylah out?' Nikau grinned now that he was sufficiently fed.

Sam didn't try and deny his interest now. 'Do you think I should?'

'Definitely! I doubt she will say no, I saw the way you two were looking at each other the entire trip, especially today. I knew that *you* were smitten, but I am pretty sure she likes you as more than just a friend.' Nikau said.

'Okay man, I trust you...do you have any suggestions?' Sam asked.

'Hmm, I always like to keep it simple. What about dinner and a movie? Something fun and light. A romantic comedy is a good place to start.' Nikau said.

'Romantic comedies, really?' Sam chuckled.

'Hey, they are cinematic masterpieces!' Nikau protested.

'Okay, okay man.' Sam laughed. 'Do you think this Friday is too soon?'

'Not at all, strike while the iron is hot, you two are in a good place now.'

Sam nodded, already nervous about what he would say but he also felt heady. Sam's blood swept through his arteries, to his heart, which even at the thought of seeing her, of hearing her voice, unfurled a little more.

Chapter Thirteen

Laylah: Logic and Love

          head. heart. logic. love.
          intrinsically we know that
logic   holds neither place nor power in love,
          yet it is a constant battle.

          so, our minds float to new worlds,
          alternate realities where we are willing to
fail(s)   to sacrifice it all, for the short-term
          pleasures of this world.

          for this alternate reality
          contains all our hopes and dreams,
          it feeds our souls. for here at least we can
          be brave. flowers bloom
when   the sun shines and sadness
          does not exist, only love.
          and the ones we love.

          so when

i see   you although logic screams,
         s*creams.* reminding me of stormy clouds,
         rain and the harshness of this world,
         my heart hums, my blood sings, my soul believes.

         so, i take
your   hand and float into love,
         not knowing whether stretches of river
         or a waterfall will come
         all i ask is; please be gentle with this
soul   won't you?

Laylah never napped during the day but after the camping trip she was out for a couple of hours, she may have even slept through the night if not for her demanding stomach.

Too tired to cook Laylah threw a smoothie together and decided to settle in with a book for the rest of the night, she had been meaning to start *And the Mountains Echoed* for a while. Smoothie and book in hand, Laylah walked back into her bedroom and snuggled under the covers in her little slice of heaven.

What felt like moments later but was at least an hour, a knock pulled Laylah out of Hosseini's world. 'Laylah?' Ariana called.

'Come in.' Laylah responded, carefully marking her position and putting the book on her bedside table.

The door opened but Ariana stayed outside. 'Sam is here, he wants to talk to you. In private,' she added with a suggestive look in her eye.

Laylah was surprised. 'Sam? Oh, okay, he didn't say what about did he?' Laylah asked as she looked at herself in the mirror in sweatpants, a jumper and a messy bun. She didn't look great she admitted to herself as she adjusted her bun slightly but after a second she shrugged at her reflection. She didn't have the energy to do anything about it.

'No he didn't say anything...he looked nervous though.' Ariana said and shook her head grinning at Laylah's dishevelled appearance.

Laylah nodded and walked into the living room where Sam sat and indeed looked very nervous. Nervous but adorable.

Laylah couldn't help but notice that he *had* made an effort. She could smell his shampoo from across the room and noticed he looked particularly tidy in black shorts and a dark blue shirt, he knew how to pick colours that matched those eyes.

Sky blue.

'Hey!' Laylah said.

'Hey! I didn't wake you did I?' Sam asked anxiously.

'Oh no.' Laylah laughed. 'I was just reading in bed, is everything okay?' Laylah enquired as she came over and sat down on the couch opposite him.

'Yes, I have something I wanted to ask you.' Sam paused. 'I know this is a bit sudden but are you free next Friday to go out just you and me? I was thinking dinner and a movie?'

'You mean like a date?' Laylah asked.

'Well...yes.' Sam said and Laylah couldn't help but notice that his hands shook ever so slightly although his face was composed.

'Sure,' she replied quickly, heart pounding. 'I mean I would love that.' Laylah corrected herself.

Sam's face broke into relief, eyes crinkling.

Sky blue.

'Okay, I will have a look and see what is in the cinema, any preferences for a movie or a cuisine?' Sam asked.

'Nope, I am easy to please, you choose.' Laylah said suddenly even more aware of how shabby she looked.

'Okay, I will leave you to it, I have an early start tomorrow.' Sam said and smiled, standing to leave. 'Oh and Laylah, thank you for listening to me the other night, that meant a lot.' Sam added.

Laylah rose to her feet and placed her hand on his arm. 'Anytime,' she said simply.

Once he left, Laylah closed the door her emotions swirling, a whirlwind. Laylah returned to the living room where Ariana sat waiting for her, barely able to contain her excitement.

'Okay, what was that about? Tell me!' Ariana demanded.

Laylah sat slowly and looked at her, still feeling a bit dazed. 'He asked me out.'

'And what did you say?! You said yes right, *right*?!' Ariana cried.

'I did.' Laylah smiled.

'YES!' Ariana said leaping up in the air.

'Calm down!' Laylah laughed. 'Nothing has happened.'

'Okay, okay.' Ariana said sitting back down. 'I knew this would happen! The moment you two met there was something there and then this weekend...Nikau and I noticed you two making googly eyes at each other! So this means you like him right?'

Laylah nodded. 'I like him and saying yes to him? Well, it just felt easy and right. Really right.'

Ariana looked at her, brow furrowed. 'Laylah, that's amazing.'

And as Laylah lay in bed that night, her thoughts consumed with this human being, she couldn't help but think it *was* amazing. He was amazing. And this definitely wasn't nothing.

Chapter Fourteen

Sam: Beautiful

The week flew by and before Sam knew it Friday had arrived. He was nervous, to say the least, but organised, he was always organised. He had booked an Italian restaurant for dinner at 6 pm and had taken Nikaus advice with a romantic comedy at 8 pm, a ridiculously wonderful, light-hearted plot about a girl going on exchange to Edinburgh and struggling with the weather. In Sam's opinion, there was no such thing as bad weather, just poor wardrobe choices. You couldn't handle Brooklyn without layers.

Sam arrived home at about 4:30 pm, showered, shaved and meticulously chose his clothes. It was still quite warm so he quickly decided on some tidy black chino shorts but the shirt was much harder. After much thought, he decided on an emerald short sleeve button down. Next was the hair, getting it to look like he had tried, but not tried that hard was always a difficult task. But even once he was finished with that it was only 5:15 pm.

Sam strolled into the kitchen, feeling like a tiny monster had taken residence inside of him, gnawing at his stomach. His hands were slightly sweaty, his breath slightly too fast. His hands slid over the marble counter, eyes wandering to the empty sink and air drying dishes, something had shifted in George since they had their chat. Sure he was still drinking like mad, still coming home at all hours with God knows who, but still there was a new sense of calm, of responsibility about him.

Absentmindedly Sam opened one of the higher cupboards and his eyes trailed over a few cobwebs. With a thumping heart and 45 minutes still to go, Sam got to work scrubbing the insides of the cabinet. As he cleaned, his hands moved rhythmically, systematically. Spray. Scrub. Wipe. Dry. His mind slowed and eventually, his thoughts wandered to James. James had always been his protector, his knight in shining armour. His big brother. And now? Sam wished James was here more than anything, wished he had his words of wisdom, his fire.

. . .

5:45 pm came, Sam stood back and inspected his handy work, he had managed four of their five large cabinets and a sense of satisfaction washed over him. Grinning to himself he pulled off the apron, spritzed on more cologne, checked for his phone and wallet before heading across the road. Sam stood, took a deep, steadying breath before he knocked on the door.

Moments later Ariana opened it. 'Come in, I will go and get her,' she said gesturing that he should make himself at home in their quaint living room.

Sam took a seat on one of their armchairs, his foot immediately, subconsciously tapping the floor. His eyes drifted around the room, taking in the homely combination of grey walls and floors paired with deep emerald couches. The walls were lined with both art and framed photos of loved ones. Sam stood wandering over to a huge, packed bookshelf. It was painted white and speckled with the blush of cherry blossoms. Small plants were dotted around the bookshelf and for a moment Sam wasn't sure if he was in a library or a forest.

His eyes swept over the books noting the familiar seven covers of Harry Potter and a couple of books by Khaled Hosseini. A large white novel caught his eyes *The Luminaries*. Sam eased the book from its place and scanned the cover.

'Take it the author is a kiwi, and it's brilliant.'

Sam turned his neck so fast that his muscles complained.

Laylah stood at the doorway, dressed simply but gorgeously in high waisted black trousers and a red shirt that she had tucked in. Her hair was pinned back on either side of her face exposing her olive tanned shoulders and strong arms, her makeup was simple, eyeliner and a touch of mascara, the whole look was tied together with a pair of simple heeled sandals that gave her a few extra centimetres. Nothing really next to Sam.

Of course, these details escaped Sam's notice, but once he had found his voice again he breathed. 'You are beautiful.'

'Oh thank you. You look really nice too.' Laylah blushed. 'And sorry to keep you waiting, it's been one of those days,' she sighed.

'Don't worry about it, are you okay?'

'Oh sure, just hectic.' Laylah smiled.

'Are you sure you don't mind me borrowing this?' Sam gestured to the book still in his hand.

Laylah smiled, 'Definitely, you will love it.'

Sam carefully placed it back to its spot. 'I will grab it later, who painted this by the way?' He gestured to the bookshelf.

'Ariana, brilliant right?'

'Incredible,' he smiled. 'Shall we?' And throwing caution to the wind he offered her his hand, which she took easily. Naturally. With great difficulty, Sam calmed his breathing and they headed out.

It was a gorgeous summer evening, the sun shone, igniting Laylah's swinging hair.

Fire.

A breeze caressed his skin and Jasmine wafted through the air from Laylah. With great effort, Sam steadied his breathing, squeezed her hand gently and said. 'So tell me about this hectic day.'

Chapter Fifteen

Laylah: Calm

                  indecisiveness has always plagued
my   mind.

neurons   stuck.
                 unable to synapse,
                 unable to connect,
                 frozen
on   a decision,
                 so, they choose indecision.

                 but then i met you
                 and you weren't hard at all,
                 so, i stepped into this
fire   blindly and suddenly
                 a connection was made,
                 a path chosen.
                 mind, body and soul; ablaze.

Everything had gone well so far. Sam was on time, early, in fact, and he was dressed impeccably. His hair was just the right amount of messy while his emerald shirt accentuated his eyes perfectly. Those eyes.

Sky blue.

They had gone to a quaint Italian restaurant for dinner which was perfect for Laylah who glanced at the menu for a second before ordering a pizza for herself. They talked, laughed and talked some more. It was easy. So easy.

They walked into the cinema now and were immediately suffocated by the smell of popcorn that hung in the air.

'What are we seeing?' Laylah asked.

'A romantic comedy.'

'Really?' Laylah sputtered.

'Hey! They are cinematic masterpieces.' Sam answered defensively.

Laylah shoved him playfully and laughed. 'I am not complaining, at least it's not a horror movie. I am just surprised, pleasantly surprised,' she grinned.

They reached the counter where Laylah insisted on paying, after all, he had paid for dinner she argued. Sam only protested for a second, but then dashed back to buy them ice cream.

'Oh no, I couldn't possibly, I am so full.' Laylah said whilst simultaneously reaching for her ice cream.

Sam shrugged and held it away from her, a playfulness lacing his eyes. 'That's fine, I can eat yours too.'

'Well let's not get carried away,' she replied quickly and standing on her tiptoes she claimed her ice cream from him. Laughing they walked into the dimly lit cinema.

'Does this have peanut butter in it?' Laylah asked once they were settled into their seats.

'Yes, but I thought you weren't hungry...' Sam teased.

Laylah gave him a withering look, but inside her heart was light and her tone even lighter, 'I don't want it to melt!' She protested, taking another few licks. 'Thank you though, this is perfect, I love peanut butter.'

'Crunchy or smooth?' Sam asked peanut butter, was, after all, a very important topic.

'Crunchy of course!' Laylah insisted.

'Agreed,' he nodded solemnly.

Seconds later, a hush fell over the cinema as the lights were dimmed and the trailers played, suddenly Laylah was very aware of his arm on the armrest, right next to her own. When it came to romance, inexperienced was an understatement for Laylah, she had never even liked someone properly let alone held hands or been kissed. So when Sam had taken her hand before they left, with complete nonchalance, as if it was the most natural thing in the world, that had terrified her, but in the best possible way. Bliss. All she wanted now was to feel that utter bliss once more.

Just do it, his hand is right there!

No, I cannot.

But you want to!

Yes! But, but, well if he wants to, he can just take my hand again!

Are you the kind of woman that waits for a man?! Come on!

The battle ensued until almost fifteen minutes had passed and Laylah could honestly say she hardly knew what was happening on screen, although the Australian protagonist, Emily, had stopped complaining about the weather and bought herself some gloves and thermals.

After a few more rounds of deliberation, brave Laylah won so taking a deep breath, attempting to calm her thumping heart she slipped her hand in his. Sam glanced down at her and gently unwound his hand from her own. Laylah's heart dropped, sinking into utter agony. Muscular fibres transformed into lead.

But it was over in a second and suddenly her heart soared, bliss, muscles contracting as they beat faster than they had ever before when she realised that he was pulling up the armrest divider. And before she knew it he had sidled closer to her and wrapped his arm around her waist. His hand rested in her lap and twisted in her own. This wasn't the first time they had sat like this, but this time, no one needed comforting, this time, his thumb was making small circles on her hand. This time, in the deepest crevice of herself, she felt something stir, come alive. This time breathing felt impossible as electricity seared through her, she was on fire. But at the same time, despite the muscle that pounded desperately in her ribcage, she felt completely safe, calm, warm.

. . .

They walked out of the movie laughing and this time their hands tangled together naturally as they headed home.

By now the sun was well and truly making its descent, the air finally cool, Laylah glanced up at the sky, it was so clear today, aqua quickly becoming indigo as night fell upon them. Laylah loved summer nights.

'What's your favourite movie?' Sam asked thoughtfully.

Laylah paused only for a second. 'The Theory of Everything.'

'Well you had that locked down,' he grinned. 'Why?'

'I have thought about it before,' she shrugged. 'Why? The soundtrack is incredible, it's filmed perfectly and the story is inspiring. I know some people think that Hart was a bit of a jerk, even if he was, you cannot deny he achieved amazing things. I always think that if he could do so much, what is my excuse?'

'I have a lot of respect for him and his work.' Sam agreed. 'I don't think I remember the soundtrack though,' he said, brow furrowed.

'Well, guess what we are doing as soon as we get back?!' Laylah grinned. 'You?'

'The Pursuit of Happyness.'

'Will Smith?'

Sam nodded. 'I guess it also inspires me, to be more, to be better, and Jaden Smith is the cutest. He also has impeccable music now.'

'It's a great movie.' Laylah agreed. 'I don't think I have heard any of Jaden's music though.'

'Well, guess what we are doing when we get back?!' Sam said mirroring her, in the growing darkness Laylah could make out the crinkle of his eyes but little more until they passed underneath a street light and suddenly they were infused with light.

Sky blue.

Too soon they had arrived at their street and almost out of nowhere Laylah suddenly felt nauseous.

'Okay music, do you want to do this at mine or yours?' Sam asked.

Laylah looked at him, her gut squeezing uncomfortably, a golf ball lodged in her throat. Before she could even think she blurted in one breath. 'Actually, let's do this some other time, I am really tired and I just realised I have a...a thing, that's right, a thing tomorrow...goodnight.'

A thing? What?! And why had her voice become so high?

'Oh, of course.' Sam said, looking disappointed. 'Of course,' he repeated. 'Well, goodnight.'

But she had already turned away and was frantically unlocking the door. Words escaped her and the silence that replaced their laughter and conversation from only seconds before hung in the air, heavy.

Finally, Laylah found the right key and with a wrench walked inside, closed the door and promptly slid to the floor. Face in hands. Her thoughts whirred. Her gut unclenched. And suddenly her vision blurred as her eyes filled with tears.

Why did she say no?! What was wrong with her?! And god why was she crying now?!

In the living room, Ariana took one look at her face and in a second was kneeling next to her, demanding. 'What's wrong?! Did something happen? What did he do?!'

'Oh he didn't do anything, it was lovely.' Laylah said, shaking her head.

'Thank god!' Ariana said and gently took her hand, leading her to the couch where Laylah promptly slumped once more.

'Okay if it was lovely, sweetie, why are you crying? What's wrong?' Ariana asked again as she settled down next to her.

'Well, he invited me in and...'

'What?! Why are you here then?! Don't you like him?!' Ariana demanded.

'Of, of course, I do. But I...I don't know, I just panicked.'

'Laylah, come on, why?'

Laylah finally met Ariana's emerald eyes, tears pouring down her face and suddenly jumbled words were falling out of her mouth, made from thoughts that she hadn't even realised existed until this moment. 'I..like him, a lot, but what if...he...no...me...and, and, inviting me in...sex, cannot, embarrassing.'

'Laylah, breathe, *breathe.*' Ariana said, her voice soothing but firm. 'One thing at a time, I am gathering you like him and you are not sure he likes you?'

Laylah nodded.

Ariana almost laughed. 'Sweetie, there is *no way* he doesn't like you. That was a date, for sure, I saw him take your hand before you left.'

Laylah remained silent.

'And you said something about sex?' Ariana crinkled her brow.

Laylah took another deep shaky breath, her voice high she said. 'Well I think it hit me all of a sudden that I haven't even known him for that long, and...and, well you know what guys expect when they invite you in and, and, what's he going to do when I say no?! What's he going to think?!'

'Laylah you just need to explain, he will understand,' Ariana said gently, squeezing her hand once more.

'But what if he doesn't?! And what if he thinks I am a prude, what if he thinks I am ridiculous?!' Laylah asked and this time she sounded almost desperate as she frantically wiped tears from her cheek.

'He will understand.' Ariana said more firmly this time. 'And he would never do that. We haven't known him for long, but I am certain of that, you are just scared.'

'Are you sure?'

Ariana nodded. 'And if he *does* act like a jerk, well I will just have to go over there and kick his butt.'

Laylah laughed and for a moment she forgot her fear.

'What should I do now? God how do people do this?! I don't know how to do this!' Laylah confessed.

'You need to go over there right now and tell him, tell him you like him and if it comes up, talk to him about what scares you, what your boundaries are.'

'What?' Laylah said flabbergasted.

'Listen Laylah, Sam is shy, him asking you out, tonight, that was a proclamation of love, did he seem upset when you didn't come in?

Laylah nodded. 'I didn't see his face but he sounded hurt.'

'Exactly. He needs to hear this, now, before this causes any distance to come in between you, you *need* to tell him how you feel. You might think you have been obvious but people can be very oblivious when it comes to their feelings. Just knock on his door and go for a walk together.'

'I don't know if I can.' Laylah said, as her heartbeat frantically.

'Of course, you can. I know you are nervous but honestly what's the worst that can happen? Come on, *be brave*. I am not leaving this room until you go.' Ariana insisted.

Laylah was silent for a few seconds as she thought over what Ariana had just said. She was right, she knew she was right. So with a pit in her stomach Laylah nodded and stood, shakily she adjusted the strap of her sandals and patted her hair.

'I am so proud of you, I will be here when you get back to talk, no matter what he says.' Ariana smiled and gave her a gentle hug.

Laylah nodded shakily. Before she could overthink anything else she walked to her room, put her headphones in her pocket and walked out of the house. She jogged across the road and immediately knocked on Sam's door trying to remind herself how to breathe. Sam opened the door, still dressed impeccably and Laylah couldn't help sighing to herself, *he was so cute.*

'Oh hey! Is everything okay?' Sam asked.

Laylah nodded. 'Yes, everything is fine...can we go for a walk? I want to talk to you about something.'

'Of course.' Sam nodded, grabbing his keys he closed the door.

Laylah's heartbeat frantically, trying to tear itself out of her chest. She felt like she was having a heart attack. *Breathe*, she reminded herself. But she couldn't eliminate her terror completely and the air felt heavy, the mood compared to just moments ago was like night and day.

They continued along the sidewalk in silence, walking under the stars and almost instinctively Laylah led them to the gardens once more, to their bench.

Laylah sat down and Sam followed suit. 'Laylah, you are scaring me, are you sure everything is okay?' Sam asked.

Laylah nodded, taking a deep breath she bit her lip and looked down at her hands, not sure how to start.

His fingers gently tipped her chin up. 'Laylah?'

Finally, she met his eyes, crinkled, this time in concern. Sky blue.

Be brave she reminded herself before she began. 'Sam, I need to tell you something...from the moment I met you I thought there was something there, you are so calm and kind, we have so much in common. I am so comfortable around you in a way I have never been around any man, and only a handful of people just in general.' Laylah paused, recollecting her thoughts for a moment. 'Tonight was amazing and...and I guess what I am trying to say is that I really like you, I mean I *like, like* you...I mean I think I am falling for you.' Laylah finished before she dropped her eyes to her clasped hands which sat twisting in her lap once more. Heart pounding.

'I am falling for you too Laylah.' Sam finally said after seconds which to Laylah's jittery heart had stretched on to eternity.

She looked up and this time when their eyes met her heart beat faster but more steadily all at the same time. She didn't know what to say.

As if reading her mind Sam gently brushed her cheek with his fingers and whispered. 'You don't have to say anything.'

'No, I do, I have to explain something.' Laylah took a deep shaky breath but this time she felt so much calmer, so much braver. 'Before, when we got back and you invited me in. I...I panicked, I know what guys expect when they invite you in after a date and I...I just am not ready...that's why I practically ran away, I am so sorry.'

Sam shook his head. 'Don't apologise! Laylah, I would never...I am not like that...'

'It's not just that. It's not just sex.' Laylah cut him off. *This was it* she thought, *this was the moment he would find out she was a complete weirdo, the moment after which he would pretend he had an early start tomorrow or that there was a family emergency,* she took a deep breath and resolutely thought, *so be it.* 'I have never even kissed anyone.' she glanced up at him wincing but to her complete and utter shock, he did not seem horrified, merely, surprised? Taking that as a good sign she continued, there was no going back now. 'My parents are conservative, protective, let's just say there weren't many dating opportunities at school and then the first two years of university I had an eating disorder and to be honest, men, dating, sex, they were the last thing on my mind. I just didn't have the energy for it. And I wanted to tell you, to say something, but I didn't want you to think I was...weird or pathetic or a prude, so I panicked. I am so sorry,' she repeated.

Sam looked at her, brow furrowed and took her hand in his, eyes filled with compassion.

Sky blue.

'There is not a single solar system, not a single timeline that exists where I think you are anything but incredible. This doesn't bother me, even slightly. I won't lie, I am surprised.' Sam shrugged. 'But honestly, you are gorgeous and I have seen how people look at you.'

'I am pretty useless at the whole flirting thing.' Laylah admitted. 'I am just a bit incompetent. Well more than a bit.' Laylah confessed.

Sam shook his head. 'You are just inexperienced and that's okay. Anyway, I don't think you missed out on much, teenage boys are idiots. Men in almost any age bracket can be idiots.' Sam corrected himself.

Laylah laughed, feeling like an enormous weight had been lifted off her chest, as if she had been carrying some huge shame, unfairly she knew, but she had been carrying it still and now she felt like she could breathe again. And god it felt so good to breathe. 'Trust me, women, too. People in general I think.'

Sam smiled. 'Not you,' he paused, collecting his thoughts. 'Are you okay now? I mean with your diet and everything?'

Laylah nodded. 'Not perfect but I try. Even when I am stressed or upset, I make sure I am eating well.'

'I am glad,' Sam said before taking a deep breath himself. 'Okay this might send *you* running and screaming and if it does I understand, completely. But I have to tell you, I *do* have history.'

'Tell me more.' Laylah said simply.

'Well when I was a teenager and in the first few years of university, I partied...lots, but I have only had two steady girlfriends. One in my senior year of high school and one when I was twenty-two.' Sam bit his lip. 'But then my brother passed and for the first few weeks, honestly I kind of lost it. I was drinking so much, with a new girl every two or three days...and it helped, helped me not to think about James. To not think about the pain. And to be honest, once I had a few drinks in, it never seemed too hard to approach someone, sometimes they approached me,' he admitted sheepishly.

'Of course, they did, look at you/' Laylah muttered sourly under her breath.

'What?' Asked Sam anxiously.

'I said I am not surprised, you are cute!' Laylah said, laughing in exasperation, his earnestness and sincerity melting her heart. 'Do you still do that?'

Sam shook his head. 'I was bad for a while after James passed, I had maybe four or five one night stands, but when

I went home and saw how much Mum, Dad and Charlotte needed me, well I got my act together pretty quickly and haven't been with anyone since. Not that there is anything wrong with it, but after a while, I started to feel numb. I barely remembered their names.' Sam shrugged. 'To be honest, I am a relationship kind of guy, I don't mind being single, but one-off things are not for me. I learned that pretty quickly.'

Laylah sat silent for a long time, digesting what he was saying and realised how insecure she felt about her own inexperience, no wonder she had blown up at him for not talking to her at the gym all those weeks ago.

'Laylah? What's wrong? What are you thinking?' Sam asked.

And for some insane reason, Laylah was honest. 'It sounds like you know so much more than I do about relationships, and that makes me feel a bit worried.'

Sam shook his head. 'You don't need to be, I have only ever had two girlfriends. Hannah, my most recent one and Sarah, during high school.'

'What happened with them?'

'Hannah was great, is great. We started as friends and when she asked me out, I thought, *why not?* But we were just never meant to be a couple. We wanted different things, we needed different things. We had different habits and values. It's like we were the same in all the ways you *don't* want to be, but different in all the ways you do. She is also super quiet, super calm and she can be very reserved. But she is a Republican and very money-oriented. Her life ambition is to build an enormous business and earn lots of money. And that's amazing, but just not what I want.'

Laylah nodded. 'And the one in high school?'

'Ah Sarah, we, we...' And suddenly he sounded incredibly ashamed.

This time Laylah squeezed his hand. 'We were destructive, I knew that from the start, she loved me and I loved her. Well, *then* I thought that was love. I was going through a rough time, one of my childhood friends had committed suicide and I was really depressed. But I couldn't show her that of course. I was a complete jerk, aloof, uncommunicative, apathetic. I was going through the motions even though I *knew* we were incompatible, even though I *knew* that we should break up.' Sam paused again but Laylah remained silent so he ploughed on. 'We were together for six months and we slept together even though I didn't want to. It was the first time for both of us, and when I stopped returning her calls, when it all got too much for me it destroyed her. That relationship is filled with regret and I hated myself for a long time. Hated myself for staying with her when I knew I should have left, for sleeping with her even though I could see the end and then for not ending it properly. For not having the guts. For leaving her at arm's length. That's why it took me so long to date again.' Sam said, and Laylah could hear the shame and hurt that laced his voice even though he looked down so she could not see blue.

Sky blue.

'Did she want to sleep with you?'

Sam nodded. 'Definitely. We were late bloomers, both more focused on sport and school. But college was coming fast and we wanted to get it out of the way. But I still feel bad, I shouldn't have done it with her, I knew we weren't going to last.'

Laylah shook her head. 'Sam it's okay, you were seventeen. Should you have broken up with her properly? Sure. But we all make mistakes.' Laylah hesitated. 'What about all those girls when James died, did you lie to any of them? Promise to date them? Promise to call them and not?'

Sam shook his head.

'That's fine then,' she shrugged. 'Sex is normal, biological, as long as it is consensual, who am I to judge?'

'Really?'

'Of course and to be honest, I understand, sure my libido was gone for those couple of years when I had an eating disorder, but...' She bit her lip anxiously before deciding to throw caution to the wind. 'Well, let's just say it's back in full force.'

Sam looked at her, disbelief painted across his face and for a moment Laylah was worried, but then he laughed, loud and strong, filling the night air and Laylah laughed with him. It was so good to laugh.

'Okay Miss Science and logic.' Sam paused. 'Are you a Ravenclaw?' Laylah nodded. 'Hufflepuff by the way.' Sam added before he continued. 'We can go as slow as you want, as you need, do you *want* to have sex?'

Laylah feigned looking around. 'Well I feel like it would be uncomfortable...and someone might walk past, but sure. I didn't pack any condoms though, did you...'

'Laylah!' Sam laughed.

'Okay, okay, sorry, sarcasm is my go-to for anxiety-inducing conversations.'

'Is it really that bad?' Sam's brow crinkled in concern.

'Actually no, nowhere near as bad as it should be,' she squeezed his hand. 'But to answer your question, if it's okay...for now...'

'Yes?'

'Can we just say that we won't? I was raised to wait, until marriage, and I mean...we don't *have* to do that...I might change my mind, but for now...can we hold off? Take our time?' Laylah stuttered, furious that she couldn't form coherent sentences but also terrified. Absolutely terrified of what he would say.

'We can wait. I don't mind, we can do whatever you want.' Sam said simply.

This time it was her turn. 'Really?'

'*Really*, I think you forget where I spend every Sunday morning, abstinence is still a big thing in a lot of Churches.' Sam chuckled and Laylah grinned, feeling her soul immediately lighten.

'But seriously, if something is not okay, just tell me and I will always check with you before doing anything.' Sam said, with complete sincerity.

'Thank you, I really, really...' Laylah took a deep breath. '*Really* appreciate that,' she paused and bit her lip, smirking. 'What if *I* want to do something, should I check with you?'

'What did you have in mind?' Sam asked with mirth.

Throwing caution to the wind once more, with bravery that Laylah didn't even know existed within her she asked blue to kiss her.

Sky blue.

Without a word he obliged, first taking her face gently in his hands before he leaned forward, his lips, inquisitive, soft yet firm on hers. Laylah slowly rose so that she was kneeling on the bench and moved closer to him, tangling her hands through his hair, which was softer than she could have ever imagined.

And then just like that, it was over and Laylah knew she wanted those lips, every day, for the rest of her life. It was magical, fantastical. Yet also the most normal, the easiest thing in the world. It was everything she had hoped and dreamed but simultaneously none of those things.

'Was that okay?' Sam asked gently when they finally pulled apart.

'So much better than okay.' Laylah smiled against his lips, knowing that she didn't need to say anything else, knowing that just like that night when he had told her about James, they did not need words.

She pulled out her headphones and phone from her pocket. 'Do you still want to listen to the soundtrack?'

'I would love to.'

Laylah plugged in her headphones and handed him an ear pod while she scrolled through the album. 'This one is my favourite, it's called, *The Theory of Everything,*' she hit play.

'Beautiful.' Sam breathed into the silence when the song was finished.

Laylah nodded. 'I have always thought that I would have it played at my funeral.'

'Funeral?'

'I am going to die one day right?' Laylah shrugged. 'I guess a wedding would also work, but who knows when or even if that will happen.'

'We can make that happen.' Sam said earnestly.

Laylah met those eyes and felt her heart stop but then start again just as quickly. She was taken aback, but also not at all worried, her heart filled with an indescribable joy.

'Sorry, that was too much...I meant...' Sam said in a hurried tone, misinterpreting her silence.

'I know and it wasn't too much, it wasn't too much at all.' Laylah said and the look he gave her melted her from the inside out. 'Not for a while though,' she whispered.

'Of course.' Sam grinned. 'Goodness for a moment I thought I had put my foot in my mouth. Can we listen to another one?'

'Sure.' Laylah said, picking up the earbud that had fallen and replacing it. 'This one is a close second, it's called, *A Brief History of Time.*'

They listened to another, then another, then SYRE by Jaden Smith. Laylah rested her cheek against his shoulder, his head gently perched on hers, their hands still clasped under the stars.

...

Time flew and Laylah was only jolted out of her reverie by her phone vibrating, Ariana anxiously checking in. Laylah flicked her a quick text that everything was okay but was shocked to realise it was 2 am, they had been talking for hours. It was time to head home.

They said goodbye with one more long, sweet kiss. And this time although Laylah still felt it was too soon, her soul felt blissfully light. This was better than if the United Nations took away the veto power, this was better than finishing exams or even getting a new personal best at the gym. Not better than chocolate though, not yet anyway.

Makeup finally washed off, in her most comfortable track pants and oversized shirt she slipped under her comforter. When her phone vibrated, she picked it up. Sam.

Tonight was spectacular, thank you for everything. Goodnight x

And it was in that moment, in the dull glow of her phone that she realised she had been lying to herself, she had been lying to him, there was no *maybe* about it, she was falling for him. Hurtling. And she could not have cared less about what was waiting for her.

Chapter Sixteen

Sam: Faith

Sam had fallen for Laylah, there was no doubt about that in his mind and she might be falling for him. It was funny because all the clichés were true, the sun was warmer, the flowers smelled sweeter and everything was brighter. Everything was so much brighter now.

Every dating instinct told Sam that he shouldn't text her first, that he needed to give her some space, some time and maybe even let her contact him. But he couldn't. A goodnight text. A good morning text. And today? A trip to the markets. Sam had no intention of playing hard to get.

At 10 am he knocked on Laylah's door and was hit with Deja vu of the prior night and everything that had occurred, the most beautiful Deja vu. Laylah answered and they headed off. The day was beautiful but she was more so. Her hair was tied in a lazy ponytail, tiny flowered shorts and a black singlet accentuated her figure. As they walked Sam couldn't help staring at her swaying hips and her full, strong legs. But he was equally enchanted by her imperfections – the callouses that roughened her hands, how her right eyebrow sat ever so slightly higher than her left, making her look constantly, slightly surprised, or the silver stripes that glistened on her thighs when the sun caught them. She was perfect in her imperfections.

The sun shone, warm and bright as they strolled along the stalls, trying different food and arguing about which Harry Potter movie was the worst, the fifth or sixth. They finally decided on crepes and found seats on a picnic table in the sun. Sam chuckled to himself as he noted that Laylah's feet trailed, not quite reaching the floor.

'How tall are you Laylah?'

'150cm, I think that's four eleven. How tall are you?' Laylah asked.

'Six foot-ish.' Sam glanced at her feet once more. 'God, you are tiny!'

'No! You are also just huge!' Laylah protested with a laugh. 'My BFG,' she said and then blushed, looking down.

Sam's heart melted and he reached over to cover her hand with his. 'Yes, your BFG,' he smiled.

Laylah looked up and smiled back. 'You are right though, I am small, kind of all over, I have small hands too,' she said and eagerly placed her palm over his, the top of her fingers only reaching the first ridge of his own.

Sam's breath caught, a small part of him acknowledged that her hand was indeed tiny, but just like last night the larger part of him was consumed by a feeling that he couldn't even explain to himself. He wasn't sure if it was having his hand clasped in hers. He wasn't sure if it was the way the sun hit her - skin golden, hair on fire, eyes crinkled, cinnamon. But all he wanted to do at that moment was kiss her. Feel her soft lips, entwine his fingers through her hair, hold her close and never let her go. Never.

He brought his face closer to hers and she softened in response, they came together like magnets. Their lips were close now, less than a hairbreadth apart when Laylah pulled back suddenly.

'What's wrong?' He said glancing around.

'Shahid,' she muttered.

Sam's brow crinkled. 'Who is that?'

But Laylah wasn't listening, and as he followed her eyes, he saw who she was looking at. A woman, tall, with olive skin, not much different to Laylah's, but covered from head to toe, with a black scarf wrapped around her hair. Sam couldn't be sure, but it looked like she was staring at them and she did not look happy.

'Who is that?' Sam repeated.

Laylah finally looked at him and took a deep shaky breath, concern etched all over her face. 'That is Shahid, I went to school with her back in Christchurch, her parents know mine. They are very traditional, living by culture and religion is all that matters to them. Well, their version of our culture, their version of Islam.'

'And I am guessing this.' Sam gestured to himself and Laylah. 'Does not fit into this version?'

'Definitely not.' Laylah sighed. 'Of course, *I* don't care, and my parents are not particularly conservative either so I am sure it will be fine, but...this is not going to stay quiet. I am so sorry.'

Sam looked up at the sky, taking in the warmth of the sun on his skin and the breath-taking arrangement of the clouds. He stayed silent for a long moment, processing what she had said.

'Sam?' She said, her voice tearful, and he glanced down, surprised to see that her eyes were swimming with tears. 'Are you okay? I am sorry,' she repeated. 'If this is too much for you if don't want this, me...' her voice broke.

'No, Laylah, god, no. There is no need to apologise, you did nothing wrong, *nothing*. I don't care about them, or what they think. People are going to think what they are going to think. I am sure some of my uncles and aunts back home probably would raise an eyebrow at us.' Sam paused and extended his hand, which after a second of hesitation, after flicking her eyes towards Shahid Laylah took.

'Laylah, all I care about is *you*, what *you* think, what *you* want. And if *you* want me. Then I am not going anywhere.'

'I want you.' Laylah said simply, but her hand squeezed his, so tight that he could see the whites of her knuckles. A moment later she stood and this time, she kissed him, it was short and sweet. Soft. But with an edge of what felt like determination. Resolution.

Afterwards, slightly breathless, Sam indicated to their plates. 'We should probably eat.'

Laylah nodded and sat.

'Tell me about your family, your community.' Sam asked once they had tackled the Crêpes which melted in his mouth. Magic.

So Laylah told him. Told him about her family, how much she loved her parents and how hard it was sometimes to balance being Arab and a New Zealander, how hard it was to reconcile those two sides of herself. Oil and water. How the community, although it meant well drove a lot of people away because of the standards they held, both people her own age and the elders, 'Sometimes it's as if they forget we live here, that they brought us here. We cannot live like we did in the Middle East. Heck people that live in the Middle East don't act like they live in the Middle East anymore.'

'That must be tough.'

Laylah nodded. 'Very much so.'

'Coffee?' Sam asked.

Laylah nodded and they wandered over, Sam ordered a Latte for himself and a Cappuccino for her. Thanking the barista, they each nursed their coffees and began strolling around the sunlit courtyard. Their hands naturally entwining together.

'Sam, I have been thinking, do you mind telling me what happened when your brother passed away?' She asked hesitantly.

So Sam told her. Told her about. Pounding music. Shots. Soft hair. Swaying hips and pillow-like lips. Tangled bedsheets. Thudding headaches. Regret. And doing it all over again.

He told her how that had all ended when he had moved back home. How he no longer had the time or energy for pounding music, shots, swaying hips, pillow-like lips and tangled bedsheets. And how his friends...how they got sick of waiting. Apparently, there was a time limit for grief.

How he started going to church with mum, initially just for support but how with time it also became *his* solace too. How he found peace in God, a God that for so long he had denied and rejected but was there, waiting for him when he chose to return. God was an explanation, a reason, a purpose. It gave him comfort, comfort that this sorrow, this grief, that all this *pain* had a purpose. That one day, as ridiculous as it sounded, hopefully, he would see James once more. But mostly? That there was a bigger plan at work. Even if he did not need to understand it. So when his parents proposed a move, a fresh start to a beautiful nation, thousands of miles away that they had visited years ago when Sam was too small to remember, where mum was originally from. Well, Sam had said yes, he had faith. In God he had faith.

Chapter Seventeen

Laylah: A World of Uncertainties

| | my night sky has always been
| | filled with stars,
| | so, at first
| you(r) | presence was subtle,
| | unimportant.
| | the first sliver of a new moon.

| | but then?
| | it grew
| | bright, round and all consuming,
| | outshining my stars,
| | for the light it
| brought | set my sky alight.

| | it grew, bringing
| me | joy,
| | laughter
| | and a soaring heart.

so how did i ever live without
kind words,
smiling eyes
and this quiet thoughtfulness that i now love.

Last night Laylah had found out that Sam had a promiscuous past, and today he had filled in the details. In all honesty, Laylah wasn't surprised, he was gorgeous, *gorgeous*, to the point that it made her feel inadequate sometimes. But she was glad that they had talked about it, glad that she felt like she knew him better now but mostly glad that last night he had not blinked when she told him about her complete *lack* of experience, how she had never been in love, never been kissed.

Well *now* she had, she corrected herself. Three times. And it was magical. Even just thinking back to those moments made her heart race. But she was equally glad that they had been so upfront, that they had discussed boundaries because once she broke down the walls of initial shyness she knew that her self-control would be questionable.

She unlocked the door having just said goodbye to Sam after the markets, he and Nikau were going to watch rugby and Laylah had no interest in sports, even if it was the All Blacks.

Throwing her keys into the bowl she turned to find Ariana curled up on the couch her hair in a maroon turban today. *When Harry Met Sally* was playing which Laylah was sure Ariana had watched at least a dozen times already this year. But as soon as she saw Laylah, Ariana hit pause and turned. They had missed each other this morning due to Ariana's early shift so there was a lot of filling in to be done.

'Sit.' Ariana pointed, curling her feet underneath her to make room for Laylah.

Laylah settled in for what she knew would be a lengthy interrogation with a smile.

'Go.'

'He was fine with it, with all of it and we went to the markets this morning.' Laylah said, smiling as she thought back to the crêpe they had eaten, she wasn't sure what was sweeter, them or Sam's lips...she cringed at herself internally, *god romance really did make a person insufferable.*

'Laylah!' Ariana's voice pulled her out of her reverie. 'Don't you even dare. Details. I need details. What did he say? What did you say? What did he wear today? What did you eat?'

'Okay, okay, but tea first,' and only once Laylah had returned, handing a disgruntled Ariana a mug of soothing Chamomile did she give her a blow by blow of the evening. 'And then we kissed...'

'You what?!' Ariana yelped, almost spilling her tea.

'We kissed! A few times actually, last night and just before.'

'Laylah! Have I taught you nothing?! You are supposed to *start* with that!' Ariana said, shaking her head, bewildered by Laylah.

'Sorry!' Laylah laughed.

'How was it?'

'Perfect, in every way,' Laylah smiled.

'Good, he looks like a good kisser.'

'*Ariana!*' Laylah laughed again and when all Ariana did was shrug, she admitted. 'Well, he is.'

'Okay, keep going.' Ariana said once they had both calmed down.

So Laylah did, she told her about their conversation, how they had decided to put sex on the back burner, but tactfully omitted Sam's past and the parts about James. That was not her story to tell. She had just started to explain how they were about to kiss today. 'And then I saw Shahid...'

'WHAT?!' And for a second time in less than ten minutes Ariana almost spilled her tea, '*Shahid, Shahid?*'

Laylah nodded.

'Did she see you kiss?'

'I pulled away, but then, I kissed him a few minutes after that and I am sure she would have seen that.' Laylah shrugged.

'*Damn* Laylah. *Damn*. I don't know what to say, aren't you worried about what everyone is going to say?'

'I was for a moment.' Laylah admitted. 'But then I decided it didn't matter, I want him, he wants me, *that* is all that matters. And to be honest? People like Shahid are going to talk no matter what. My Muslim and Arab friends, the ones whose opinions I care about, like you, they won't mind.

Ariana nodded. 'Good for you. God, I am so happy for you two.'

Laylah smiled. 'I am happy too.'

Ariana took her hand. 'I can tell. Now, do you want to finish this movie with me?'

Laylah settled in. 'Has Sally showed him the fake orgasm yet?' She asked.

. . .

The weekend ended too quickly and Laylah was once more flung into the week, it was one of the busiest with two assignments due on Wednesday and a test Thursday afternoon she barely saw Sam. It didn't take her long to start missing him immensely.

Laylah walked out of her test on Thursday, exhausted but so relieved that it was over. *That had gone well*, she thought satisfied. She had to ramp up her writing speed a bit in the last fifteen minutes to finish her second essay but she was satisfied with both.

A breeze rustled a lone tree and Laylah rubbed her arms, feeling the cold, it was definitely starting to get cooler. Already in tights and a sports bra, she headed to the gym for a much-needed sweat session alone. As much as she usually loved company she needed this. She needed to sweat off the late nights and the exhaustion of the week that had just been. The frustration and odd satisfaction from all those assessments.

At the gym, Laylah pulled on her headphones and made a beeline to the squat rack, her blood already pulsing.

. . .

An hour later she was done, drenched in sweat, heart racing, but done, she walked home in satisfaction.

At home, Laylah stepped under the hot water of the shower and just let herself soak, allowing the water to gently caress her skin. Her taut muscles began to unwind.

Skin first. Laylah reached for her coconut scented soap and as she scrubbed her olive skin she mused how golden it was right now. How it would return milky and pale in winter. That was a shame. Her skin had always been one of her favourite parts of herself. Even more so when it was sun-kissed. It reminded her of Syria. It reminded her of her ancestors and that no matter how long she lived in this beautiful land, no matter how much *this* became home too, she should never forget her roots. It made her feel connected to her past and more certain of her future in a world that most of the time was anything but certain.

Hair next. Laylah massaged her scalp with a shampoo that smelled of Jasmines like the ones that had grown, climbing the walls of their garden in Syria. Her first real home. Ahh, *home* she sighed, what a funny concept.

Finally, Laylah dragged herself out of the shower, wrapped snugly in a towel she walked into her room and noticed her phone light up. A text from Sam.

I hope your test went well, I have missed you so much. If it's okay, I am coming to pick you up at 8:00 pm. And before you ask, no I cannot tell you for what, it's a surprise. Dress warmly, see you soon. x

Dress warmly? She thought, what on earth were they going to do.

...

A couple of hours later in her favourite purple turtleneck, a pair of simple black jeans and flat boots she opened the door to Sam who was in his own black jeans, Chelsea boots and a light blue sweater that matched his eye almost frighteningly.

Sky blue.

He also held a bag, *interesting* she thought and although she yearned to ask where they were going she held her tongue.

Sam leaned forward and kissed her forehead before he took her hand. 'Let's go.'

Chapter Eighteen

Sam: Blood Red

Sam was impressed by Laylah's self-control, she had not asked where they were going once even though he was sure that every fibre in her body would want to know. But she remained silent and had simply accepted his hand as he led her out of the door.

Sam glanced at his watch every few seconds, as they walked along darkened streets. Hopefully, they would not be late.

They smelled the gardens before they saw them, the air drenched, infused with the sweet scent of roses and flowers. Sam led her past the chair they had sat on only a few days ago but they didn't stop, not tonight. It was a strange thing wasn't it, that something could simultaneously feel like it was happening an eternity ago, but also like it was happening right now. Time was funny like that.

Sam flicked on his phone's torch as he led Laylah to an unlit incline, a side trail he had discovered on a run the other day. As they climbed, the shadows of the trees on either side, danced in the torchlight like their own personal guardians, they were alive.

Ten minutes later they were almost there and light began to filter through an opening in the trees allowing them to glimpse the canvas of the night sky. And painted on that canvas? The moon. Beautiful. Blood red. Fire. Just like Laylah.

'Sam!' She whispered up at him before she let go of his hand and ran towards the moon, her hair silver in the darkness.

Sam found her like that, standing on the lookout as the city lights winked below, drenched in moonlight. He placed the bag down and from behind her slipped his arms around her waist. She leaned back into him and it felt so natural, the sway of bamboo in the breeze. He held her tight.

'It's called a blood moon, a lunar eclipse,' he whispered. 'The next one won't be for another fifteen years,' he hesitated. 'It's rare, it's beautiful, it reminds me of you.'

Laylah's eyes turned to meet his and without a word she turned and looped her arms around his waist, burying her face in his chest. 'Thank you,' she said.

'Did I ever tell you that my name means night?' She whispered into his chest a moment later.

'Really?'

Laylah nodded and pulled her head back, she took his hand and traced something, a drawing. 'Laylah,' she said.

'And this is Sam,' she said tracing a new sequence, a new pattern onto his hand.

Sam finally understood, this was Arabic. 'You will have to show me how to write that out properly,' he said. 'You know what?'

'What?'

'My name, Sam, is actually short for Samson, it's Hebrew. My parents chose it because when I was born James wanted to name me Sun.' Sam chuckled.

'What?' She laughed.

'He was so little, I am not sure why. Maybe because he loved the Teletubbies and the sun was a baby in that show? When we were older he said that it was because I was the light of his life, he had wanted a little brother for so long.' Sam chuckled.

'Anyway, my dad suggested Sam, short for Samson. In Hebrew, it means the sun.'

'Sun and night.' Laylah said. 'This is either meant to be or a complete disaster.'

'Definitely meant to be.' Sam said and leaned down to kiss her forehead.

Sam pulled his arms away from her, opened the bag and pulled out some food, a tarp for them to sit on and a blanket before he sat down and extended his hand for Laylah to sit. She nestled herself between his legs so she could watch the moon, leaning back into his chest.

As they sat, under the stars, he pointed out the constellations. It had taken a while for him to learn them, the sky here was different from what he had grown up seeing. *This was better,* Sam thought. So much better and the blood moon above, in all its majesty, Sam was sure it agreed.

Chapter Nineteen

Laylah: A Life of Sin

	they preach that to love him is a sin,
	but how so?
	for did not
god	place this love within me?
	from the day my heart first beat,
	at just six weeks?

	but he believes, he reads
	and he prays to you almighty,
	if only in a different tongue,
	in a different home.
	but...he is home.
is	that not enough?

	because these men, these
	men that they insist i
love	they do not pray at all,
	they do not read. they do not believe.
	they are not home.

Friday morning, Laylah and Sam sat in their favourite café, both sipping their coffees before Sam drove Laylah to the airport, she was going home to visit family for the weekend.

'Do you think your parents would like me?' Sam asked teasingly, but with a level of earnestness just below the surface.

'Of course, how could they not?' Laylah laughed. 'You would dwarf everyone though, honestly, I am the shortest, but no one in my family would be described as *tall* either.'

'Wait, even shorter than your eight-year-old sister?' Sam teased.

Laylah frowned and feigned anger. 'Sir you are playing a dangerous game!'

'I am sorry, I am sorry.' Sam laughed and clasped her hand from across the table in his. 'I am going to miss you,' he said, his playful tone becoming serious.

'I will miss you too.' Laylah said and squeezed his hand in return. 'What are you going to do?'

'Some marking, go to the gym with Nikau, but mainly finish up my proposal. It's due Wednesday.'

'Sounds busy.' Laylah smiled.

'Well, I should get as much work done as I can since you aren't here.'

'Are you calling me a distraction?!' Laylah asked in mock horror.

'Yes, but I am not saying that's a bad thing. You are the *best* kind of distraction.' Sam grinned.

'Good.' Laylah said knowing she was going to miss him immensely, more than she was willing to admit.

...

As the engines of the plane whirred, Laylah's mind wandered, thinking about the best way to tell her parents about Sam. Logical Laylah suggested silence, that it was too early to tell her parents about someone that she had only known for such a brief period of time. But her heart disagreed and even the logical side of Laylah, flustered as it was by the events that had unfolded recently could not deny that Sam certainly wasn't just *someone*. Couldn't deny the feelings that were blossoming, blooming for him. Sam was important, her soul *knew* that he was important. This wasn't something that she could hide and even if she wanted to.

Still unsure Laylah slipped into a weary sleep. As the plane flew towards its destination, like a pendulum she swung between the moments of sheer joy that she had spent with Sam and nerves at her parent's reaction. She had never told them about a boy, before Sam, there hadn't been anything to tell. *It will be fine* she promised herself and forced herself to breathe.

...

The plane landed with a gentle thud and then within moments came to a halt. Almost immediately people began to unclasp their seatbelts and gather their bags but Laylah remained in her seat, avoiding the queue that was quickly forming while they all waited to be able to leave the plane. Instead, Laylah opted to enjoy the view outside the window, the sun blazing in a clear sky.

Fire in sky blue.

Once people started moving Laylah quickly and efficiently, grabbed her carry-on and strolled out of the airplane where *Mama* and *Baba* were waiting for her. They weren't difficult to spot. Laylah was almost identical to her *Mama*, long red hair, now streaked with grey, that fell down her back in waves, a small gentle face embedded with emeralds and skin like ice with just an undertone of olive. *Baba* was more traditionally Arab looking with caramel skin and what remained of his balding hair midnight. Laylah could have not looked more different from *Baba* if she had tried, except the eyes, they both had the same cinnamon eyes.

Laylah embraced them both, noting with a bit of frustration that she was indeed shorter than both of them, apparently she took after one of her great grandmothers in height.

As they strolled to the car, *Mama* chatted away in Arabic about how excited Ayat and Dina were to see her, how they were at home now, cooking lunch and how Yousuf would drop by too, he wanted them to go to the gym with Laylah.

Mama continued her steady stream of conversation in the car, which cousin was engaged, which had broken a leg and who had upset the precarious state of a middle eastern family politics. All the while *Baba* remained mostly silent, shooting her a smile here and there about something that *Mama* would say. Laylah's mind flitted in and out of the conversation, making sure to say the right things at the right time, *Walahi?* Really? *Mashallah!* Praise be to God! *Inshallah.* If God wills. But Laylah was distracted as they entered her childhood home, a city that had crumbled as the earth stretched, groaned and rearranged itself with no concern for the humans that lived upon it. But that was the nature of the earth, of the world. Sometimes it comforted them, gave *exactly* what they needed. And sometimes it brought callous destruction.

The earth trembling, bricks, walls, furniture collapsing. Lives lost, forever. Laylah remembered the earthquake vividly, she also remembered every aftershock that had followed. Every aftershock that had caused them all to tremble, just as the earth did.

Now, the earth had calmed, fallen back into its slumber. The aftershocks were rare, months of sleepy calm punctuated with tiny snores. Now, the city was being rebuilt, slowly, but surely. Murals had popped up everywhere, as people turned their despair, their horror, their grief into art. Trying to make sense, to bring brightness and light to what can be such a dark, dark world. Bike lanes were being installed everywhere and their public transport would soon be unrivalled. Christchurch, she was rising, giving everyone hope that *yes* we can crumble, but we can all rise too.

...

Soon they were home and Laylah walked into her childhood house, the memories flooding in. A place filled with laughter and memories. *Baba* had recently repainted the exterior she noted and the garden was filled with the heady scent of roses, *Mamas* pride and joy. As a child, she had hated being pulled into these tasks, but she almost missed it now.

Dina ran to the door and Laylah enveloped her first and then Yousuf in a hug before she gave Ayat a gentle shove. She strolled into the kitchen, the main hub of the family, kitted out with every gadget and appliance that you could ever possibly want or need. The living room was just ahead and Laylah felt the familiar, though still odd sensation that she was transported back to the middle east. Lush carpets covered all of the wooden floors, the colours of jewels. Rubies. Sapphires. Emeralds. The walls were lined with sketches and watercolours of olive trees, dates and Arabic calligraphy. In the centre stood an enormous watercolour of *Al-Aqsa,* the golden-domed mosque of Palestine which only her mother had ever been lucky enough to visit. She touted it as one of the best days of her life. Finally, every inch of every surface was covered in ornaments, made of wood, copper and steel.

She was home, in so many, many ways, she was home.

...

It was a good day, lunch of hummus, falafel and fresh from the oven pita bread was followed by a gym session with Yousuf and Emma which was followed by some family time. Naturally, Laylah's attention was pulled in a million directions as she flitted from conversation to conversation.

Dina jabbered endlessly about school, her friends and the new art project they were doing in class. Ayat badgered her with questions about university, the anxiety that plagued her because she had no idea what she wanted to do and had just over a year to decide. Yousuf boasted about the gym, his new deadlift weight and whether or not he should get into CrossFit. She discussed the political climate with Emma and *Mama* chatted about her new job caring for the elderly, how although she found it exhausting, it brought her endless satisfaction and joy. *Baba* told her about his job, he was a physics teacher and was contemplating how best to teach his young students about Newton's three laws without boring them.

Suffice to say that by dinner time Laylah was exhausted, happy but exhausted, in one day she talked as much as she did in a week back home.

Emma and Yousef joined them for dinner and without even asking *Mama* had made Laylah's favourite meal, semolina dumplings in a yoghurt sauce. It sounded strange but it was delicious and Laylah had three helpings, only stopping when her jeans were beginning to feel slightly too tight. It was perfect. The food was amazing, the company even better.

Once dinner was done, Emma and Yousuf went to the living room to choose a movie while the rest of them cleaned up.

Mama sighed and shook her head at the living room. 'Yousef was hanging the washing earlier, I told him though, that's what happens when you marry a white girl, they don't know our ways.'

'*Mama*...' Laylah sighed. 'We have talked about this, there is nothing wrong with Yousef doing his share and besides, it is *none of our business*.' Laylah said firmly.

'I know, I know, sorry *habbibty*. Do you know your cousin? The one in America? Well, she is engaged to a *Shia* man.' *Mama* said.

'Oh that's awesome, I will have to give her a call and congratulate her.' Laylah said excitedly, she had never met her cousins in America but she had always sensed they would get along.

'Awesome? Laylah, *habbibty*, your aunt is distraught.'

'Why?'

'Well she is much more traditional your aunty and she is worried that her grandchildren will be raised with *Shia* principles. I know they are Muslim but they are just...*different*.' *Mama* shook her head.

'What about a non-Muslim, say a Christian or a Jew?' Laylah asked tentatively, trying to appear, nonchalant.

'For a man? We allow it. But for a woman? *Astaghfar Allah,* it is *haram*.' *Mama* said and shook her head almost violently with a shudder.

Laylah remained silent, truth be told the religious element had never occurred to her. She had assumed that because her parents had accepted Yousef's relationship, begrudgingly, sure, but they had, that they would accept hers too. Especially since they had lived in New Zealand for almost her entire life. In the last few years especially, Laylah had separated her spiritual side from Islam almost entirely but the rest of her family were not particularly religious or traditional either. Laylah's aunty that lived in the United States was the only one who wore the *hijab* and although her father studiously went to every Friday prayer, most of her family only attended the mosque a couple of times a year for *Eid*. Where were all these rules, all of this religious conviction coming from?

Laylah remained distracted throughout the entire film, all she knew was that there were a lot of explosions and flashing lights. A very typical Yousef film. A couple of hours later the film finally finished, Yousef and Emma headed home and everyone else when to bed. Laylah, exhausted, pretended that she was not tired and as soon as *Mama* kissed her goodnight she went to the bookshelf in *Baba's* study, her fingers trailed along the spines of all the books, over her father's old Physics textbooks, his bound Masters dissertation, all embossed with gold lettering. Finally, she found it, her father's Quran, passed down, from his father and his father before him, one of the oldest things in this house. Gently she pulled it from its place, stroked the black leather, filled with an intricate mass of gold Arabic calligraphy. Slowly she opened it, sitting cross-legged on the floor, she couldn't even remember the last time she had opened a Quran.

Half an hour later she had given up, her Arabic was average at best but the verses of the Quran were long and complex. If only there was a control *find* function. Carefully replacing the Quran, she knew what to do next, she should have thought of this from the beginning.

Google. Thank god, thank *Allah* for Google.

It didn't take long for Laylah to find scholar after scholar after scholar who all agreed that it was okay for a man to marry a non-Muslim woman, but not the other way around.

Laylah's heart deflated. Even though she was not practising, even though her parents were not that devout, when it came to something like this, to *haram, halal,* to sin, there was little room for *ifs, buts, maybes* and *exceptions*. In the eyes of the community, there was right and then there was wrong. There was black and then there was white. Except the world wasn't black and white, it was a kaleidoscope, a whirring combination of wavelengths of different spectrums. At the very least, it was a world of grey.

Laylah sighed and finally closed her laptop, she would have to talk to *Mama,* be open, honest and hope that her parents who she had always seen as so progressive, so liberal, would understand. *Surely they would understand and want her to be happy.*

Teeth brushed and in her most comfortable set of track pants, Laylah finally settled into bed in her childhood room. Posters, Harry Potter, Green Day, Red Hot Chili Peppers and so many more were still draped across the walls.

Her phone buzzed, a sweet text from Sam, asking her how her day had been and wishing her goodnight, he missed her he said. She missed him too but a pit had formed in her stomach. The beautiful lake that was their love was now tainted, finally after almost an hour of worry, of tossing and turning, Laylah fell into a tumultuous, restless sleep.

...

Laylah was up before the rest of the family so she wrote, it was funny but poetry, good, bad, soft, hard, hopeless and hopeful came so much more easily now. It was as if her blood was made of words. So maybe this assignment wouldn't be so hard after all?

Laylah felt calmer, pouring her soul into paper gave her hope, as did the bright sun and the brilliance of the sky outside.

Sky blue.

Her phone vibrated on the table and Laylah glanced at it, a smile stretching the muscles on her face, warming her heart.

Good morning, I am helping Nikau at his father's Avocado farm today, I will make sure to bring you some. I hope you are having a good time with your family, miss you! xxx

Her sky blue.

Laylah closer her eyes and enjoyed the bliss of having someone *miss you*, a completely foreign, completely heart-warming feeling that she wanted to savour.

. . .

Half an hour later, *Mama* walked into the kitchen in her big, fluffy, purple robe, hair pulled back into a bun. Laylah had inherited her mother's hair but not her eyes, *Mama* had gorgeous green eyes that were a sea of softness in her fire. And *Mama* certainly was fire, she had left her home, everyone she loved and entered an alien country for the safety of her children. The first years were hard, she had been ridiculed for her halting English and getting a job was difficult, even once her English had improved, all the employer had to do was glance at her name. Worst of all were the rare occasions when people had said things to *Mamas's* face.

Go back to your own country. How when it was nothing but rubble?

But *Mama* had survived. Beautiful. Strong. Soft. Hard.

Laylah made *Mama* a cup of tea and they chatted mindlessly for a bit before Laylah decided to brave the topic. '*Mama*, you know the whole women marrying non-Muslims, men can, why cannot we?' Laylah asked.

Mama remained silent for a long moment. 'Men and women are not the same *habbibty, Allah* made it so.'

'But why does it matter?'

'Laylah, the man is the head of the household, if a man marries a Christian or a Jewish woman, his children will still be Muslim, but if a Muslim woman does, her children won't be.' *Mama* explained.

Laylah frowned, trying to contain the feminist within her that screamed at the injustice and instead put herself within the historical context. 'But does that matter today? Some children have two Muslim parents and don't become Muslim, some children have a Muslim father and become Christian...look at Ariana,' Laylah argued.

'Exactly, look at Ariana, the children are lost *habbibty*.' *Mama* said.

'No, Ariana isn't lost, she's just...' Laylah protested but *Mama* interrupted.

'Laylah, *habbibty,* it is not our place to question the scholars and the scholars have deemed it is not permissible for a woman to marry outside of her faith. It is a sin and any woman who goes through with it will be living a life of sin. Her children will be the product of sin...' *Mama* shuddered, shaking her head she said a prayer.

'But we do not wear *hijab*, you let Ayat date that Pakistani boy in her class, why is *this* so important?'

'We are not perfect...' *Mama* started, brow furrowed, she understood the card Laylah was playing. 'But this is too much. As Muslims, it is our *duty* to do everything in our hands to ensure that our children are Muslim, that we pass the faith to them.'

Laylah remained silent. She hadn't prayed for years and neither had any of her siblings. None of them considered themselves religious, a fact she was sure deep down her parents knew. Laylah's parents had made a lot of changes and adjustments but on this topic, Laylah could tell that *Mama* would not budge.

'Laylah, why are you asking all of these questions?' *Mama* asked quietly.

Laylah took a deep breath, her heart racing she thought of Sam and decided to be brave, to tell *Mama* the truth. 'Well, I met someone, his name is Sam, he is half American and...' Laylah paused, wondering how she could sum up the love that had blossomed within her already...*wait she loved him?!* And it took only a second for Laylah to agree with herself, *she did love him*. But how could she make *Mama* understand?

'Laylah.' *Mamas* voice was ice, cutting through her thoughts. 'Laylah, don't tell me that you *love* him, don't do what your brother has done to me, don't, don't...' *Mama* said, her voice beginning to rise.

'*Mama*, I, I...' but Laylah couldn't lie, neither to herself or *Mama* who didn't appear to be listening anyway.

'After everything we have done for you, everything we have sacrificed, a *kafir*?! Worse, an American?! Do you know what they have done to our people? To Muslims everywhere? Oh, the shame. The shame! *Astaghfirullah*. I should just go back to Syria now, you don't need me, you don't care about my opinion here anyway,' *Mama* cried.

'*Mama*, stop.' Laylah said and held her arm firmly. 'There is *nothing* happening between us, we are just friends and I was curious,' she said firmly.

A tear slid down *Mamas's* cheek but she was beginning to calm down. '*Walahi?*' She asked.

Laylah sighed, and although she could feel her own heartbreak, shatter into a million pieces, she nodded.

'Laylah, *habbibty* if you are interested, if you want to marry, we know plenty of nice, young Muslim men that we can arrange for you to meet, Ahmad for example, he is a nice young man...' *Mama* began.

But Laylah shook her head, she had gone to school with Ahmad. Sure he was a nice young man when it suited him when his parents and the community were watching, but Laylah also knew for a fact that he spent half of his lectures high, the other drunk and every weekend he was at a different club. And that wasn't even what Laylah's objection was. She knew that when the time came Ahmad would marry a *good Muslim girl,* who had never so much as touched a man. The hypocrisy infuriated her. 'It's okay *Mama*, honestly, I am too busy with university for men.' Laylah said.

Mama nodded. 'Good, you are too young for all of this anyway,' she said, resting her hand on Laylah's cheek.

Laylah smiled and nodded but inside fury and frustration joined her breaking heart. *Too young?* How could Laylah explain that her body had yearned for another for years? *Years*. How lonely she was some nights, how she wanted, *needed* companionship. But she didn't. She couldn't. No matter how liberal or progressive your parents were, you did not discuss sex in an Arab household. Instead, her generation did whatever they wanted while their parents looked the other way.

...

Soon the rest of the family was awake, for *Mama* the conversation was forgotten, but Laylah could not forget it. It was seared into her soul and now Laylah felt as if her heart had torn in two. Where did her duty lie? To herself? To her own happiness? Or to her parents? Her parents who were the kindest people in the world, who had given her so much, sacrificed so much. For all of them. No, she couldn't disappoint *Mama*, couldn't bring shame onto her family.

And Sam? She loved him so much, loved him enough to know that he didn't deserve this either. He deserved a kiwi girl, one whose parents would meet him happily, who would not speak a foreign tongue in front of him. Who would happily let them marry in a church and would not make him fight. He shouldn't have to fight. She loved him too much to ask him to fight.

As her family gathered for breakfast, *Zaatar* with Olive Oil and bread fresh from the oven, Laylah poured cement into her heart. She felt it seep into every crevice, every atrium, every artery, every capillary, every vein. And then it hardened. This was not meant to be. Better that she knew this now than later. Sam would be hurt, yes, but he would move on, he would be fine. He would find someone better. Someone who belonged in his world.

Chapter Twenty

Sam: World Crumbling

The weekend had gone by so slowly, Sam couldn't believe how lonely it was without Laylah, how she had become such a permanent fixture of his life so quickly. But Sam ploughed on, spending a day out with Nikau at the farm, finally getting started on his literature review and resisting the temptation to bombard her with texts so she could spend time with her family. Suffice to say he was partially successful.

'What are you doing tonight?' Nikau asked on Sunday afternoon as they worked on their assignments on the family dinner table.

'Laylah should be back from Christchurch so I am cooking us dinner.' Sam said.

'Ahh, you two lovebirds.' Nikau grinned and then wrinkled his brow. 'I was thinking the other day, do her folks know about you by any chance?'

Sam paused and looked up from his laptop. 'My parents know about her...I was even thinking of inviting her over in a couple of weeks but I don't know what she has told her parents.'

'Okay...I wonder how her parents will take it.' Nikau said.

'Do you think it will be a problem?' Sam frowned.

'Honestly, I don't know man, I have met her parents a few times, they are cool, super nice and they love Laylah more than anything in the world, you can tell.' Nikau paused. 'Even though they aren't super religious, people can be funny about these things, they can cling to their faith and culture in these situations.' Nikau shrugged. 'My whole family will insist that they aren't homophobic but when I came out, well a few uncles and aunties had things to say.'

'What should I do?'

'Talk to Laylah and hey, maybe I am projecting, maybe I am way off base, I hope so. But there is no harm in bringing it up, although I am sure it will be fine.' Nikau reassured.

Sam nodded absentmindedly, worried for a moment before he shook his head, it wasn't the 1900s, it would be fine, he was sure it would be fine and Laylah had said that neither of her parents were that conservative anyway.

'How is your assignment going anyway?' Sam said, closing his laptop, he couldn't read another article from Google Scholar if his life depended on it.

Nikau sighed. 'Not bad. You know I am thinking of moving though?'

'Really, why?'

Nikau shrugged. 'Uni is full-on this year and I am spending half my time in the library or on my way to the library. I cannot afford to spend so much time commuting. I feel like I have no time for a proper social life. Do you know when the last time I went on a date was?!'

Sam shook his head.

'Well only a couple of weeks ago.' Nikau admitted sheepishly and Sam fought a grin.

'But seriously man, it's just getting a bit too hard.'

Sam nodded, there was a time when his commute was almost an hour in New York and he had *detested it*. Sure you could fill the time with podcasts and good music, but when you felt like you didn't have much time in the first place, having so much taken from you was painful.

'I will keep an eye out, if anyone is looking for a roommate, I will let you know.'

'Thanks, man.' Nikau smiled. 'Also...Kiwis say, *flatmate*, otherwise it sounds like you are sharing a room with someone.'

Sam crinkled his brow. 'Right, *flatmate.*'

Nikau shut his laptop with a sigh. 'Do you want to go for a walk, I don't think I can stare at the screen anymore.'

Sam nodded and they set off into Nikau's beautiful farm. Rolling hills, sheep *everywhere*, and fresh air that New Yorkers only dreamed of.

...

After he left Nikau's house, he made a quick trip to the grocery store before heading home. As he walked through the front door, groceries in hand for homemade chilli, he was surprised to see George on the couch.

'Hey Sam, do you have a second?' George said and gestured to the seat next to him as soon as Sam walked in.

'Sure.' Sam said, dropping off the bags to the kitchen before joining George. 'How are you going?'

'Good, actually, really good. But I have some news, I am moving out. Back to Wellington.' George paused. 'That conversation we had a couple of weeks ago stuck with me. I am going, to be honest with you, I am *useless* at business, I have failed half my tests and only scraped through the other half. So I have decided I don't care what anyone thinks, I applied to nursing school and well, I got in.'

'Oh my god man! That's so awesome, good on you!' Sam slapped his shoulder, a huge grin spreading across his face. 'Where will you live?'

'My parents have a little unit with its own bathroom and kitchenette. It's still attached to the main house but I have my own entrance so I can come and go as I please and most importantly, I get Newt back,' and the biggest smile engulfed George's face like the rising sun. 'I miss him so much, and I am going to need him with all the late nights I am sure are coming.'

'Have you told your dad?'

George shook his head. 'He finishes work in an hour so I will call then, but Mum knows, and she was *very* happy for me. I will just be honest with Dad, tell him I cannot be this person who he wants me to be and, and I am sure he will come around.'

'Well, I will be sorry to see you go.'

'I am going to miss you, honestly, I don't know what I would have done if you and I hadn't had that chat and I know we haven't had the chance to hang out heaps but seeing you running or going to the gym, getting your ass to the library, well it made me realise that I need to get my life together. That I cannot waste three years and thousands of dollars just getting pissed. Thank you.' George said, his brown eyes solemn, sincere.

'I am glad to have helped and honestly, you are going to be amazing at this. Hit me up if you ever need anything.'

George nodded. 'You too man, and of course I will keep paying rent till we find a replacement.'

Sam nodded. 'When do you fly out?'

'Tomorrow, pretty early so don't worry about waking up.'

'Are you sure?'

George nodded. 'You have already done so much.' They both stood and hugged, the awkward, one-armed hug that men often did. Then with one last smile, George strode into his room to finish packing and make his phone call.

Sam walked into the kitchen and noticed how clean everything was. George. He grinned. Sam started on the onions and garlic, he would miss George. They hadn't had the chance to hang out hugely, their schedules were just so different, but he had still loved their kitchen chats, joining him on the couch while he watched the rugby. George had thankfully spent a good afternoon explaining the rules of this strange game which was just like football but without the safety equipment. Sam swept the onions and garlic into the already hot pan and heard the satisfying sizzle as they hit the olive oil. The smell was intoxicating. Sam moved on to chopping the carrots and celery and admitted that he was very happy for George. Happy that he was going to do what he loved, despite what his dad thought.

...

A few hours later, dinner was finished, Sam was exhausted, yet satisfied, he checked his phone, it was almost 7:00 pm, Laylah should be back by now. He had just finished setting the table when he heard a knock on the door.

Quickly, he whipped off his apron, wiped his hands and made sure he smelled okay – mainly like onions and garlic which wasn't *bad* – before opening the door. Immediately he enveloped Laylah in his arms and the wave of calm, of affection that passed through him made him realise once more just how much he had missed her. How much it had felt like something was missing when she was gone. They stood for a few moments, neither quite ready to let go before finally Sam pulled back, she was beautiful as always in a simple blue dress.

'We better head inside, dinner will be getting cold,' he laughed.

Laylah gave him a half-smile and nodded.

They sat down and Sam began filling her plate with the chilli, a tortilla wrap, guacamole and a salad before filling a plate for himself, Laylah thanked him but did not touch her plate.

'Sam, we need to talk about something,' she said, her voice quiet.

Sam looked up immediately, sensing that something was not quite right and only then did he notice the dark circles under her eyes and her expressionless face. Stone.

'Is everything okay?' He asked and put down his own fork.

Laylah nodded. 'Sam, I...I...I think we should just be friends.'

Sam slowly shook his head. 'What? Why? Did I do something? Did something happen?' He asked fighting to remain calm.

'Sam, no of course not, you did nothing wrong. I have just been doing a lot of thinking this weekend and...well this could never work, we come from different worlds, let's stop now. Let's stop before this goes too far before it's too late,' she sputtered.

From the depth of his despair, Sam registered that she was fighting to keep calm too, but he was fighting harder, his mind whirred and his heartfelt too heavy to bear. 'I think it is already too late...' He whispered. 'Come on, we can make it work, please, just tell me what you need, tell me. Anything. I will do it. I...I love you.' Sam said and although this was the first time he had said those words, he knew that they were true. That nothing could ever, would ever be *more* true. And for a moment he thought she felt it, thought he saw something in her eyes. A flicker. Could it be *warmth*? But the moment passed as quickly as it came and her face became emotionless once more. And her eyes, those eyes that had always been so warm. Cinnamon. They were now hardened pools. Charcoal. Emotionless. She wasn't going to budge.

Fire had turned to ash.

'I am sorry Sam,' she said and stood to let herself out.

Sam sat in silence. His hands shook. His world crumbled. His heart tore. He didn't know what to do. Wasn't even sure he remembered how to breathe.

Seconds later a knock on the door startled him and like a zombie, he walked over, opened the door to Nikau who stood, ice cream in hand and a look of compassion on his face, he knew what had happened, he knew everything, Sam could tell.

Nikau put the ice cream down and without a word pulled Sam into a hug. Sam gripped him, so hard he was sure it would have been uncomfortable. But Nikau did not move and they stood there for what could have been hours until eventually, Sam pulled away.

'Do you want to talk about it?' Nikau asked.

Sam shook his head, too numb to even respond.

Chapter Twenty-One

Laylah: A Good Arab Wife

                it's 9 am on a saturday
                and screams echo through aisle ten,
                the home of biscuits and tea.
                a weary toddler
                sits on a throne,
                face beetroot
screaming   for chocolate chip cookies.

                an
over   weary parent looks on,
                dark bruises an eyeliner of exhaustion,
                desperation,
                as bystanders hurry by, eyes down,
                grabbing biscuits and tea.

                but i? i stand in the centre of the home of
                biscuits and tea,
                look the child dead in the eye
                and inside i am demanding answers.

you think you have a reason to scream do
you?

but on the surface, I am quiet,
calm as I stand in the aisle of
biscuits and tea,
mouth closed,
breath steady and no one knows,
not a single person knows that inside,
i am   screaming too?

Laylah closed the door and threw herself onto the couch, tears streaming she finally allowed her concrete heart to crack. This was for the best she reminded herself, she had done the right thing. But the tears that fell, swiftly and threatened to never stop – well they argued that this wasn't for the best. Not even slightly. Not at all.

Worse still? Sam. She had broken him, that much she could tell. Thank god she had the foresight to call Nikau. But she knew she would never forget his eyes in that moment, they would forever be seared into her conscious.

Sky blue turned to ashen grey.

Her sobs grew louder and she found herself wishing that Ariana was home, but she was on night shifts and wouldn't be back till late. So Laylah lay on the quickly dampening couch for what felt like hours, fearing that she would never move. That she would never want to, that she would never be able to.

The jangle of keys signalled that someone was at the door and Laylah sat up as Ariana walked in, a look of complete frustration on her face, her midnight hair in a sensible bun, frustration that melted instantly with one look at Laylah's face. 'Are you okay?'

Laylah drew her knees to her chest and held herself in a tight ball as if she hoped she could somehow keep herself from falling apart through sheer grit, her fingernails dug into her arms, almost painfully, she shook her head. 'I am fine,' she whispered.

Ariana walked over and held her in silence. Because sometimes nothing needed to be said, sometimes nothing could be said.

Once Laylah had returned to some semblance of calm Ariana explained that Nikau had called her, told her what was happening, that she had left work early, rushed home. Laylah explained what had happened at home, the conversation that she had with *Mama*.

Ariana sat quietly, listening, she could tell that Laylah would not budge, at least not for the moment. Laylah had chosen her parent's happiness and with that shattered her own.

...

Laylah woke the next day and despite her red-rimmed, swollen eyes, despite the hours of crying she was determined to be positive, determined to move on. She had to.

Laylah's phone rang and she sighed, trying to make herself sound human before she picked up. 'Salam *Mama*, how are you?'

'I am good *habbibty*, good, how are you?' *Mama* responded.

'I am okay.'

'Good, good. Now *habbibty* I have a favour to ask of you, *Khalto* Aza's sister just moved to Dunedin with her family, they are a very good Arab family. They have a son your age studying at university and I promised *Khalto* Aza that you would help him find his way around. Is that okay?' *Mama* asked.

Laylah sighed internally. She knew what this was, this wasn't the first time *Mama* had tried to set her up. A good Arab boy from a good Arab family, someone that *she* would approve of. Maybe she had mistaken her questions about marriage last weekend as interest?

'I am sorry *Mama* I am so busy right now with training and assignments. I don't think I have the time.'

'That's okay *habbibty*.' *Mama* said although the disappointment in her voice was evident.

After a few more minutes of exchanging pleasantries, Laylah said goodbye. She felt exhausted, her heart heavy from having to fake normalcy.

But as the day continued, Laylah could not push the interaction out of her head. When *Mama* had tried to set her up in the past and she had said no she had meant it, she had no interest in marriage, at least not in the traditional sense. But the longer Laylah thought about it, the more she realised if she was to ever meet someone that her parents approved of, this would be how it would happen, how it had to happen. So why not? Would it really hurt to meet this person? Maybe this would help her forget Sam, *oh Sam*.

Her eyes filled with tears which she angrily wiped away and before she could overthink it she called *Mama* back and arranged to meet this good Arab boy from a good Arab family. *Mama* was overjoyed and they agreed that Laylah would meet him for lunch tomorrow. His name was Amir.

'Okay *Mama* I have to go now, but I will talk to you later.' Laylah said.

'*Inshallah* oh and Laylah?'

'Yes, *Mama*?'

'Make sure that you dress *appropriately*.' *Mama* said.

Laylah paused for a moment and if it was possible her heart became even heavier. Finally, she responded. 'Of course *Mama*,' she didn't have any fight left in her and *Mama* was right, most Arab men would take issue with how she dressed. If she planned to be with a good Arab boy from a good Arab family, she better start practising how to be an Arab wife.

A good Arab wife.

Laylah shook, and this time she did not wipe away the falling tears, her heart so heavy she could barely stand at all.

...

The lunch date came faster than she thought it would. Laylah had barely slept and now she stood, looking over herself one final time in the mirror, smoothing her long-sleeved blouse nervously and reassessing her trousers. *Were they too tight?* A moment later she sighed to herself, this was the best she could do.

Not wanting to be late, Laylah headed off to the cafe where she had arranged to meet Amir, she had been careful to choose one outside campus not wanting anyone, especially Sam to see her, even Ariana didn't know at this stage.

Laylah arrived early, as usual, and reminded herself to *breathe*. But the moment she sat down her foot as if it had a mind of its own began tapping the floor anxiously.

Amir arrived, a few minutes late and Laylah rose to greet him. With the ease and smoothness of Arab etiquette, he apologised profusely.

They both sat down.

Immediately Laylah registered that Amir really was the epitome of an Arab male, about average height, dark brown hair and eyes that were set against surprisingly pale skin. He wasn't bad looking, not her type, but not bad. He was also impeccably dressed in dark chinos and a branded t-shirt with meticulously styled hair. Speaking of clothes, Laylah couldn't help noticing how his eyes lingered a little too long on her pants. *Damn, they probably were too tight.*

After she had directed him to the best stores for clothes, groceries and other purchases the questions naturally turned to each other.

'So Laylah, what are you studying?' He asked.

Laylah took a deep breath and reminded herself that this was the whole point. 'Law and Politics,' she answered.

'How are you finding it?' Amir asked.

'Honestly, it's pretty hard work. I love it though and I am pretty much guaranteed a job overseas or at least one with lots of travel.'

'Oh, that's a shame?' Amir frowned.

'A shame?' Laylah responded in surprise.

'I mean, I assume that you want to settle down in a couple of years, stay close to home, close to your family, have a few kids...' Amir stammered.

Laylah shook her head. 'Not at all, I would love the opportunity to live overseas or at least travel often. And I don't plan to have children anytime soon.' Laylah shrugged.

'*Oh.*'

Immediately Laylah kicked herself, she had said too much.

'What do you like doing in your free time?' Amir asked after a pregnant pause.

'A bit of everything, I like writing, going to the gym, cooking.' Laylah responded.

'Oh cool, I go to the gym a couple of times a week!' Amir grinned at her.

An awkward pause filled the air once more.

'Do you read?' Laylah asked as she pushed herself to make an effort.

'Not really, honestly, I spend most of my time studying and playing COD.'

'COD?' Laylah frowned.

'Call of duty, it's a computer game.' Amir responded.

'Oh, I see.' Laylah said before another awkward silence filled the air.

Finally, the conversation moved to family, something at least all Arabs could talk about at length. Amir eagerly pulled out his phone and showed her his entire family, two older sisters and a younger brother, Laylah couldn't help noticing that both of his sisters and his mother wore the full hijab and long *abayas.* Her pants were definitely too tight for this family.

After a few more questions, a few more awkward silences, coffees finished, they said goodbye.

As Laylah walked away her emotions swirled and the moment she closed the door of her flat, all the pent-up emotions, all the control she had tried to maintain, left her and the tears began to flow freely. She sobbed. Amir had been a nice guy. That was part of the problem. But the comment about her staying close to the family and settling down, his family's very obvious religiousness and as silly as it seemed even the fact that he seemed more interested in computer games than anything else told her that they were different. Very different.

Laylah took a deep shaky breath and her gaze landed on one of the few family pictures she had from Syria. Her mother stood, hugging *Teta* and *Sedoo* outside the brick walls of her grandparents' house where Jasmines entwined and climbed up to the heavens. This was taken mere months before they had left for New Zealand, the last time *Mama* had seen either of her parents. She had to try, she had to.

Laylah straightened up and walked to the bathroom. She sighed at how blotchy her face had become, not a great look with her hair before she washed her face and gently dabbed her puffy red eyes. Compromise she reminded herself was a normal part of a relationship and if she was to be a good Arab wife she would most certainly have to compromise. *For Mama*, she thought.

Slowly Laylah pulled out her phone and text Amir;

It was great meeting you today, let me know if you want to grab coffee or dinner at some stage.

Chapter Twenty-Two

Sam: Fragments

Sam wasn't sure if he was truly okay or if it just hadn't sunk in yet. Why? That had been his biggest question.

Ariana had briefly explained. Religion. Choosing between her family and him. Sin. But Sam still didn't understand. All his conversations with Laylah had proved to him time and time again that their faiths, faiths that had warred against one another time and time again for *centuries*...these faiths? They were truly two sides of the same coin. Two shafts of light from the same source. So a sin? How could love be a sin?

As for her family, Sam understood that, understood their importance but she hadn't even tried, hadn't even asked.

So Sam circled round and round his mind on this destructive, seemingly endless merry go round. But he refused to come to the most logical conclusion. A conclusion that with time seemed to be perhaps the only one; *she didn't care about him and perhaps she never had.*

No. Sam refused to allow himself to believe that, refused to believe that this had all meant nothing. *No!*

These thoughts whirled inside his head as he walked home after a long day at the lab and as Sam walked into his house he forced himself not to glance at her door.

Inside it was brightly lit and clean but also homely. Since moving in Nikau had quickly injected his own flair into the apartment and Sam had to admit, he had a real eye for it. The pieces of art that hung on the walls, the grey comforter and cushions – grey was Nikaus favourite colour - artfully strewn on the couch were just a couple of the touches that Nikau had made. Sam was infinitely grateful for Nikaus presence, it had been one of the few things that had kept him going in the last few days. The only bit of hope, a silver lining in this seemingly endless stormy night.

Light streamed through the open window and the curtains – you guessed it, grey – danced in the wind. Sam wandered almost instinctively towards the light and as he approached, the cool breeze caressed his skin whilst the sun warmed his face. He sighed and closed his eyes, momentarily forgetting his worries, momentarily being. Just being.

Sam made the snap decision to go for a run, he needed to calm down, needed his brain to slow down. To stop.

Moments later, shoes on, he was out the door and after a quick stretch, his feet pounded the pavement. Almost immediately he felt his mind begin to settle just as his heart began to race. Sam's feet led him to his favourite trail almost subconsciously, he had only been in Dunedin for a couple of months but he was beginning to know it quite well.

On the trail, his senses became alight.

The soft earth beneath his feet littered with roots that had carried the feet of hundreds of wanderers since before

Sam was born. The scent of sun-kissed pine wafting through the air, filling it with a heady scent. The crunch of twigs and early fall leaves beneath his feet, the rustle of the branches above and the twitter of birds excitedly having a conversation. A language all of their own. And slowly ever so slowly Sam felt his mind return to a place of calm. That's what nature did, it took him out of his head, reminded him that despite his troubles time would march on; flowers would blossom, leaves would fall, nature would be. Despite everything, nature would be. *Always.*

He heard the voices before he saw them and immediately he recognised one of them, Laylah. And another voice...a male? His heart stopped.

Sam's fears were quickly confirmed when he saw them come around the corner. His eyes met Laylah's large cocoa ones before she quickly dropped her gaze. She looked good in her all black attire of tights and a hoodie. Her rust coloured hair pulled back in a pony tail. Although Sam couldn't help but notice how pale she looked, was she usually this pale?

But Sam's attention was quickly drawn to the guy that she was with. Even in that brief moment Sam knew two things. First, he didn't like him. Second, they weren't just friends. The way he looked at Laylah, well it was the way he used too.

Worse? He was good looking. Not only was he classically dark and handsome, he exuded confidence, was dressed impeccably - despite the hike - and lacked the awkwardness that Sam knew was inherent with his long limbs.

All these thoughts whirred inside his head, a flurry of snowflakes in a snowstorm as he forced himself *not to stop.* As he ran, Sam's body shook. His heart rate quickened and his face flushed but it wasn't from the run. It took him a moment, but he quickly recognised this emotion. Anger.

The thought that he had tried to push down for days, that she didn't care, that she had never loved him was now rising to the surface, molten lava. His vision blurred so much that he wasn't sure how he got home. But he did.

Still shaking he slammed the door behind him and was so distracted that he bumped into the table on his way to the kitchen, knocking a plate to the floor. Sam stopped, sighed and with shaking hands bent down to pick up the plate and return it to the kitchen. As he straightened he caught sight of his reflection in the window. His eyes were round, his face blotchy, red and...wet? *When had he started crying?!*

No. No! He was better than this. He would show her. He should show them all.

Without thinking, Sam slammed the plate into the ground and it shattered. Whole pieces becoming fragments. Some large enough to cut. Other's so small that they were almost dust

And at that moment? Sam's world, his mind also shattered.

Fragment. Shaking hands, shards swept and then dropped into the bin.

Fragment. Shower, shave cologne, confidence.

Fragment. The local bar.

Fragment. A drink that burned like acid but numbed like heaven.

Fragment. Another drink. Then another. Then another. Then more. Ten? Fifteen? More?

Fragment. Slurred words. Blue eyes. Blonde hair. Long legs. Short skirt.

Fragment. A hand on the waist.

Fragment. A hand on his thigh and then higher.

Fragment. Arms around him. Pulling him away from the blue eyes. Blonde hair. Long legs. Short skirt.

Fragment. Fists raised.

Fragment. More arms. Restraint. Cannot. Move.

Fragment. A bucket of water. The icy sharpness of reality.

Fragment. An arm around his waist, half carrying him. Nikau?

Fragment. Head down the toilet. Retching. Bile. Fire.

Fragment. Warm water. Shaking limbs. A towel.

Fragment. A warm bed. The release of darkness. The sweetest nothing of all.

Chapter Twenty-Three

Nikau: Broken

It was pure luck really that Nikau had run into Laylah - also clearly a mess - who had blurted out something about Sam being upset, something about his feelings being hurt. Laylah had asked if he was okay and when Nikau said he hadn't seen him all day she asked, no, she *insisted* he found Sam. Almost hysterical. No, not almost, she was *definitely* hysterical.

But Sam didn't reply to his texts. Sam didn't reply to his calls. Alice didn't know where he was and neither did Sandy. Nikau wracked his brain trying to think *where could he go* and slowly a memory had emerged from the fog.

'Honestly man, there was a time when I was drinking so much that I was probably an alcoholic...I don't go near the stuff now if I can help it.'

Whatever had happened was serious; so maybe, just maybe alcohol was the answer. With a heavy heart Nikau had entered the local bar and with an even heavier heart, had seen Sam chatting up a gorgeous blonde.

'Mate, where have you been?' He had asked as he approached Sam.

Sam met Nikau's eyes. They were glazed, misty and immediately answered Nikau's question, that bottle of beer was not his first, probably not even his tenth. He was smashed.

Nikau had tried to pull him away gently but immediately had to duck a flying fist. It took the help of two bouncers to wrestle Sam into submission and get him home. Finally vomit cleaned, Nikau had managed to get a sobbing Sam into bed. He was a mess.

...

The next day, Sunday, Nikau had skipped church to keep an eye on him. At around midday, Sam staggered into the living room where Nikau was finishing up an assignment. Wordlessly Nikau grabbed him some water and two Panadols which Sam gulped down like a parched man before he slumped onto the couch. He looked terrible. Hair rumpled. Eyes bloodshot. Wrinkled clothes.

'I am so sorry. So, so *sorry*.' Sam whispered his voice hoarse.

Nikau sighed and put his laptop down. 'That's okay, but man, what *happened?!*'

Sam looked down his face flushed again, anger? Embarrassment? 'I, I...' He stuttered.

'It's okay, you can tell me.'

Sam sighed, taking a deep breath he looked up, his normally clear blue eyes glazed over in pain.

'I saw her with someone else.'

Nikau didn't even have to ask who *her* was.

'I was running and I saw her with this *guy*...'

'Maybe he was just a friend...' Nikau started.

Sam sat up almost violently and shook his head. 'No, I saw the way he was looking at her...' He paused and slumped back down, deflated once more. 'It's the same way I do, the way I did,' Sam paused.

Only then did Nikau notice Sam shaking from the strain of trying to contain his emotions. He was a dam. A dam that was about to break.

Sam took a deep breath. 'I got so angry...how could she, how?! Did I mean nothing to her?! Did *we* mean nothing?! I haven't touched alcohol since James but I just couldn't stop. It was the only thing that made me feel normal, made me...' Sam sobbed.

The dam broke.

Nikau moved closer to him and placed his arm on Sam's shoulder. 'Take a breath, focus on sounds. What can you hear? Your own breath. Inhale. Exhale. The birds outside. My voice. Breathe. Inhale. Exhale. *Breathe.*'

Sam's breathing slowed a little.

'It made me feel like I was something and then that girl came.' Sam half sobbed. 'And she definitely made me feel like I was something.'

The dam broke again and this time Nikau wasn't sure if it would ever stop.

'I am so sorry Nikau, I am so sorry.'

'It's okay man, you *will* be okay.'

Sam shook his head. 'I don't know if I ever will be.'

Chapter Twenty-Four

Sam: Wings

Sam woke, it was 5:00 am on a Sunday but he couldn't sleep, his thoughts whirling around in his head. A tornado.

It had been a week since Nikau had picked him up from the bar on the verge of a decision he would have regretted forever, no matter how beautiful she was. Two weeks since it had all happened. Since it had ended. The week had gone by quickly, luckily work and the looming deadline of his literature review had taken up most of his time. But the weekends, the evenings, they were harder. Restless, exhausted and tired of whirling thoughts that rotted his heart Sam rose and got dressed to go for a walk.

As he stepped out into the brisk morning air, still warm compared to the land that had been his home for so many years beforehand, his mind wandered.

'Mom I'm home,' he called, slamming the door behind him he dropped his bag of washing on the floor.
No response.
'Mom,' he called again but still no response. He sighed and walked up to his childhood room where he promptly crashed on his bed. His phone was dead but he couldn't be bothered

charging it. Who cares he thought, he would do it later. Right now all he wanted to do was sleep off the late-night he just had trying to get that assignment in. Honours was a bitch. Quickly, he slipped into oblivion.

Hours later he stirred. It was dark outside, getting cold, but the house was still eerily silent.

Sam rolled out of bed, plugged his phone in and wandered around the house. Nobody was home. Maybe something was wrong?

No, of course not.

Sam shrugged nonchalantly and returned to his room to see his phone vibrating.

16 messages and 20 missed calls from Mom. Something had happened.

'Where are you?'

'Something has happened.'

'Call me as soon as you can.'

'Please call me.'

'God, where are you?'

Hands shaking Sam picked up his phone and called his mother. She picked up immediately.

'Sam where have you been?!'

'It doesn't matter, what's wrong, what happened?' Sam asked, straining to keep the panic from his voice.

'It's James. There was a shooting at his school and, and...please just come,' she sobbed.

She didn't have to finish, Sam knew. James, his big brother, who was so kind, so brave, so god damn stupid. James who loved those kids more than anything else. James who had always thought he could save the world. Somewhere deep within him he just knew, James was gone.

'Where are you?' Sam demanded.

'I am at the hospital, your dad, your dad didn't take the news well, he had a minor heart attack, he is okay but please come,' she whimpered.

'I am coming.'

Sam didn't know how he made it to the hospital but he did. He ran faster than he ever had. He made every green light. He arrived at the Subway just as a train pulled in. It was as if the universe knew there was somewhere he had to be. It was as if God gave him wings.

Sam only slowed when he arrived at the hospital, shaking, he followed the nurse to his father's room and opened the door. There his mother stood, shoulders slumped she swayed. His mother who had always been so strong, who had always been able to carry the weight of the world on her shoulders at that moment looked minuscule.

His father was if possible worse. Pale as death, connected to a million monitors that tracked every tiny signal from his body. The green blip a comforting reminder that despite his closed lids, he was alive.

Oh, thank God he was alive.

But mostly he looked at Charlotte, tiny in moms arms, her face pale, eyes round like pennies. She had no idea what was happening.

Sam walked towards his mom and enveloped her in his arms as she sobbed. Stroking her hair he soothed her as his world fell apart, as their world fell apart.

The room went out of focus his eyes covered by a waterfall of tears. Would they ever stop?

Sam wasn't sure how, but he had ended up at the gardens, his feet subconsciously taking him to where it had all begun.

He thought of James, thought of the hole left in his life after he died. No one told you how hard grief was, maybe because no one could. Those who haven't experienced it did not know. They were the lucky ones, stuck in oblivion. An oblivion that would inevitably shatter. And those that *had*? With time they had learned to mute the pain. The hard feelings. For you can only be stuck for so long. Only be sad for so long, in a world that insisted on moving forward. On a world that insisted on forgetting.

And then he thought of Nikau's words last weekend. *'She definitely cares man; she is the one who found me, she asked me where you were, asked me to check you were okay, she was hysterical...hysterical.'*

Sam stared up into the heavens, the sun was beginning to rise now, it warmed the earth with its lingering touch and coloured the sky. Brushstrokes.

Sam thought of James, thought of Laylah, thought of his journey here, to this beautiful land that was now home. He had already lost James and with him, he had lost so much love. But he wouldn't lose Laylah even if all they could be was friends. That would be enough. It had to be.

Chapter Twenty-Five

Laylah: Compromise

i	want to cry,
	scream,
	and shout.
	i want to cut,
	tear, bleed and
don(t)	scars.
	i
want	to listen to sad music,
	be melancholy
	and watch the clouds.
	i want
to	write,
	words scratched in the dead of the night,
	as my body
talk(s)	to my soul.

　　　　　i want to look up at the sky
　　　　　and wonder
about it and the thousands of lives, it has seen unfurl.
　　　　　does it see me?
　　　　　see me cry, scream, shout,
　　　　　cut, tear, bleed, scar, be melancholy
　　　　　and write, write when nothing,
　　　　　nothing else makes sense.

Laylah was on her way to meet Amir's family today. It was only their second date and while that may seem rash in New Zealand it was perfectly acceptable, expected really in Middle Eastern culture.

Amir had offered to pick her up but Laylah had politely refused, she wanted to walk, to calm her nerves and at least attempt to digest everything that happened in the last few weeks. And as soon as she let her mind begin that process it strayed to her first official date with Amir. That time Laylah had suggested they go for a walk in one of the nearby trails. Not to the gardens, no, that was her and Sam's place.

Laylah stopped and shook her head, reminding herself that there was no *Laylah and Sam* anymore. That was her fault, she had decided that.

Laylah forced herself to move past that now and focus on the date itself which she admitted hadn't been great. It had started off badly when Amir had arrived dressed in chinos, a shirt and dress shoes. Not exactly activewear and naturally he was complaining within the first five minutes. Apparently, his shoes were getting scuffed. Laylah had shaken her head but managed to stop herself from sarcastically asking him what he had expected in a forest.

Worse still he seemed to have gained confidence since the last time. He talked louder, was more expressive and he had even tried to hold her hand. Laylah admitted to herself that at least their conversation wasn't stilted like last time, but it also wasn't a conversation either. Amir had just watched a documentary and was declaring how the United States was really the source of the worlds political problems. Laylah didn't disagree completely but then again he hadn't asked her what she thought, despite the fact that she was a politics major. But as Laylah was quickly learning that was Amir, you didn't really have a conversation with him, he had a conversation with himself and you just listened. That was not to say he wasn't nice, he was lovely, but he was just a bit much. Laylah sighed internally he was just being himself she reminded herself. And *Arabs, after all,* were passionate people by nature, she knew she certainly was at times. But she couldn't help thinking how much Sam *wasn't* like that. When you talked to Sam he listened, he...

Laylah stopped herself again. It hurt too much and what was the point? *He wasn't Sam.*

Speaking of Sam the worst part of the date, the absolute worst part was when he had run past them. Laylah's heart had stopped. Days later, Laylah hadn't forgiven herself for that oversight. She should have known that they might see him if not that day then at *some* stage. She should have said *something* to Sam about Amir. *Anything.* But Laylah had been avoiding Sam because she did not want to look into those eyes.

Sky blue.

She knew those eyes would cause her resolution to falter, to fail. Sam had her heart, wholly, she could not deny that even to herself. And on the trail, by the time she had seen him, seen the hurt painted across his face. He was long gone.

Sky blue turned ashen grey once more.

And Amir? He hadn't even noticed. Laylah thought back to how she had immediately excused herself, shaking hands she had called Sam, once, twice, a third time. He hadn't picked up. How she had run to the apartment. Frantic. How she had only found Nikau, how she had begged him to find Sam. *Begged.* How finally Nikau had found him, at the bar, drunk of his face, but okay. Thank *Allah* he was okay. That was a week ago now.

Laylah sighed and went to run her fingers through her hair, as she often did when she was anxious and was surprised as usual when her fingers abruptly stopped just above her shoulders. She had cut her hair not long after that day at the forest, it had been a spur of the moment thought. An act of pure impulse. Her hair had always been long and she had always liked it that way. But when the thought crossed her mind she walked into a salon and just did it. At least this was one thing, one area in her life she still had control over.

Glancing at the letterbox's she realised that Amir's house was the next one. She gave herself a final look over, she had chosen a plain black skirt and a pale pink button-up shirt. Her uncovered hair and a glimpse of ankle, her only two signs of defiance, as her rebellious spirit screamed.

Screamed.

Laylah took a deep breath and frantically tried to remember the conversation she had with *Mama* about Middle Eastern protocol.

Do:

- Shake hands and kiss the mother and sisters; two kisses or three on the cheek.
- Say *salaam alaukum* and *alhamdulillah* when appropriate.
- The mother will serve food, eat it and compliment her on her cooking.
- Help the mother after with the dishes and clearing up, even if she insists you don't.

Don't:

- Shake hands with the dad or brother.
- Bring up feminism.
- Speak too much.

Laylah took one more breath and knocked on the door. A moment later Amir answered and gave her a sweet smile that crinkled the corners of his eyes.

'Laylah! *Salam*, come in come in,' he said and escorted her to an immaculate living room. Plush maroon cushions arranged perfectly on beige couches that matched both the lush carpets and the curtains.

'Take a seat, I will go and call them over.' Amir said before walking out of the room and leaving Laylah to take a couple of deep breaths alone. *Calm down, you are okay, you are okay!* she said to herself.

'So this is *Laylah!*' A voice exclaimed, a thick accent accentuating every syllable of her name.

Laylah looked up and quickly stood as Amir's mother entered, she was a small woman but her presence was that of three. She spoke loudly as most Arabs did but it was more than that. Amir's mother wore a beige headscarf conservatively tied so that it covered her breasts, a black loose skirt that pooled elegantly to the floor and a black shirt. Her makeup was minimal and her wrinkles showed a hard life, her eyes although kind, cocoa not that much different to her own had a firmness that could not be missed. She was unyielding, she was strict, that much was obvious.

Laylah extended her hand out. *'Salam Khalto,'* she said as she was drawn into a kiss, then another, then another. Three on the cheeks she noted.

Out of the corner of her eyes, Laylah noticed Amir's two sisters walk in. Thankfully they weren't wearing headscarves indoors and one of them even had pink lipstick on but they were both dressed in loose-fitting shirts and skirts that made Laylah instantly self-conscious of her own bare ankles and waist hugging blouse.

As Laylah greeted the sisters in the same fashion, *Sumya* and *Rawan* she was acutely aware of Amir's mother who looked her up and down, making an assessment. Her face gave away nothing, of course. His mother would be very well versed in Arab social politics and social politics deemed that you did not speak poorly of the guest, at least not in their presence.

'Sit down *habbibty*.' Amir's mum gestured. Laylah obliged and Amir sat next to her, although a good arm's length away. Laylah was surprised by how much his presence was a comfort to her, especially as his mother chose to sit directly opposite them.

Moments later Amir's sisters began to set the table, ahh this was the meal her mother had warned her off.

'So Laylah, you are studying Law?' His mother asked.

'Law and politics.' Laylah corrected.

'Ahh I see, what do you hope to do once you have finished?'

'Probably family law initially but I would really love to work for the United Nations woman's congregation.' Laylah said and only just stopped herself from going on a feminist tirade about the importance of women's rights especially in the east.

'Hmm, that will be difficult to balance with a family no?' She asked.

'Well I don't really want children for a while, I mean I am only twenty-one.' Laylah stuttered unsurely. 'And I am sure I can still do both when the time comes,' she concluded lamely.

Amir's mother raised an eyebrow but luckily at that moment the food arrived and Laylah was saved from further interrogation.

Without asking Amir's mother piled a plate high for Laylah insisting that she ate more, 'You are too skinny, a woman needs a bit of roundness to carry children,' she shook her head. 'Amir told me that you lift weights, that is not for us women. You should stop that,' she offhandedly commented.

Immediately Laylah glanced at Amir who shrugged amicably, apparently, his mother's comments about her weight and lifestyle didn't bother him.

Laylah took a deep breath, bit her tongue and luckily the conversation moved to more pleasant things, food, family and culture. Laylah even started to relax. Clearly, her values didn't line up with his families completely, but they weren't *too* conservative. Anyway, she would be dealing with him, not his family and Amir was already relatively liberal like many young Arab men in the west.

After his mother threatened to leave the house if she helped clean up, coffee was served although Laylah couldn't help but notice that Amir himself made no attempt to help clear up, his sisters doing the brunt of the work. Clearly, he was a *mama's* boy.

'So Laylah.' Amir's mother began sipping her coffee. 'I assume that *inshallah* you intend to wear the *hijab* soon?'

Laylah quickly looked at Amir once more, this time he dropped his head and remained silent, not meeting her eyes. He knew how important her freedom of dress was to her. 'Um no *Khalto*, I don't...' Laylah said at a loss for words.

Amir's mother frowned and was silent for a moment before she slowly said. 'But it's *haram*, you must cover. You must, especially once you move in?'

'Move in?' Laylah asked, her voice high, laced with confusion.

'Why yes dear, we have a room for you and Amir. *Inshallah* if things work you will be wed by next year. This house is large, you two will have a room to yourself and *inshallah* when the children come soon after there is space for them too.'

Laylah sat shell-shocked as dread slowly seeped in. Laylah could handle the comments about her eating, the gym, even being dissected by his mother's eyes but not this. No.

Children? Moving in? Her clothing? No!

Laylah slowly shook her head as she quickly realised, Amir she could live with, but his family? No, and he seemed to have no autonomy. His bowed head and silence was evidence of that. If this was how things were now what about if they *did* get married, what then?

Laylah abruptly stood. '*Shukrun* for the food *khalto* but I have to go.'

Without waiting for a response she walked out of the door, *just hold it in, just hold it in* she begged herself but she was struggling to breathe. She managed to get out of the door and onto the sidewalk when a voice called after her. Amir.

'Laylah, Laylah wait! What's wrong?'

Laylah spun to face him. 'I can't do this?'

'What? Why?!'

'I can make compromises Amir, I can, but my career, my lifestyle, my children, where I live, how I dress?! I cannot, I just cannot. I won't.'

'Oh come on Laylah this is the way things are done,' he paused and said with uncertainty. '*Maybe* we can move out? Let's talk about this.'

'This is the way things are done? No Amir. And 'maybe' moving out isn't good enough.' Laylah shook her head. 'Amir, we might both be Arab but we are too different and as I seem to remember you didn't say a single thing while your mother was talking even though you know how much this all means to me...or at least you should.' Laylah finished sadly.

'Laylah...' He started.

'I am sorry, I tried, I really did,' she said before she turned and walked away no longer able to fight the tears or her breaking heart. Let them see, *let the world see.*

Laylah didn't know how she got home but by the time she had closed the door behind her and collapsed on the couch the tears still hadn't stopped. Perhaps it was simply not meant to be, perhaps her happy ending didn't exist, perhaps she simply wasn't made for love?

An hour or so later the door rattled and Ariana walked in, scrubs and all. One look at Laylah's face, she dropped her bag and immediately rushed to the couch.

'Laylah, sweetie, are you okay?!'

Laylah shook her head. 'I don't know if I ever will be.'

April

Chapter Twenty-Six

Sam: Missing Her

James,

Oh god, I am writing to my dead brother, I must be losing my mind. But honestly James, I don't know what else to do, everything hurts, almost as much as when I lost you.

Laylah decided to end it between us and well let's just say I didn't take it well, I am pretty ashamed of how I acted, at first, I was so angry. But then I realised I was just hurt, so completely hurt by the whole situation. I have talked to Nikau and Ariana since, honestly, I do understand her reasons, what we are trying to do, it isn't easy. But it's not impossible. We could have made it work, oh god I know we could!

But I guess it doesn't matter what I think, it doesn't matter how I feel and what I want because she would be the one facing her community not me, facing her parent's. All I know is that I don't want to lose her. I cannot lose her. I cannot lose someone else.

The mid-semester break is coming up anyway, she is going away, home for a few days and then up north to Wellington for a mooting competition. I know the space will be hard but it will also be good for us I think. I need time to reframe, time *to heal, time to make sure that my feelings for her are friendship and nothing more.*

I am also going home for a couple of days but I have to get back here to put the final touches on my Literature Review. I am so excited to see Mum, Dad and Charlotte, I wish you could be here.

Love you, miss you every single day,
Sam

Chapter Twenty-Seven

Laylah: To Be Numb

	what
would	you say if i told you i crave,
	a heart of ice,
	a mind of metal,
	empty eyes
	and a wisp, the mere memory of a soul.
	because my heart?
it	bleeds when i feel.
	i spiral in thought,
	i am blind.
	and to love is to
be	hurt.
	so perhaps it would be
easier	to freeze this heart,
	dismantle this mind,
	hollow out these eyes,
	and burn this soul.

no heart, no blood
no mind, no spirals
no eyes, no sight
no soul, no hurt
but can you still be human,
if you so yearn
to be numb?

May

Chapter Twenty-Eight

Sam: Coloured by Her

James,

The second half of the semester has officially kicked off and I am swamped. I am glad that I only went home for a couple of days, now that my Literature Review is done I need to actually start writing my Method and god that is going to be a mission. James, how can I write about the stars when every time I look at the night sky I think of her? Honestly, sometimes I think I am losing my mind. But the time away was good, she landed yesterday and we went out for coffee she looked tired but beautiful as always. She cut her hair, it sits just above her shoulders now. I liked her long hair James, but I like this too. She looked fierce.

During coffee she explained about that guy that I saw her with, he was someone that her mother set her up with, she told me about how much they had clashed and how she had ended it soon after I saw her. She was so apologetic, I am not exaggerating James, she apologised again and again and again for not telling me, for not running after me. She said that she didn't know what she was thinking.

I told her it was okay, that she didn't owe me anything and I meant it. I love her James, I don't know if I will ever stop. But I also know that I want her to be happy and if that happiness involves someone else then that's okay. I am happy for us to just be friends. I told her so James and I meant it. That doesn't mean I don't miss her, during that week, wandering around campus, everywhere I went I remembered her, remembered us and the precious memories we already have together. James; the stars, the moon, the gardens, it's all coloured by my memories of her. Just like Brooklyn will forever be coloured by you.

Love you, miss you every single day,
Sam

Chapter Twenty-Nine

Laylah: The Ways A Heart Can Die

              it's funny isn't it,
              how many ways a heart
will   die, can die.

              sometimes
it   shatters,
              quickly,
              unexpectedly
              and painfully.

              other times it is slow,
              tiny pinpricks that slowly destroy you
              as you bleed out
ever(y)   single drop of life.

              or perhaps it is malicious,
              intentional, a slow deliberate tear.
              so how can i ask for it to
heal?

          but the heart is a muscle
          and
i   know that just like any muscle,
          to grow it needs to be destroyed.
          to heal, it must shatter,
          bleed, tear. perhaps then it can love and
hope   more fiercely than ever before.

June

Chapter Thirty

Sam: The Easiest and Hardest Things

James,

Laylah and I have been spending more time together, it's so easy, just like before and if there is one thing I now know it is that I don't think I will ever stop loving her.

We run, when Nikau is busy we lift weights, we go out for ice cream and have hour-long conversations. She tells me about her dreams, how she wants to make a difference in this world, how she shudders at the thought of living an ordinary life. We talk about children, she wants five (some adopted of course) and I want three, boring I know. We talk about names. We talk about the future and our perfect days.

It's the easiest thing in the world, but it's also the hardest thing because even though I can push my emotions for her to the side, James, sometimes I will see her and she will have her hair done differently, or she will be wearing a shirt that complements her skin, or she will furrow her brow in concentration or she will laugh...and I will think about just how darn cute she is and how much I want to kiss her.

God, what is wrong with me?! I don't know what's wrong with me.

At least she seems to be okay, although James, she is looking awfully thin, awfully tired, I think she is pushing herself too much, maybe I should mention it to Ariana? Yes, I think I will.

Love you, miss you every single day,
Sam

Chapter Thirty-One

Laylah: I Miss You

                  i miss
you.   it's been months,
               but i do.
               when i see the moon rise
               when i feel the warmth
               of the sun brushing my skin.
             or when i visit the places your soul touched,
               the places our souls touched,
               together.

               every day you
are   haunting me.
               penetrating every part of my life.
               filling my thoughts,
               and my dreams.

               so, in the midst of an
everywhere of sadness,
               when sleep calls to me,
               an old friend,
               a lover,

i come. for it brings me comfort,
it brings me peace.
and at least in dreams,
i can be with you.

July

Chapter Thirty-Two

Sam: Control

James,

Ariana and I talked the other day, our first real talk in months. I asked her about Laylah's health and she told me about Laylah's eating disorder. Laylah did mention it to me once, but she didn't really go into it, didn't really explain. But Ariana did. She told me that this is what Laylah does when she is miserable, when she feels out of control in her life, she controls her eating and exercise instead. I asked Ariana why she was miserable, she replied 'Why do you think?' and pointed at me. That cannot be true though James, she was the one that broke it off not me, she must be stressed over college.

I asked Ariana if we should say something, do something and she said no, the best thing we can do is make sure she doesn't go too far, feed her when we can and just be there for her. I hope she is right James.

Love you, miss you every single day,
Sam

Chapter Thirty-Three

Laylah: Haunted

                it is 2 am and i lie awake,
                in these darkest hours of the night
                whilst
You   and the rest of the world slumber peacefully.

                mind racing.
haunt(ed), i am unable to silence cruel thoughts,
                hard feelings.

                so, the darkness, she watches
me   sit,
                writing words upon tear-stained paper,
                hoping that from all of this pain,
                at least some beauty may come.

August

Chapter Thirty-Four

Sam: Change

James,

The North Island is just as beautiful as the South Island, just different. Wellington was busy, Nothing like Brooklyn, but a world apart from Wanaka or even Dunedin.

We were only in Wellington for a couple of days but it was spectacular, I could see myself living there James and I know you would have loved it. It was kind of like a less old and much cleaner SOHO.

We went to a museum called Te Papa, walked along the pier, took the cable cars to the top of the city, went to the planetarium and even spent an evening at the sauna which was bliss. And my god the food and coffee was incredible. I will say this, coffee in New Zealand is miles, miles better than back home. You know sometimes I miss home, I miss the churning streets of Brooklyn, the blossoms and snow in Central Park. But by god, this is a beautiful country James and it's becoming home, I just wish you were here to see it.

Laylah was perfect too, as usual, it was like our first camping trip in the South, a different season, a different location *but it was as if nothing had changed between us. Except I guess everything has changed.*

Love you, miss you every single day,
Sam

Chapter Thirty-Five

Laylah: Pay My Bills

                seconds turn to minutes,
                minutes to days,
                days to months
                soon - months to years,
does(nt)   it fly?

                you see
time   passes and,
                day, by, day, i seem able to
                get out of bed, pay my bills, and live,
                with this previously elusive,
                emotional stability.

                but then for reasons,
                reasons i cannot
really   explain i become blue,
                photos bring pain,
                places unleash tears,
                and songs? songs are unbearable.

                i wish i could explain my weaknesses,
                or put a timeline on emotions,
                that make me feel, a fool.
                but i cannot, so instead, i pray for
heal(ing)   for peace, for patience.

                because for now,
                it is
all(?)   i can do.

September

Chapter Thirty-Six

Sam: Over You

James,

The break is over now so it's back to the real world - although it honestly wasn't much of a break for me anyway! It is nice having everyone being back on campus though, it brings a sense of normalcy back and it definitely makes it easier to focus.

Nikau talked to me about trying to set me up the other day, he said that maybe it was time. But I cannot James, I just cannot, at least not right now. I am not over her, and even though the scientist in me, the logical part of my mind, knows it isn't true, sometimes my nearsightedness gets the best of me and I don't think I will ever be over her. How can I? How can I possibly find someone better James? I don't know a lot of things James but I do know this I am not ready for anyone else. I am not sure if I ever will be.

Love you, miss you every single day,
Sam

Chapter Thirty-Seven

Laylah: Flesh of My Dreams

how   can i explain that
          you were the flesh of my dreams
          the fulfilling of a longing i have always had.
          an ache i
can   not rectify.

          a hole
i   cannot fill.
          a breath of air i was gasping for;
          gasping.

          but you took my heart,
          and tore it to shreds, with
          a whisper, a hope,
          a future that could
(n)ever be.

          so why was it you that my heart chose?
          why *you?* god, why didn't you

stop	this?
	but...you were kind and
loving	you were honest and true, for
you(?)	ripped my heart to shreds yes,
	but blindly and with kindness.
	so perhaps i should say thank you,
	perhaps i should say *thank god it was you.*

October

Chapter Thirty-Eight

Sam: Moments

James,

Do you know what's crazy? We still have moments. We still have moments where I brush against her shoulder, where I steady her when we train, where our hands touch as we walk and I want her. So badly.

Will this ever stop James? Am I crazy? Sometimes I think I am, truly.

Love you, miss you every day,
Sam

Chapter Thirty-Nine

Laylah: In Another Life

              perhaps in another life, we will meet again,
              a life where we are both wiser and braver,
              where the world is less harsh and
i   never have to let you go.

              for when i saw you, all my
will   dissipated into nothing. as if it
never   existed at all.

              for even
be(fore) my mind knew yours,
              instinctively, my soul recognised your soul,
              loved it. my soul was
ready   for your soul's presence.

              i cannot fight the harshness
              of this world anymore,
              so, i have surrendered
to   my forever yearning soul,

     ceased the battle of hopelessness
     against these tears,
let   them fall i scream.
     let them fall.

     i met a scientist once who told me of
     alternate realities, a certainty she promised,
     so, i comfort myself. that in another world,
you   and i will meet again and this time?
     my soul will never have to let yours
go.

November

Chapter Forty

Ariana: Stuck in Orbit

The alarm shook Ariana awake, pulling her from dreams. Shower. Clothes. Breakfast. On autopilot, Ariana prepared for her morning shift at the hospital in silence careful not to wake Laylah who was thankfully sleeping. *Good*, Ariana thought, knowing how poor Laylah's sleep schedule had been in the last few months, she was still a mess, no matter how much she denied it.

Laylah thought that Ariana hadn't noticed how little she was eating or her protruding collarbones. Thought she hadn't noticed how she was almost killing herself at the gym. Thought she hadn't noticed the bruises under her eyes, now a permanent feature of exhaustion. Thought she hadn't noticed her haunted expression in the moment's when she thought no one was watching. But she had, of course, she had.

And Ariana? She was helpless. She had tried to talk to her but Laylah was stubborn, so stubborn.

In the last few months, things had gotten a little better, mostly because Laylah and Sam were back to being friends.

At first, Ariana had been wary, Laylah was clearly not over him yet and he definitely wasn't over her. Why were they torturing each other? But slowly Laylah gained a little weight, slowly she ate more, slowly she calmed down at the gym, slowly the bruises faded a little, slowly she got better. A tiny bit better. So perhaps their friendship wasn't a terrible thing after all? Although Ariana still caught the haunted expression on her face now and then, still heard her sobs late at night. And every single time her heart broke for her sister.

...

After her shift, Ariana stopped at home briefly for another shower, grabbed her pre-packed bag, hugged Laylah and set off to the airport. It was her dad's birthday and she was going home.

The engines screeched and the plane sighed as the pilot gently landed the plane onto the tarmac. Her voice came in on the overhead speakers. She thanked them for flying with Air New Zealand and gave the weather forecast for Christchurch. Clear blue skies. A beautiful day.

Parent's murmured. Toddlers screeched. Couples nuzzled. Everyone was eager to get off the plane, Ariana too.

Carry-on bag securely over her shoulder Ariana looked for her parents in the myriad, in the sea of love she saw before her. Because that's what airports were, love. Tearful hellos. Even more tearful goodbyes. Loved ones coming together and parting. Like the movement of the tides. The flow of life.

Finally, Ariana caught sight of her mum who even in age was a beauty. Silky, midnight hair streaked with silver that reached her waist, gorgeous golden skin and emerald eyes. Ariana was the image of her mother. Except for her height,

Ariana had inherited that from her dad who was comfortably six foot. But that's where the similarities ended with her dad. His midnight hair was now mostly silver; comets filling a night sky. His skin was dark as were his eyes and his shoulders broad. With a grin, Ariana still remembered sitting on those shoulders as a child and feeling like she was on top of the world.

Ariana waved and walked over, seconds later she was enveloped simultaneously by both her parents.

'Darling, how are you?' Mum asked as she kissed Ariana unabashedly.

'Mum!' Ariana chuckled in feeble protest before she returned her kisses. 'I am good, how are you? Dad, how are you?'

'Good my dear, good.'

They both nodded, smiled and reassured her that they were doing well before Dad insisted on carrying her single bag to the car. Laylah would have refused but Ariana didn't mind and on the walk over they caught up on each other's lives. Dad, predominantly a pianist, had a concert coming up in a few months as well as a few new students who showed some serious promise. Mum was swamped with job applications, as a partner it was her job to make hiring decisions and it was definitely her least favourite part of being a lawyer, in her perfect world she would be in the courtroom all day.

As they chatted on in the drive home, Ariana couldn't help grinning as she looked at her parents. They were an unconventional couple and she? She was an unconventional child. A potion, the result of the merging of two faiths, two worlds, two cultures. When they wed everyone had insisted it wouldn't work, insisted that they were too different but they had loved each other and love? Love was stronger than those voices. At least their love was, then and now. Sure they had fights, sure they had disagreements. But they had survived, they had survived better than so many of the naysayers and for that Ariana was grateful. The only thing missing from their little family was a little brother or sister for Ariana but complications at her birth had meant that this was impossible. When she was younger she had longed for a younger sibling, someone to talk to, play with, teach. But now she was content, content in her own little family, her own little family that was so filled with love.

...

That night Laylah's parents were invited to dinner, their parents were also good friends.

Ariana greeted Laylah's mum at the door. 'Aunty, how are you?' She beckoned as she directed her and Laylah's dad to the couches.

As her parent's bustled in the kitchen Ariana entertained, her main job ensuring that Laylah's mum relaxed and didn't help.

'Isabella!' She exclaimed to Ariana's mum. 'This won't do, let me help, you have been at work all day.'

Ariana's mum laughed. 'So have you! Rest, the food won't be much longer. In the meantime, tea or coffee?'

The tea arrived and soon after they were all sitting down for a meal. Ariana's mum and dad were entangled in a conversation with Laylah's dad about the state of Palestine, the usual.

Ariana glanced at Laylah's mum and for the first time noticed that she did not look well, in fact, she looked tired and worried. 'Aunty are you okay?'

Laylah's mum turned her brown eyes to Ariana, they were almost identical to Laylah's. She sighed. 'Not really *habbibty*, I am worried, something is wrong with Laylah but she won't say, she insists she is okay, but she isn't. She has lost weight, she is always tired, she looks like she did when she was sick,' her voice was thick with worry and sadness.

Ariana understood. Ariana had been there when Laylah was at her worst when her desire for a healthier lifestyle became an obsession when her diet ruled her life. Oh, Ariana remembered it all too well. The meticulous weighing of food. The tiny portions. The cutting of bread, chocolate, cake...all the things that made life good. The daily hours and hours of exercise. The collarbones and protruding hips. The skeletal arms and tiny legs. The sharp shoulders and cheekbones. How she was constantly cold.

Constantly.

But mostly Ariana remembered the comments, Laylah's complete and utter denial that she was thin, how she would pinch her tiny thighs and insist that they still needed work. Those days were hard. Some of the hardest. How did you tell someone that they were blind? That their perception of themselves was wrong? Sure you could just say it but they didn't listen because it wasn't just Laylah's body that was sick, fading and wasted. It was her mind.

Ariana sighed. 'I remember Aunty. But don't worry, Laylah is okay. I think she is a little stressed because of her coursework, but she is okay.'

'Are you sure, I don't know, she doesn't tell me things anymore. A while ago I gave her the number of this boy called Amir, a nice Arab boy, from a good Arab family and I know she went out with him, but then she stopped and I don't know why. I worry that something happened...' She said, now on the brink of tears, her distress so apparent that she had managed to pull the other parent's from the hole that was politics of Palestine.

'Nehad.' Laylah's dad said and gently placed a hand on her shoulder.

'I am sorry Issa but Laylah isn't okay, she hasn't been since she came to see us all those months ago in February. I don't know what to do, I just don't,' she despaired.

Luckily Ariana's mum swooped in. 'Nehad, listen, Laylah is a smart, accomplished woman, I am sure she is okay. She is probably just stressed like Ariana said,' she reassured and Ariana thanked the universe for her perceptive mother.

'Maybe.' Laylah's mum slowly nodded.

'Definitely, she will be okay. Anyway, Nehad, tell me, didn't one of your nieces in America just get married?' Ariana's mother said deftly steering the conversation away from Laylah.

Hesitantly at first but then with vigour Laylah's mother launched into the story of her niece, instantly Ariana recognised this story. This was the niece that had caused Laylah to end it with Sam. Laylah's mother told of the scandal, the shame of the family, the persistence of the couple and finally how in the end it hadn't been so bad. Even if he was a Persian, Shia. Ariana was shocked, sure she rolled her eyes at the Sunni-Shia divide, it was exhausting and only caused harm, but for Laylah's mum to say that it was okay...well that was progressive, that was more than progressive, that was a miracle. Maybe people could change.

. . .

After Laylah's parents left her mum and dad grilled her. Ariana was reluctant, this was not her story to tell. But her mum was insistent and in the end, Ariana told them everything after making them promise not to speak a word, especially to Laylah's mum. Maybe they could help? After all their situation hadn't been that much different.

Ariana's mother and father looked at each other with sad eyes. 'No wonder she is so upset, no wonder she cannot say anything to her parents,' her dad sighed. 'It was hard enough for me and I am a man.'

Ariana nodded. 'Yeah, I think Laylah thought she could get over him easily, I think she thought he would get over her...but neither of those things has happened and if anything they are more entangled in each other's lives than ever. I honestly cannot see either of them moving on anytime soon, they are both miserable but at least a little less when they are together, even if it is just as friend's.'

Ariana's mum had been silent until that stage. 'I think they should try.'

'Bella...' Her dad started.

'Muhammad, wait, trust me, I understand the Islamic and Arab communities and I am not pretending this is going to be easy. Not at all. But can it be done? I think so. If they both want it, I think so. Especially in a country like New Zealand.'

Ariana looked at her parents, the life they had built, the love they had and for a moment saw Laylah and Sam in their place. They were both smart, kind, logical people. If anyone could make it work, it was them and lord whatever slack they got from the community would be better than this. Better than their misery. Better than their yearning.

Ariana had spent months in the hospital now, seen life bloom and wilt over and over again. One thing she had learned time and time again was that that life ended, life truly ended and death came when we stop. Laylah and

Sam? They were planets in their very own solar, for months now they had been stuck. Stuck in orbit. And now? They were dying.

Chapter Forty-One

Laylah: As Simple as Gravity

i

wish i had held you
when i had the chance.
wrapped my arms around you,
and pulled you close.
listened to your heart beat more,
a frantic tune now seared into my soul.

want(ing)

i wish i had spent more time with you,
watched the
sun leave this earth, a kiss goodbye
before the moon rises to take its place
in a sky speckled with stars.

you

speaking of kisses,
i wish i had kissed
every day. been brave enough
to feel your lips on mine,
one more time, run my hands
through your soft hair

and stare so deeply into your eyes
that i would never forget them.
never.

our souls embrace was brief,
merely a fleeting moment,
a second in the
forever   that we call life.
but still, i wish i had held you
when i had the chance.

Once a month Laylah hated being a woman and today was that day. She lay in bed, uterus cramping, on the verge of tears. As nausea rolled over her all she could do was pray that the Ibuprofen would kick in before she threw up.

Oh no!

Suddenly her mouth became a lake, she gulped quickly, trying, to fight the increased inflow of saliva, but she knew that it was futile and ran to the bathroom just in time.

Acid. Bile. Relief.

Afterwards, Laylah sat on the bathroom floor feeling very slightly better. Her periods weren't usually this bad but Laylah knew that she had only herself to blame, the stress from university was bad enough but she wasn't looking after herself. And although poetry calmed her mind in sleepless, tear-filled nights, it did nothing for her body which yearned for rest as she pushed herself harder and harder at the gym. Trying, desperately, hopelessly to forget.

The tears started up again but this time it wasn't from the cramps that still plagued her. Laylah wished Ariana was here, at least then she would have a distraction from the pain that ravaged her body and soul but Ariana was home for the weekend.

Eventually Laylah took a deep breath, grit her teeth and forced herself to her feet, still hunched over, she hobbled to the kitchen, downed another couple of Ibuprofen and crouched on the floor as the jug boiled, hopefully, a hot water bottle and some Chamomile tea would help.

Tea and hot water bottle in hand, Laylah hobbled back to her room but a knock on the door stopped her in her tracks.

Who on earth was that? Ugh, I cannot face anyone today, hopefully they will just go away...

Laylah continued her shuffle and placed her favourite Harry Potter mug down carefully on her bedside table. But the knocker was undeterred and if anything had become louder, more insistent until she sighed and clutching her hot water bottle slowly made her way to the front door.

What did they want? I swear to god if it's just a sales person...

Laylah opened the door, preparing herself to firmly but politely tell someone to buzz off, only to find Sam at the door, hand raised ready to knock again.

'Oh hey, are you okay?' He asked, concern etched along his face.

Only then did Laylah realise how she must look, shivering in a ratty singlet, oversized track pants and fluffy socks. Her hair literally had knots in it, desperately in need of a wash, and her face was still streaked with the remnants of tears. Suffice to say she didn't look great.

Laylah nodded, lacking the energy to even care that she was such a mess. 'Yeah I just got my period this morning and it's a bad one.'

Surprising her Sam nodded as if the female reproductive system wasn't a foreign concept to him. 'My mum gets really bad cramps too, come on, let's get you back to bed,' he said and took her by her elbow, marching her to her room.

Laylah was shocked, Sam was never this firm about anything, but she obliged, too exhausted to protest.

Steadying her, Sam helped Laylah get under the covers and nodded approvingly at the cup of Chamomile. 'Have you had anything to eat?' He asked, eyes crinkled in concern.

Sky blue.

Laylah shook her head. 'I just threw up.'

'Give me a minute,' he said and walked out of the room.

Once he was gone, Laylah quickly looked at herself in the mirror and confirmed that she did indeed resemble a hot mess. *Oh god.*

A few minutes later Sam was back, laptop in one hand and a steaming bowl in the other which he carefully handed her.

'That smells amazing, what is it?' Laylah asked.

'Soup, it's been cold so I made it yesterday and had some leftovers. It's dads recipe, downright the best thing for when you aren't feeling too great. Do you mind if I join you?' He asked, indicating to the spot next to her on the bed.

Laylah shook her head and Sam slowly, careful not to nudge her or the soup, climbed in next to her.

'Thank you for this.' Laylah said.

Sam's eyes smiled back at her and Laylah couldn't help noticing how light and clear they were.

Sky blue.

'It's nothing, have some, it shouldn't be too hot. I was thinking we could watch a movie.' Sam said and nodded to his laptop. 'That's all I like to do when I am feeling unwell.'

Laylah took a sip and let the warmth of the soup fill her to her toes. 'That sounds lovely, this is amazing by the way,' she said. Her appetite picking up now, she devoured the soup.

Sam smiled. 'What do you want to watch?'

'Anything.'

'Well why don't we watch Harry Potter, it seems appropriate,' he nodded to her mug.

'That sounds perfect.' Laylah said and turned to place the now-empty bowl on the floor. She overbalanced, leaning too far and began to slip off the bed. Immediately she felt Sam's hand on her arm as he steadied her.

'Try not to die,' he teased before he frowned. 'Are you cold?'

'A little.' Laylah admitted.

Without a word, Sam took off his jumper and handed it to her. Laylah began to protest but Sam shook his head and she stopped. He wasn't going to listen and being sick really took the fight out of her. Laylah loved the jumper on Sam, the way the purple brought out richness and texture of his brilliant blue eyes. But as she slipped it on she relished in its warmth, in its softness, in the pleasure of being wrapped in his scent. Laylah's heart sighed.

Sam set the laptop between them, starting the movie and almost immediately, for the first time in a long time, Laylah felt calm. Perhaps it was the familiarity of Harry Potter, the Ibuprofen kicking in, the comfort of having Sam next to her, or simply her exhausted mind and body but within half an hour her lids became heavy and she drifted off to sleep.

Time passed, Laylah slowly opened her eyes and rejoined the movie just in time for Harry's last epic duel with Voldemort for the Philosopher's stone. Or as Sam called it, *The Sorcerer's Stone.*

Sam looked down at her. 'Hey sleepy head.'

Laylah laughed, only slightly embarrassed, but quickly her attention refocused on Harry and his defeat of the dark lord.

Movie over they sat in silence for moment.

'How are you feeling?' Sam asked.

Laylah nodded. 'Much better...Sam, thank you for this, the company, the soup, god I am such a mess. I look terrible!' Laylah moaned, catching sight of her reflection in her wall mirror.

'You aren't a mess, you are beautiful.' Sam said, simply as if it was a fact like that the acceleration of gravity was 9.8ms-2 which was ironic because at that moment Laylah felt like she was floating. Eyes like Lake Taupo, calm, quiet, yet filled with a quiet strength that demanded attention he added. 'And Laylah? Anytime, truly, anytime.' Now Laylah really felt like she was floating.

Floating in sky blue.

...

Sam stayed for the rest of the day. He made her more food, they talked endlessly, watched another movie, played cards and he even ran to the store to buy her sanitary products. Laylah was happy but also? Calm, like she always was when he was near.

Too soon night fell, Laylah began to yawn once more and Sam stood reluctantly knowing this was his cue to leave. Laylah sighed to herself, wishing every day could be like this she began to take off his jumper, but his hand on hers stopped her.

'Keep it,' he said.

'No, I cannot, it's yours,' she protested.

Sam shook his head. 'I know you love purple, it's yours now,' he smiled.

Laylah's eyes filled with tears, she couldn't quite comprehend his kindness and surprising them both she leaned in and hugged him. 'Thank you,' she said into his pounding heart.

Slowly Sam put his arms around her. 'That's okay.'

Face buried in his shirt, his scent intoxicating, Laylah realised this was the first time they had hugged in months.

Throwing caution to the wind she took a deep breath and she whispered. 'Do you have to leave?'

Sam was silent for so long that Laylah's heart sank; *she had crossed the line, they were only friends, of course, he couldn't stay the night.* But then Sam whispered back, his voice shaking ever so slightly. 'Not if you don't want me too...I could stay.'

Laylah pulled her head back, her arms still around him and looked into his eyes. 'I would like that,' she said to sky blue.

While Sam went across the road to get ready for bed Laylah dragged two spare mattresses and blankets into the living room. Having extra linen on hand was a must with a large family that loved to spontaneously visit.

Ten minutes later, Laylah had just settled under the covers when Sam arrived pillow in hand, looking adorable with wet hair, an old blue t-shirt, track pants and a punnet of blueberries in his hand. 'I forgot I had these,' he said chuckling at Laylah's expression.

The blueberries disappeared quickly between the two of them and teeth brushed they settled in their respective mattresses talking until Laylah couldn't keep her eyes open.

...

The next day, Laylah woke, ravenous having barely eaten anything the prior day despite Sam's best efforts. Immediately she noticed that Sam was gone, his mattress put away, linen neatly folded. Laylah wandered to the kitchen in search of food and found a piece of paper on the table:

Laylah,

Sorry, I had to leave before you woke but I had church and you seemed so peaceful I didn't want to disturb you. I made some pancakes, they are in the oven, hopefully, you have a bit more of an appetite today.

I will drop by after church, if you aren't sick of me, maybe we can go for a walk, or the gym if you are up to it?

See you soon, Sam

Laylah opened the oven and indeed found a stack of warm pancakes on a plate waiting for her, she carried them to the table before sinking into a chair. But instead of joy her heart was drowning in the eerie silence of the flat, flooded with a terrible sadness. Tears threatened. How unjust was the universe, to bring someone this beautiful into her life, only to hold them, tauntingly, just beyond arm's reach, so close but never close enough.

And in that moment, as she sat his scent enveloping her, tears falling faster than she could bear, she knew that she would never be able to forget Sam, there would be no one better, no one kinder, no one whose presence filled her so wholeheartedly and whose absence left her feeling so very alone.

Chapter Forty-Two

Sam: Love is Patient

Sam and Nikau walked into church, Nikau was, as usual discussing his favourite topic; what on earth he would do once he graduated next year. 'I mean I could leave the nest altogether and go to Aussie or the States but then again I would have to start paying interest on my student loan and when I think about it I could easily get a job here in Dunedin. That way I get to keep the world's best flatmate right?' Nikau grinned at him.

Sam nodded and smiled absently.

'Sam? What's up?' Nikau frowned.

'Nothing, nothing.'

Nikau shook his head stubbornly. '*What's wrong?*' He insisted.

Sam sat heavily on an empty pew at the back of the church and bit his lip, silently.

'It's Laylah isn't it? Did something happen last night?' Nikau asked taking his place next to Sam.

Sam sighed heavily. 'No, we just, we...'

'Tell me.' Nikau said simply.

So Sam did, he told him how magical their day had been, but how much he knew it had set him back, how destructive it had been to his efforts to detach his feelings from her. 'But it was so hard Nikau when she slept, looking so peaceful all I wanted to do was hold her. When she was beating me in Scrabble she would bite her lip and all I wanted to do was kiss her. When she held me and asked me to stay I, I...'

'You didn't want to let her go.' Nikau finished simply.

'Never.' Sam nodded with a pause. 'When I was little I thought there were three types of love, Family. Friends. Romantic. But the older I get the more I realise there are a million other types of love. There is Laylah.' Sam sighed

'You love her.' Nikau whispered, not a question, a statement.

Sam nodded sadly. 'Even after all of these months,' he shrugged. 'You know, I am a scientist, I don't believe in *the one*. I know there are billions of people in this world, and I know that I will meet someone else, but...but I don't think that will mean I will ever stop loving *her*.' Sam bit his lip so hard it almost bled before continuing heavily. 'But I also know that one day *she* will choose someone else and I will let her go...I love her enough to know that I will let her go so that she can be happy.'

'Even if that happiness doesn't include you?' Nikau asked, his brow furrowing.

Sam looked down at the wooden floors and nodded. 'Of course, even if it destroys me.'

Sam felt Nikau's hand on his arm, squeezing it tight. Only then did he have the strength to look up and meet Nikaus jade eyes which were filled with furious compassion.

Only then did he realise that his own eyes were blurred, glistening with tears.

'Pull away from her.' Nikau insisted.

Sam shook his head. 'I tried, that was worse.'

'Well, then you have no choice but to keep loving her for now. But Sam, I promise that with time your feelings will soften, that they will be carried away. This is just another storm that the universe is sending your way and it sucks, but you will get through it.'

Sam sniffed and nodded. 'Why is love so hard?!' He lamented knowing full well he sounded a tiny bit pathetic.

Nikau shrugged. 'It's because love is the great truth, the great constant of our world...but at the same time, it's so multi-dimensional that we don't truly understand it. It is feeling, a hope, a wish a dream. It's anything but logical. Anything but simple.'

Sam nodded and opened his mouth to respond but at that moment they were interrupted by Ailsa walking in, wearing relaxed trousers and a dress shirt. She nodded good morning at them with a smile before continuing down the pews, stopping to chat to families, vivacious groups and nervous individuals alike, leaving smiles on everyone's faces, joy blossoming within every soul she touched. Finally, she arrived at the front of the congregation, the church quietening immediately.

'Today's topic is the easiest and hardest thing on this planet. Love,' she said simply.

Nikau turned to Sam and squeezed his arm once more.

'Love is humanity's biggest strength, but also our Achilles heel. It can bring us ecstasy but also great pain. Poets, philosopher's and humanity at large have tried to define love for thousands of years. The famous Greek philosopher Aristotle once said that love is a *single soul inhabiting two bodies*. But love is so much more than that.' Ailsa paused.

'In times of hardship it is easy to deny love, for love is not logical, love is vulnerable. But whilst our minds may try to fight it, our bodies, our souls *cannot survive without it*. For love is bigger than all of us. Love is what makes us look up at a star-filled night and search for the moon, it is what makes us dance in the street and sing out loud. It is what softens our heart when we hear the cry of a newborn,' she said, slowly making her way down the pews once more, looking into the eyes of each and every single one of them. She stopped, her cocoa eyes meeting Sam's and at that moment he felt like she was staring into his soul as she said. 'It is what makes us want to hold those dear to us so tightly that we never want to let them go.'

Sam felt his breath catch but then the moment passed and she walked past him, continuing her sermon. 'Love takes our mind on journeys, makes our heart flutter and gives our souls a reason to *exist,*' she said, her voice barely a whisper, but in the utter silence of the church, it carried and penetrated Sam's mind and heart.

'Jesus *loved* love. Jesus *is* love. So I ask you all to go out, give love and receive love with an open heart. Let us read Corinthians 13:4-8 together.'

The Church hummed with their voices, high and low, young and old, weaving into one another as they read yet another sentence that attempted to encapsulate love. They all finished at slightly different times but once the church was quiet, Ailsa whispered. 'Enjoy your Sunday.'

As people began to empty out of the Church Sam turned to Nikau and pulled him into a hug. Sam held Nikau tight and whispered fiercely. 'You are the best friend I have ever had. My second brother. I love you.'

Nikau held him, just as tight and nodded. 'I love you too.'

After what could have been forever they finally let each other go and stood. As they made their way to the door, they passed the Ailsa. 'Goodbye,' she smiled and in that gentle smile, Sam felt that she said everything that ever needed to be said.

They stopped at the threshold of the door, a man in his forties with a dramatically receding hairline knelt, blocking the exit as he tied the shoes of his little girl. His wife stood next to him, hand resting on a growing belly. The father glanced up at Nikau and Sam. 'Sorry,' he said abashedly with kind eyes.

Nikau smiled at them gently. 'No rush.'

The man smiled back and stood, brushing the dirt from his trousers, he took his daughter's hand and looked adoringly at his wife before taking hers also.

His wife? She was on fire.

Together, the little family walked off into the brilliance of the day, a gentle breeze rustled past, the sun was warm, but inside Sam was freezing, his hands shaking.

Behind him, Nikau placed a steady hand on his shoulder, Sam turned and faced cinnamon skin, emerald eyes and knew he didn't have to explain. Gently Nikau whispered;

'Love is patient. Love is kind. It does not envy, it does not boast, it is not proud. It does not dishonour others, it is not self-seeking, it is not easily angered, it keeps no record of wrongs. Love does not delight in evil but rejoices with the truth. It always protects, always trusts, always hope, always perseveres. Love never fails.'

Sam glanced up at the endless sky before looking back at Nikau, taking a deep breath he smiled sadly. 'Love never fails,' he whispered.

Another lifetime passed before Sam smiled once more, this time, his heart lighter, 'Blueberry pancakes?'

Nikau grinned. 'I thought you would never ask.'

Chapter Forty-Three

Laylah: Bones

we   are born into this world,
glorified in our nakedness.
big,
small,
it never mattered,
we are simply enveloped in beauty.

but then...something changes
and suddenly the world says that our legs
are   too big,
our breasts too small,
our flesh pockmarked.
so, confidence and comfort are replaced by
imperfections and insecurities.

i have breathed long enough
for the sun to have journeyed
around this earth twenty-two times.
but only now do i stare at this naked flesh
that envelopes muscle,
flesh, bone

and this brilliant mind.
entranced,
only to realise that
big?
small? we are all
beauty.

Laylah stepped into the shower and shivered but slowly, ever so slowly the water warmed her, to her bones. She lathered her shoulders with coconut body wash and then massaged her scalp with her jasmine shampoo. Their scents, coconut and jasmine filled the steamy air of the bathroom, heady in their richness and strength.

Suddenly Laylah was no longer in her little shower, no longer at home, but watching the blood moon, Sam's arms wrapped tight around her. But then just as suddenly she was back, the water no longer felt warm. In fact, she was freezing, alone. A sob escaped. Her throat began to close. Tears mingled with the water of the faucet. So much had changed since then. Her skin was no longer golden, oh how she missed the sun. And Sam? Well, everything had changed. But at the same time, she admitted to herself, nothing had changed, she still caught herself watching him, imagining herself in his arms. When she received important news, he was the first person she wanted to call, even before Ariana. But more than anything she found herself so often lost in the calm abyss of those eyes, an abyss that followed her everywhere, even in dreams.

Sky blue.

Laylah took a few deep, steadying breaths, stepped out of the shower, wrapped herself in a gloriously soft towel and walked to her room to get changed. But she stopped her reflection in the large mirror that hung on the inside of her closet catching her attention. She straightened and stared, entranced, realising that she had not looked at her reflection properly in months, hadn't been able to, hadn't wanted to, hadn't cared. But now she looked, as if for the very first time, as if at a stranger and she *could not* look away. Her face was more angular than usual, dark circles had blossomed, bruises beneath her eyes and her collarbones peeked out above her towel, against paper-thin skin.

Without thinking, she dropped her towel and stared at her reflection. Almost scientifically she tilted her head to the side. An examination. Thigh gap. Visible ribs. Jutting collarbones. Laylah shook, but no longer from the cold and the flashbacks began once more.

It had all started well enough, she had been a little chubby at high school, uncoordinated, bad at sport and then her big brother, her well-intentioned big brother got her into the gym. Naturally, she threw herself into it. She was sick of being chubby. Sick of being *cute*. Sick of men looking past her. It had begun as five days at the gym and more fruit and vegetables but then gradually escalated. As soon as she started seeing results, her mind sunk its teeth in and refused to let go. Five days for an hour became seven days for an hour and a half. Suddenly bread was no longer okay. Then pasta. Then cake. And then, maybe she should be weighing cabbage? She wrote everything down, was meticulous as her weight dropped. And dropped. And dropped. Soon? She was barely recognisable. Jutting hips. Bruises. Hair falling out. All skin and bones. Bones.

It had taken her months, years to wrestle free, to tame the beast. But now as she looked at herself Laylah realised the beast was licking its lips and getting closer once more.

She traced her collarbones. Traced her ribs. Traced her hips. This was how she took control. And suddenly, all the hours at the gym, all the skipping meals, all the *just coffee for me* hit her like a ton of bricks.

A ton of bones.

She was exhausted, she was ravenous and she would let herself eat. Finally, she would let herself eat.

Chapter Forty-Four

Sam: Perhaps I do Love You

The day of Alice and Dee's joint birthday party had finally arrived. Unsurprisingly, Alice had been stressing about the details for months and since Sam spent so much time locked in a room with her marking, he had heard it all. The only deviation from the original plan was the location, initially, Alice had her heart set on them all going to a bar in Queenstown until she realised that hiring out that much space was going to cost a small fortune. Alice and Dee's place, an immaculate but tiny studio apartment was not going to do either and she point blank refused to have it at a local bar. So Sam and Nikau had offered their house and now as Sam stood back and surveyed his unrecognisable living room he wasn't sure if that had been the best or worst decision he had ever made.

Rainbow flags were draped artistically over every surface, the walls were plastered with the faces of iconic men and women. Maya Angelou. Helen Clark. Barack Obama. Dr Martin Luther King. Jonathan Van Ness. Dr Brené Brown. Kate Shepard. And oddly enough Justin Trudeau.

Sam had to admit it looked spectacular and that if anyone, literally *anyone* else had attempted this it would have been ridiculously tacky. But Alice and Dee knew what they were doing. Oh and Laylah of course, who had recruited them all into making the piles of food which now sat on the slightly sagging dining room table waiting to be consumed.

By 7:00 pm most of the guests had arrived and Nikau was already mingling, smiling, chatting, unleashing those green eyes and natural charisma on everyone, strangers and friends alike. Alice glowed in a form-fitting, full-length Fluro pink gown with Dee on her arm in a floor-length silver skirt and fitted crop top, swirling with a rainbow of colour. And then there was Laylah who had *nipped across the road to throw something on.* Sam's fingers had fumbled on the buttons of his shirt and he could not stop his mouth from sitting slightly ajar when she had returned. A dark blue dress with a plunging neckline showed off her beautiful olive skin, only slightly paler now despite months of winter. Her hair was arranged in a perfect, intricate but somehow carefree knot, the ends curling slightly and just brushing her bare shoulders. She was, as always, perfection.

More people arrived, they mingled, made small talk and danced for *hours*. Sam was having a fantastic time although he had to actively remind himself to not stare at Laylah as she held Ariana, or Nikau or sometimes him, swaying to one dance track or another. Her face lit up in ecstasy, hair whirling. On fire.

She was always on fire.

But as with all good things it had to come to an end and as 1 am quickly approached, Alice and Dee turned down the music and stood in front of them, hand in hand.

'I just wanted to thank everyone for being here. For celebrating this day. Dee and I have so much love for all of you.' said Alice.

'We love you too!' A voice called from the crowd and they all grinned, nodding in agreement.

Alice laughed. 'Thank you! Lots of love to Sam and Nikau for graciously offering up their flat and letting us transform it, you are truly stars. Thank you also to Laylah and Ariana, queens of the kitchen, without them, we would have all starved and trust me I am *hangry*.' Laughter rippled through the crowd once more. 'And finally, thank you again to all of you for showing your beautiful faces. Now Dee just wants to say a few things.'

The crowd's eyes swivelled to Dee who looked nervous but determined. 'I would like to add my thanks and love to everything Alice said. Thank you all for being our safe space, for being our chosen family. It's not easy. We walk around in a world that even in New Zealand is screaming that we are wrong.' Dee began to shake ever so slightly and took a pause but Alice squeezed her hand and even from across the room Sam saw her draw strength from that tiny gesture. 'The wrong gender, religion, race, sexual orientation. Thank you all for loving us, for choosing love,' she said before she turned to Alice, gave her the most tender of all looks and then kissed her, unabashedly, unapologetically, to the whoops of the crowd around them.

Sam's heart sighed.

Finally, they broke away and once everyone calmed down Alice said. 'One last song for the night and then we will start packing things away if you can help that would be amazing but get home safe. We love you!'

Dee turned up the music, Adele's angelic voice echoed around them. Alice took Dee in her arms and they began swaying to the music, in a world all of their own.

People began to pair off all around, couples, friends, strangers. But Sam's eyes roamed through the crowd, searching for one face. The only face that mattered. He didn't have to look far because she found him, face streaked with tears Laylah tapped his arm.

He cupped her face tenderly, wiping another hot and fast falling tear, he whispered. 'Are you okay?'

She nodded and silently, gently she removed his hands and placed them on her waist before she wrapped her arms around him and nestled her head squarely in the centre of his chest.

They swayed to the haunting melody and as Sam held her, longer than he had been able to for months, his heart was simultaneously bliss and despair.

But that too came to an end and before he knew it, Sam reluctantly removed his hands from her waist. Still concerned he glanced down at her face once more, but Sam didn't have a chance to ask her if she was okay again because before he knew it Alice had assigned him to dishes and kitchen duty. Thankfully lots of people hung around and they very quickly got the flat back into shape. When only the chairs were left to rearrange, Sam waved everyone, including Dee and Alice away with a smile.

'Sam you are a dream.' Alice said with a grin.

'Don't mention it,' he said waving to the pair of them as they also flitted off into the night.

Sam returned to put away the last of the dishes.

'Where does this belong?' Laylah called a chair in her hand.

'In my room.'

Arranging the last of the dishes carefully on the drying rack, Sam dried his hands and pulled off his apron so that he could give Laylah, Ariana and Nikau a hand.

'What can I do?' He asked and turned only to see the three of them, standing in his doorway, unmoving. Nikau's emerald eyes were crinkling around the corners, but he wasn't smiling, his eyes, his face, they were an endless pool of empathy. Ariana was biting her lip, looking uncomfortable, but there was something else in her face that Sam could not quite read – was it triumph? And then slowly, painfully, Sam let his eyes fall on Laylah who was clutching a piece of paper. And in that moment, despite there being fifty-odd pieces of paper floating around in his room, Sam knew what she was holding. Something he has scrawled out right before the party, his heart aching. Laylah's face was pale, unreadable, and she refused to meet his eyes.

'Laylah...' He started but did not know what to say, did not know how he could possibly explain.

'We are going to go now okay?' Ariana said, interrupting his thrashing thoughts, he had forgotten all about her and Nikau. 'We will just be across the road if you need us.' Ariana said kindly, her eyes flitting between Sam and Laylah before she grabbed Nikau's hand. Nikau flashed him an encouraging smile before the two of them headed out of the door.

As soon as they left Sam's eyes immediately fell back to Laylah, to where they always wanted to return. He walked towards her, hand outstretched, she placed the paper in his hand, still refusing to meet his eyes;

My heart has always been a fortress,

guarded by walls of silence.
But when you walked past and for
some reason, I let you in. I let you in
and since that day my life has never
been the same. Because you filled me with
ecstasy, yes, but also pain, so much pain.
So despite my denial, it seems that perhaps
I do love you, or at least I love you as much
as I know how. I love you as a friend.
and I love you for the possibility we could have
morphed into more. Impossible the
world decided. Because as hard as it is
for me to admit, you do not love me
and you never did, at least not in the way
I want you to. Not in the way I need you to.
Perhaps I should have walked away,
all those months ago when you said no?
Perhaps I should have protected myself
from heartbreak? But I remained.
Stubbornly I remained, insisting that
these emotions, these hard feelings
had passed, that your friendship was
enough, for I could not stand the
thought of losing you.
But the more I learned of the intricacies of
your soul, the more I slipped. I slipped, only
to find that I have fallen for you all over again.
I have fallen and with that, I handed you my
heart to tear into pieces once more. tiny pieces,
and then smaller still.
We are friends so I cannot let you know my pain,
so I hate myself. I hate myself for my feelings,

*my anxieties and my fear. For the months that
have passed but the pain that has remained.
For the mask of silence, logic and strength that
I wear when I am weak, flawed and emotional.
For the walls that have now rebuilt, higher than
ever before. But mostly? I hate myself
for hopelessly falling in love with you again,
every day, every single damn day.
So despite my denial, it seems,
perhaps I do love you, or at least I am
as close as I have ever been.
for what could hurt this much if not love?*

Sam looked up, and finally, her cocoa eyes met his. Unreadable. His heart sank.

Chapter Forty-Five

Laylah: We Were Made to Love

	they diagnose pessimism. wrong.
i	will always water the buds,
	of love. for
was	i, were *we*, not made
	for the love of love?
	but *my* garden is no more,
	buds have
not	bloomed for months,
	weeds have grown rampant.
	my sun? gone. forever.
	they ask about healing,
	but how can i explain how much this hurts?
	how much this bleeds?
	how my soul yearns?
	my mind, futilely avoiding memories,
	a future
made	into nothing but a whisper, a dream.

for love

        perhaps if i told them how my heart cracks,
in song, in places his soul and mine,
shared time. or how
my soul returns to Him,
every night,
because at least in darkness
i can come home.

Before the party:

Exhausted from a day of cooking Laylah decided to go for a walk, Jaden Smith blasting through her headphones. It was getting warmer, and the radiance of the sun, the tiny blossoms, the smell of nature, lifted her heart. As did the memory of Sam, earnestly listening to her instructions for making tiny, handheld pizza's. Laylah's heart sighed as she walked further still, letting her legs lead the way.

Suddenly Laylah stopped, realising that lost in thought her legs had taken her to unfamiliar territory. She glanced around and finally recognised a building up ahead. The local mosque. Laylah hadn't been inside a mosque in years because although she had many Muslim friends, the crowds that congregated at the mosque were often conservative, rigid and completely closed to any version of Islam that wasn't their own. It was too black and white in a world that Laylah was finally realising was a Kaleidoscope of colour. So she had found God, *Allah,* in other places, in other ways and that worked for her. But today looking at the mosque, something called to her, something called and she listened.

Tentatively Laylah pulled the door open. Thankfully, it was empty. She wrapped her arms around her waist as she felt tiny goosebumps erupt on her bare arms, as her body adapted to this new climate after the sun-soaked brilliance of the day outside.

As her eyes roamed the room Laylah's mind wandered to the mosques she had seen in the Middle East, the majestic turrets, the intricate calligraphy on the walls and the handwoven mats, soft like the sands of Arabia. But mostly her mind remembered the colours, seared into her conscious.

Rich blues, golds and reds. The colours of life.

This mosque was not quite that majestic, from the outside it looked like any other building, brick walls and not a turret in sight, the only giveaway was a sign outside. But on the inside, it was beautiful, modest, but beautiful. Laylah had been to many beautiful Churches but they were nothing like Mosques. Architecture and design in the east was so very different to the west.

Laylah walked across the mosque, took a headscarf from a shelf and laid a softly woven Turkish rug on the floor, in preparation for the customary two *raqas* that one did when they entered a mosque.

It had been years since she had prayed, but instinct took over. Standing straight she raised her hands touched her ears with the tips of her thumb before resting them, one hand on top of the other on her waist. She said a prayer.

She bent forward, hands resting on the top of her thighs. She said a prayer.

She stood once more and then knelt, palms flat on the lush mat below, forehead resting gently in the middle of her hands. She said a prayer.

She knelt, palms resting softly on the top of her thighs. She said a prayer.

She rested her forehead on the floor once more. She said a prayer.

She rose and repeated it all over again.

The practice of prayer was both physical, mental and spiritual. Often Laylah felt like she was going through the motions, felt like she was murmuring meaningless words, but today was different. Today *felt* different. Today Laylah felt calm. She didn't worry about the future or the millions of things she could not control, instead, she had faith. In *Al-*

lah, in God, in the universe, in whatever you wanted to call it, she had faith.

Laylah finished her prayers and then took a Quran from the bookshelf before she settled on the floor, feet tucked underneath her body. Immediately, her hands caressed the cover, traced the beautiful gold lettering, ancient Arabic calligraphy that had stood the test of time. Intricate. Mesmerising.

Laylah opened the Quran and gazed at the letters. The Arabic language, ancient, was both beautiful and complex, it was poetry all on its own. Not only did the words look like art, beautiful brushstrokes, but the language itself was intricate. An accent enough to change the meaning of an entire word, the entire tone. Language was powerful and never more so than in Arabia.

Almost instinctively Laylah flicked to the verses that had changed the course of her life, her hand trembling, she traced the lettering. And at that moment despite the beauty of the book she held, the history it carried, despite the lush carpets below her feet and the brilliance of the sun that shone just beyond these walls, despite it all, sadness and pain settled in her soul once more. A lingering cough that she could not shake. Laylah's breath became ragged and she felt she would burst. Even within this peace, she could not forget Sam.

Laylah stood quickly, she carefully put the Quran and the headscarf she had borrowed away, and then she hurried, almost running out of the mosque, back into the brilliance of the day. Her eyes blurred, clouded with tears, she collapsed onto a bench just outside the mosque. Her tears now streaming.

'Excuse me, sister, are you okay?' A voice, gentle, broke through her thoughts.

Laylah looked up and tried, hopelessly, to wipe the waterfall of tears that now soaked her face. She saw an elderly man, perhaps in his sixties, with soft, kind twinkling blue eyes and lines that showed a life of happiness. A life lived well.

Laylah nodded, unable to speak, he was the spitting image of her great uncle who had passed only a few years ago in Syria.

The man walked towards her and gestured to the space on the bench. 'Can I sit?' He asked softly.

Laylah nodded.

'What is your name?'

And unsure why she was speaking to him, a stranger, but sensing a deep calm settle over her she replied. 'Laylah.'

His eyes crinkled. 'Laylah, oh what a beautiful name. The night sky, ahh but you are so fair.'

Laylah smiled softly. 'Yes, it's a bit of a running joke in our family. But I love the night,' she whispered, her voice still frail.

He nodded. 'The night is beautiful, it brings out our souls. Without the judgment of the day, we can just be,' he said, his face solemn but with a twinkle in his smiling eyes. Those eyes.

Sky blue.

They sat in an unhurried, gentle silence for what could have been forever and slowly Laylah's tears slowed and then stopped.

'Child, what is bringing you such sadness?' He asked.

Laylah bit her lip and hesitated, she didn't know this man, didn't know anything about him, but he was kind, he was gentle and mostly? He made her feel calm in a way only one other stranger ever had. 'It just doesn't seem fair...' She hesitated. 'It doesn't seem fair that even when you meet someone you love, even if they mean the world to you, you cannot be with them, you cannot be with them because they pray slightly differently because they speak a different tongue because they visit a different house of God...'

Laylah stopped. Her tears began to flow again, her heart, a hummingbird's wings. She felt hysterical. *Hysterical.* He extended his hand, an invitation. And without even thinking she took it and immediately felt a tiny bit calmer. His hands, soft clouds, so different from her own taut, smooth, calloused, palms. She held on tight and he did not let go.

'Breathe,' he instructed. 'Listen to your breath. *In and out. In and out.* Good. Can you hear the birds outside? Listen to them sing. Can you hear the wind? Listen to it rustle the leaves. Breathe. Good. Inhale. Exhale. *Breathe.*'

And so Laylah breathed, she listened to the birds sing, the rustle of the leaves, his soothing voice all while she looked into his eyes.

Sky blue.

All while she clung to his hand as if it was the only thing keeping her on this earth. Perhaps it was? And slowly, ever so slowly, her breathing slowed.

'I am okay,' she finally whispered but did not let go of his hand.

'Laylah, why do you think *Allah* created us?'

Laylah did not hesitate, this had been drilled into her from the moment she said her first words, earlier really. 'To worship him.'

The man tilted his head to the side quizzically. 'Perhaps, Laylah I have studied the Quran for years, I found solace in it when my parents died, when my grandson passed after only a few days of life and as my country, my home, Palestine is being destroyed. Perhaps *Allah* created us to worship him, but *Allah* also created us to love. Love Him. Love ourselves and love one another.'

Laylah was silent but she listened.

'Why else would love still exist, why else would we still love even in the harshest of circumstances? Even in the face of death?' He asked. 'Humanity has continued to love and ask for love because that's what *Allah* made us for, He made us for love.'

'But...but we can only love Muslims.' Laylah said.

To her surprise, he shook his head. 'No one can say who we can love, who we *should* love. And a Muslim one day is not a Muslim the next. A non-believer one day is not a non-believer the next. Only *Allah* knows the faith, knows the love in a person's heart. Only *Allah* can judge and *Allah* is fair. *Allah* is always fair.'

Laylah was silent, she hesitated for a moment, eyes to the ground she confessed. 'I love this man, I love him, *so much*, he is a good man, the best I have ever met...but, but he is a Christian and my *Mama* says it is a sin, that my life will be a sin, that our children will be sin...' Her eyes filled with tears once more.

'Love is never a sin,' he interrupted.

Laylah, astounded by this gentle, kind man, looked up and met his eyes.

Sky blue.

'What do you believe?' He asked.

'I don't think it's a sin, how could it be? How could *we* be? Why would *Allah* bring him to me if it was? Why would he put this love into our souls?'

He nodded, his eyes twinkling.

'Laylah, I cannot tell you what to do. We will all face *Allah* alone and He will judge us for our actions. But *Allah* loves beauty. *Allah* loves happiness. *Allah* loves to love. Do what brings beauty, happiness and love into your life and *Allah* will be fair. If this man is as good as you say, *Allah* will know his soul already and will guide you both.'

Laylah was dumbfounded, this was so different, *so different* to everything any Muslim had ever told her And at that moment Laylah felt peace and calm return to her in the midst of those eyes.

Sky blue.

Only then did she realise she still hadn't let go of his hand. '*Shukrun,*' she whispered.

'Thank *Allah, alhamdulillah.*' He responded standing and pulling her up to her feet with him.

'*Alhamdulillah,*' she whispered.

Gently, he let go of her hand and stood. 'We were made to love,' he said as if it was that simple.

Maybe it was, thought Laylah.

And then he was gone. Laylah opened her hand shaking and clutched in it were prayer beads, each one engraved with one of the 99 names of *Allah* in beautiful, intricate Arabic lettering. Each of the beads was blue. Blue like the old man's eyes. Blue likes Sam's.

Sky blue.

She glanced up to thank him, only to realise he was gone, she hadn't even asked him his name.

· · ·

Laylah walked out of her room, ready for the dinner party in her favourite blue dress, this was her confidence dress. No matter how she was feeling, in this dress she could conquer the world and that was a feeling she desperately needed right now.

Ariana was already in the living room and gave a low whistle when she saw her, Laylah rolled her eyes and laughed, it felt good to laugh.

Ariana grinned and indicated to the couch. 'Laylah, sweetie, we need to talk,' she said, her voice serious.

Laylah sat down and frowned, this must be important.

'You and Sam need to talk…' Ariana started.

'No.' Laylah cut her off.

'Laylah, I have been your friend for years, I have let you two wallow for months and I haven't said anything, you don't have to do what I say, but you have to hear me out.' Ariana insisted.

Laylah sighed and nodded, Ariana was right. 'Sorry.'

'Laylah, you two are miserable, don't try to deny it, I know you are, don't think I haven't noticed how little you have been eating…god even Sam has noticed.' Ariana paused. Laylah was surprised but didn't interrupt so Ariana ploughed on. 'You know how I went back to Christchurch last weekend? Well, my family went to visit yours and you know what your *Mama* told me? She said she was worried about you, that she noticed you were different and that she didn't know what to do…Laylah, she started crying, in front of my parents!'

Laylah remained silent but tears filled her eyes.

'Laylah, your parents love you, they love you more than the world and they *will* be okay with this. Maybe not initially, but they will, especially once they meet Sam and realise how lovely he is, how happy he makes you. And you know your cousin? The one that started all of this? Well, even your *Mama* admitted to mine that it isn't such a terrible thing, that the family had overreacted.'

Laylah shook her head. 'It's too late anyway Ariana, he has moved on...' The tears now flowed freely.

Ariana wrung her hands in exasperation. 'No, he hasn't! Are you so blind that you don't see how he looks at you?! When you are there Laylah no one is, *no one!*'

Laylah shook her head, she was so confused, so tired. 'This shouldn't be this complicated, look at you, you are not in a relationship and you are one of the happiest people I know.'

'Yes, Laylah you are right. I am happy and there is absolutely nothing wrong with not being in a relationship. But you *aren't happy*!' Ariana said, forcing herself to remain calm.

'You are right, I am such a mess.' Laylah said, struggling to breathe.

'No, you are not.' Softening, tissue in hand Ariana gently wiped Laylah's cheeks. She was at serious risk of ruining her perfect eyeliner. 'Laylah you have cried for months, hurt yourself for months, made all of these *sacrifices* for months. Promise me, promise me that if the chance comes for you to be happy with Sam, tonight, in a few weeks, months, promise me you will take it. Promise me you will let yourself be happy.'

Laylah remained silent but her mind was going at a thousand miles per second and suddenly she saw her life unfold before her eyes. Two paths.

Laylah fumbles in her handbag for her keys before she opens the door to her house. It is beautiful with a porch swing in the front and a backyard full of vegetables, fruit trees, herbs and of course, a blueberry bush.

The door swings open and Laylah puts her handbag on the kitchen counter. 'Sweetheart, are you here?' She calls.

A bob of oak hair, now thinning slightly walks down the stairs, in his arms a giggling toddler with brilliant hair on fire, pale skin and eyes?

Sky blue.

Laylah takes her out of her dad's arms and nuzzles her as Sam puts an arm around her waist and reassures her that his day at work was good and that dinner would be ready soon. Laylah stands on her tiptoes and kisses him, as entranced by him and her own little family as she was that first day she met him.

Laylah fumbles in her handbag for her keys before opening her apartment. Her cat Tonks comes to the door and greets her with a purr, but otherwise, the apartment is silent.

Laylah puts her bag on the kitchen counter and turns on the TV as she starts dinner for one.

After dinner, Laylah looks around her home, looks at the giant TV, the plush carpets, all the high tech gadgets that money can buy and her enormous library. But she cannot help thinking that it isn't enough, that nothing ever would be. She misses sky blue.

But he moved on, married, had his own little ones.

Laylah had tried, truly she had and was even engaged at one stage. But she couldn't do it. They weren't him. Not even close. So she filled her life with travel, friends, family, she had lived, lived well. But nothing, nothing could fill the hole of what could have been. If only she had been brave enough. If only.

'*Laylah...*' Ariana said.

Laylah pulled herself out of her reverie and nodded. 'I promise,' she whispered, her voice hoarse.

Ariana hugged her. 'Okay, now let's go party,' she said and pulled her to her feet and laughed.

But Laylah couldn't stop thinking about the two paths, had she already chosen? Was it already too late?

Chapter Forty-Six

Sam: Fireworks

'How dare you?!' Laylah cried.

Sam's heart sunk, his stomach turned to stone. Terrified. God, she knew. She knew how much he still liked her. What if she didn't want to be friends anymore? He couldn't lose her.

'I am so sorry, I can control my emotions I promise, this isn't your problem, it's mine and if I ever make you feel uncomfortable you just have to tell me. Don't worry, I know that you don't feel this way and nothing will ever happen, I am sorry. So sorry!' Sam fumbled frantically.

A tear ran down Laylah's cheek and Sam's heart sunk further but then it stopped abruptly, frozen in its descent as Laylah walked towards him and without a word she wrapped her arms around him. Tears running down her face, unrestrained.

Sam's mind was a blur of confusion but she held him, held him so tightly and at that moment something stirred within him, was it hope? But no, he couldn't let himself. Wouldn't. It would hurt too much. So he simply held her, the front of his shirt steadily becoming soaked by her tears.

A full minute passed before Laylah pulled back. 'Stay,' she whispered, her hand pressed on his chest before walking out of the door. A moment later she returned, a small notebook in her hand that she passed to him. 'Open it,' she said, her voice hoarse from the tears.

Sam did and found...poems, love poems. Initially, they were filled with hope tainted with confusion but soon they are riddled with sadness, despair and anger. Sam felt as lost as ever.

'Laylah, I don't understand...' Sam said and looked down at her tear stained face, now on the verge of tears himself.

Laylah took his hand, led him to the couch and climbed on so he could look directly into those cacao eyes. A moment passed, then another, she remained silent. Sam's anxiety climbed, he needed to know that he wouldn't lose her. He *needed* to know. 'Laylah...'

'Stop.' Laylah interrupted, placing her hands on either side of his face she rested her thumbs on his lips.

'I am not upset by the poem, it's beautiful actually. I am upset because for some ridiculous reason you think I don't love you.' Laylah said.

'But...'

'Didn't you read those poems?' Laylah interrupted again. 'I didn't say no because I don't love you, I said no because I *do* but I don't know how to tell my family. I said no because I don't want to put you through the fight, the uphill battle that is my community, because I knew that if I let myself keep falling for you, I would choose you, I would choose you every single time. But I hoped you would move on, I didn't realise you cared so much. So don't you dare think for a moment that I didn't love you. *I did. I do!*' Laylah exclaimed, tears now rolling down her cheeks once more.

'I don't know what to say.' Sam responded, his soul swirling with emotions.

'You don't have to say anything.' Laylah said before she hugged him again, this time their heads rested against one another and she coiled her fingers through his hair.

They stood there for what could have been a lifetime, held each other, both terrified, both uncertain of the future and what it may hold, but certain of each other and that nothing was as important as this. Nothing was as important as them being together.

Eventually, Sam pulled back, his eyes wet too and Laylah gently wiped the tears that escaped his long dark lashes with her thumb.

Sam caught her hand, looked deep into those cinnamon eyes and almost subconsciously leaned in. 'I really want to kiss you.' Sam whispered, his voice hoarse.

'I really want to kiss you too,' she whispered, leaning forward to meet him.

Their lips met. No fireworks, no sparks, but still perfection. Gentle, soft, filled with uncertainty and fear, yes, but also hope and love. Brimming with love. The kiss lasted both a lifetime and a millisecond. Eventually they pulled away, resting their foreheads together once more.

'Okay let's try, it's going to be hard, we have to talk about *everything*, but I am willing if you are.' Laylah said.

'I always have been.' Sam responded and kissed her forehead before he sat, with her in his arms. And so he held her, held her, barely able to believe that they were together once more.

Chapter Forty-Seven

Laylah: Sand and Ice

as the sun colours my skin,
from the white hues of snow,
to the gold of the desert sands,
i think of my ancestors,
and their journey. in
a   land so different from my own.

and then i think of you.
pale as snow,
sky blue,
and your journey,
to this
new   land. the land of the
long white cloud.

for if i am heat you are ice.
hard and unyielding.
but in my
world,   in my desert,

ice becomes water.

don't you see,
i am parched,
and you?
you are the last drop of water,
for miles, so perhaps
together   we can survive.

Laylah clenched her hands together so tightly her knuckles whitened as she sat in front of her parents. 'Mama, Baba, I need to tell you something.'

They exchanged looks, filled with terror, complete and utter terror before *Baba* nodded, inviting her to speak.

And so Laylah began, began the tale of how she had met a man who she loved dearly, almost more than life, a good man, someone Laylah would be proud to call her husband one day. A non-Muslim. A Christian man.

Baba's face remained unreadable but *Mama* looked almost beside herself, Laylah knew what she would be thinking; *her Laylah, her perfect child?!* But before they could say anything, Laylah ploughed on, she told them how she had ended it, months ago, how she had tried to stay away, but how all that had done was make her miserable, more miserable than she ever had been. How she had eventually realised that she couldn't live without him, that she didn't want to. 'Mama, Baba, I love you, I know what you have sacrificed for me, for us...but I love him and last week...' Laylah's breath caught in her throat but she thought of Sam and courage seeped through her veins. 'Last week I chose him and I have never been happier.' Laylah finished, tears now streaming down her face.

Without a word *Mama* stood and walked out of the room, her face unreadable. '*Mama,* no!'

Laylah stood to follow her but felt *Baba's* gentle hand on her shoulder stopping her. 'Laylah, *Mama* will be fine, give her some time,' he said.

Laylah sat back down and *Baba*, his eyes more serious than they had been her entire life asked her two simple questions. 'Do you love him? Does he loves you?'

'More than I can say, *Baba*,' she responded to both and her eyes filled with tears once more, heart pounding, hands shaking as she wondered whether she was about to lose her parents.

Baba took a deep breath, looked down at his own hands and muttered in Arabic. '*Hasal Khayer* – this is a blessing,' he looked up at Laylah, his cinnamon eyes, so much like her own filled with compassion. 'Laylah, this is not the path I would have chosen for you, you two will have many challenges, but if this is what you want if this is what makes you happy, then I am happy and *Mama* will be too,' he said.

Laylah was in shock, her brain barely able to comprehend what she had just heard, but slowly she found her words. 'Thank you, *Baba*,' she whispered and held him more tightly than she ever had before.

...

The engines of the plane roared as they glided through the air to Christchurch, Laylah glanced at Sam who had dozed off beside her, *he is going to need all the rest he can get* Laylah thought to herself and gently squeezed his hand, their fingers intertwined.

Not long after, the pilot announced they were about to land and Laylah gently shook Sam to wake him. Once they had landed, Laylah and Sam remained in their seats, the other passengers caught in the predictable rush of collecting their carry-on luggage although the doors had not even opened. Laylah squeezed Sam's hand and made small reassuring circles on his palm with her thumb. 'I wish we could stay here forever,' she said.

'But then you would never see Times Square,' he said, smiling and squeezing her hand. 'It will be okay, I know it will,' he promised.

Eventually, they got off the plane and strolled into the airport, it didn't take long for Laylah to spot her parents, *Mama* immediately zeroed in on their clasped hands of course. But Laylah refused to let it faze her and hugged both her parents before she made the introductions. Sam shook both of their hands politely and despite the tension of the moment Laylah couldn't help but laugh internally at how Sam towered over both her parent's. He truly was her BFG.

The car journey home was awkward and silent, penetrated only by the occasional question lobbied from *Baba* to Sam.

Where are you from in America? Do you watch American football? What about basketball? What do you think of the new president?

But despite his inherent shyness, Sam responded to *Baba's* questions confidently, calmly and Laylah squeezed his hand, knowing how much he was trying. She appreciated it more than she could say.

Finally, they arrived home and Sam was greeted, much less awkwardly and much more lovingly by Dina and Ayat - thankfully Yousef was out of town. They were both very excited to meet him, especially Dina who assaulted him with the most important questions in life like his favourite flavour of ice cream, his favourite colour and which Harry Potter house he belonged to. Chocolate. Green. Hufflepuff, just like Dina. Laylah smiled to herself, *it was going to be okay.*

That night at dinner, the table groaned from the weight of all the dishes *Mama* had cooked. Laylah turned to serve Sam only to find that *Baba* had already piled his plate high. Sam grinned at her and even had the know-how to compliment *Mama* on the food. *Maybe he would survive Arab politics after all?* Laylah thought with a smile.

'So Sam, tell me about your God.' *Mamas* voice interjected the first thing she had really said to Sam yet. Her eyes flashed.

Dina's eyes became as round as pennies, Ayat looked flabbergasted and *Baba* grim. *No!* Laylah thought her heart sinking. She began to protest that now wasn't the time but Sam stopped her. 'It's okay Laylah,' he said and squeezed her hand.

Laylah sat back and looked at her plate of food, heart thudding against her ribcage.

'What do you want to know?' Sam answered, the epitome of politeness.

And so the interrogation began. *Mama* lobbing questions at Sam and him answering. Politely. Calmly. Confidently. He even had the perfect response when *Mama* asked him if he would convert, a question which actually did make Laylah stand and protest.

But Sam placed a calming hand on her arm. 'I am happy to learn as much as I can about Islam, but no, I have no intention of converting, my faith is just as important to me as yours is to you,' he responded and miraculously *Mama* nodded.

In that moment Laylah knew. She knew how hard was pushing himself this weekend, all for her. She knew that most men would not have the courage to do what he was doing. But mostly? She knew that she had made the right decision choosing him and those patient eyes.

Sky blue.

After everyone had eaten their fill, and then some, they tidied and cleaned the kitchen. It did not take long however for the yawns to start rolling in and everyone agreed to call it an early night. Laylah lay in her childhood bed, Sam, of course, set up on the couch, her gaze skimming the walls, filled with posters and photos. These walls, which for most of her life she had shared with Ayat held so many memories, some bad, most good. Like the time when she was ten and their playfighting had woken Dina, an infant at that stage, seconds after an exhausted *Baba* had managed to get her asleep. *Baba* had furiously banished them to their room for hours. Or the time in high school when one of her friends had kissed the boy she had a crush on and sixteen-year-old Laylah had cried into her pillow for hours wondering if anyone would ever love her like that. But now she was making new memories, she thought as she nestled into bed and wondered if ten-year-old Laylah would be proud of her? If sixteen-year-old Laylah would be proud of her? Of the life, she had chosen? She hoped so.

...

The next day Laylah decided to take Sam to one of her favourite places, the town library a place of quiet energy. Like Sam.

There were quaint spots where you could sit to read or study quietly, other nooks where you could have a coffee and other's still where toddlers giggled as they read picture books and drew.

Sam and Laylah settled into two armchairs in a small alcove facing the window, it was warm and cosy. Private but not secluded.

'Sam, I was thinking, we should probably talk about some things, some big things. I have questions.' Laylah hesitated and pulled out a list.

Sam chuckled at the list but nodded. 'I have some questions too.'

'Good, we don't have to decide on everything today but I think we should at least think about these things.'

Laylah hesitated but thankfully Sam swooped in. 'I can start if you want?'

Laylah nodded gratefully.

'My parents would like to meet you, are you okay with that?'

'Of course, I would love that.' Laylah smiled, she had spoken to his Mum on the phone and she had seemed *so* lovely.

'Can I come to church with you?'

Sam nodded with a smile. 'Definitely.'

'When we get married, would we do it at a church?' Laylah asked, blushing furiously but knowing that he wouldn't flinch at the *m-word*.

And he didn't. 'I would like to, but I am not opposed to doing it somewhere else.'

Laylah smiled.

And so they continued like they were in some fast-paced, godly tennis match, each lobbying questions to the other.

'Christmas?' Sam asked.

'I *love* Christmas! Do you know what *Eid* is?'

'No idea, but if it involves food I am here for it.' Sam grinned.

Laylah smiled back. 'Of course, it involves food, have you learned nothing?' She teased.

'Can we visit the Middle East together? Meet the rest of your family?' Sam asked.

The smile slipped from Laylah's face and she bit her lip. 'We can visit the middle east together but meeting my family? Probably...probably not. I am so sorry Sam, they just wouldn't understand. Would never accept us.' Laylah sighed sadly.

Sam nodded and reached for her hand. 'It's okay, I understand.'

'This is so hard.' Laylah exclaimed.

Sam agreed. 'It always is when you are trying to merge two forces that are so powerful,' he hesitated. 'I was thinking, do you have any Qurans at home? I would like to read one. I know you aren't religious but this was an important part of your life. It is important to your parents and there is so much I don't know.'

Laylah chuckled.

'What's so funny?!' Sam asked defensively.

'Oh no, I am not laughing at you, sorry! It's just ironic, *Baba* wanted to give you one but I said no.' Laylah explained.

. . .

At home, Laylah led Sam to their little library. *Baba* pulled out the Quran that he had wanted to give Sam. Laylah remembered him telling her that he had bought it the day after she had told him about their relationship. It was made in Syria. Their home. A land that now wept.

Like all Qurans, it was beautiful with intricate lettering sweeping the blue cover.

Sky blue.

On the inside, it contained the verses in Arabic and sitting parallel next to them the English translation. It was the meeting of two worlds. Just like her. Just like them.

Baba handed Sam the Quran. 'It's yours,' he said simply.

'It's beautiful, thank you.' Sam whispered.

Baba tilted his head and left, unlike *Mama* who would have certainly dawdled.

Sam carefully took it in his hands and Laylah watched as his palm stroked the blue cover and his long fingers traced the gold lettering. 'It really is beautiful,' he whispered again before he took a seat and opened it slowly as though it was delicate. Breakable.

He flicked through the pages, his eyes scouring the contents. 'I want to learn, to learn Arabic,' he said after a moment and looked up at Laylah with those earnest eyes.

Sky blue.

Laylah sat next to him and looked at the sky. '*Mama* is a good teacher. If you want, I can ask her?'

Sam nodded, 'I would like that.'

As Laylah watched him, brow furrowed, reading, she realised that not only was this a foreign language to him. It was a new world. And even though she did not practice, even though she had built a relationship with God outside of Islam, this was still part of her world. This language, this faith, it was part of her and she wanted Sam to know that. She wanted him to know *every* part of her soul.

Chapter Forty-Eight

Sam: Sun, Moon and Three Stars

Laylah was coming to Wanaka this weekend and both Sam and his parents were ecstatic. In fact, that might be an understatement.

Sam glanced at Laylah who was engrossed in yet another re-watch of FRIENDS as the tiny plane carried them through the heavens. Sam knew that Laylah was nervous, but it barely showed and Sam had to admit to himself, anything would be easier than last weekend. Laylah's mum had been discerning and not easy on him in the slightest, although by the end of the weekend she had insisted he call her aunty and had sent them off with some of her delicious homemade Pita bread. Both good signs, Laylah had assured him. And then there was Laylah's dad, he was nice but quiet, difficult to read. It was the first time that Sam understood what people meant when they said that about him.

But regardless, Sam was glad he had made the trip with Laylah, glad he had the chance to meet her siblings and parents, glad that he now knew a whole new side of her. He wanted to know *every side of her*. But mostly last weekend had meant that Sam had come to understand her decision all those months ago as well as her parent's reservations because even from the brief time he had spent with her family he could tell they were close, he could tell they loved her. Immensely.

Sam squeezed Laylah's hand now and she glanced up from yet another of Joey and Chandler's antics. The sun streamed through the window and hit her face causing her eyes to shine, cinnamon in its light, hair, on fire.

'I love you,' he mouthed.

...

After a patchy landing that made Sam never want to fly in such a small plane again, they arrived. Shakily, gripping Laylah tight he walked down the stairs, off the plane.

'Are you okay?' Laylah laughed.

'Fine, fine.' Sam muttered, focusing all of his energy on not falling down the stairs.

Finally, after lots of deep breaths and more shuffling steps they walked into what was one of the tiniest airports Sam had ever seen. This sure as hell wasn't JFK. Almost immediately they spotted Sam's parents, they would have been difficult to miss. Sam was a replica of his dad who was tall, broadly built and blue-eyed whilst his mum was *slightly* smaller with brown hair, green eyes and an athletic build. And then there was Sam's little sister, Charlotte, who immediately sprinted towards them and threw herself into her big brother's arms. Charlotte was a miniature version of him.

Sam finally released Charlotte from a bear hug and her eyes immediately fixated on Laylah.

'Charlotte, Laylah. Laylah, Charlotte.' Sam gestured.

Charlotte vivacious as ever extended her arms out and Laylah did not even hesitate, wrapping her arms around Sam's little sister. Sam grinned to himself, they were the same height he noted and quietly added that to his arsenal of teasing, but later because his parents had walked over, eyes also glued to Laylah. It was time for more introductions.

'Mum, Dad!' Sam enveloped them in a brief hug. 'Meet Laylah.'

Sam's Mum immediately turned to Laylah, brushed aside her extended hand and swept her into an embrace. 'Laylah, we have heard *so* much about you! It's so nice to finally meet you!'

'It's lovely to meet you too Mrs Hart! And should I be worried?' Laylah laughed.

'Anna, please,' she insisted. 'And not at all...'

'Our boy here is just smitten.' Sam's Dad finished for his wife with a smile. 'Peter,' he added as he took Laylah's hand and shook it vigorously, a smile plastered across his face.

'Smitten?' Laylah smirked, raising her eyebrow at Sam.

'Cannot fight it.' Sam shrugged smirking straight back and taking Laylah's hand.

'Should we head off?' Sam's mum asked.

'Sam?' A voice called. He felt a tug on his sleeve, and looked down, meeting huge blue eyes and a pout that could melt souls, halt armies.

'Sorry, how rude of me!' And he promptly got to his knees, allowing Charlotte to climb on before rising with a groan. 'Soon you are going to have to start carrying me.'

'I could carry you.' Laylah grinned, her eyes dancing in merriment.

'We can test that.' Sam promised.

They began making their way out of the airport and as Sam's stomach finally settled he felt his heart rise. Here he was, on another brilliant South Island day, listening to an endless stream of chatter from Charlotte about her new classmates whilst the love of his life was laughing with his parents, his dad excitedly questioning her about her knowledge of the Arabic language. *'I have always wanted to learn!'*. Sam's heart rose even higher. This was going to be fine. So much better than fine.

The brief drive to his parent's house was much the same, an endless onslaught of questions and laughter, luckily Laylah was an extrovert and was more than up to the challenge.

Sam's parents dropped them off at the house, promising to return and start on dinner once Charlotte had finished her drum lessons. Backpack in hand they walked up towards the house and Sam opened the door, feeling a sense of excitement set in, he hadn't seen the house at all, just pictures of the renovations. And immediately he could see why this place had fast become his parent's pride and joy.

'This is incredible!' Laylah exclaimed as soon as they walked in.

'Dads an interior designer and Mums an architect.' Sam explained. 'I have to say though, they have outdone themselves!' He said as they moved into the living room which looked like it had been taken straight out of an architecture magazine. Three of the walls were painted eggshell whilst the third was crimson, an immaculate fireplace in the centre. The walls were decorated with family photos, drawings Sam, James and Charlotte had done as youngsters alongside valuable pieces of art. Chic black couches and a coffee table were arranged perfectly, and in the corner, a tiny table, filled with miniature succulents. It was perfect. Now they just needed a dog Sam grinned to himself.

'Did you draw this?' Laylah called.

Sam wandered over to where she stood and standing behind her he slipped his arms around her waist, holding her close. Laylah nodded at the artwork that had caught her eye, a *masterpiece* by four-year-old Sam. A family portrait outside their first home in New York City. Wobbly lines captured skyscrapers perfectly, whilst three people who looked more like blueberries than human beings stood next to a little boy wearing what looked like a brilliant blue dress.

Sam nodded with a laugh.

'I love the linework, it really captures the sweeping skyline of New York City.' Laylah said her voice dripping with sarcasm.

'Hey, it's a work of art!' Sam protested with a grin.

'I said I liked it!' She laughed but then suddenly her face became serious and as Sam followed her eyes he realised they had fallen on one of his favourite photos.

'James?' She whispered.

'Yes.' Sam said, his voice shaking as he held her more tightly than ever. Laylah stroked his hand comfortingly as they both studied the photo taken mere weeks before his death. James, brown hair, exactly the same shade as mums, shining in the afternoon sun, his brown eyes crinkled in joy as he knelt, surrounded by his pupils.

'He looks so happy.' Laylah whispered.

'He was, he loved those kids, loved his job.'

'Do you miss him?'

'Every single day.'

Sam felt Laylah lean further into his arms and for once Sam allowed himself to feel his grief, feel his sorrow, hold these emotions and give them the time they deserved. The time that James deserved.

What could have been a lifetime later, breaking the tension Sam led her to one of the couches. 'How can you smell this good all the time?' He protested.

Laylah smiled and leaned in to kiss him with an enthusiasm that took him by surprise. Their heart rates rose and Sam braided the fingers of one of his hands through Laylah's fiery hair whilst the other gently cupped her face. Laylah pulled him onto the couch with her as she entangled her fingers through his hair. Kneeling above her, Sam slipped his hand from her face, stroking all the way down to her arm and then back up again before settling on her waist. As their kiss deepened his hands scrunched the edge of her shirt, Laylah's hand moved from his hair to his back. They hadn't been alone for a long time.

When they were almost gasping for air their mouths broke apart and immediately Sam's lips moved to the edge of her face, slowly kissing her jaw. He continued down her face, to her neck and down to her collarbone which his lips caressed dearly, tenderly. She moaned and her eyes turned molten as his lips returned to hers and he kissed her deeper still.

Her hands travelled down the front of his chest and her fingers trailed along the skin that peeked in the gap between his jeans and shirt. He shuddered as she pulled his shirt off, her hands immediately on his bare skin, tracing every contour, slowly, with feather-like touch.

Sam's heart pounded and his muscles rippled as he also continued to explore. His hands crept down her neck and skimmed her collarbone. His fingers shook ever so slightly as he began to unbutton her shirt when her hands stopped him.

'Sam, we need to stop...what, what if your parents come back?' She panted her eyes still molten but traces of logic beginning to return.

With difficulty, Sam pushed himself off her and they sat side by side, breathing hard.

Laylah reached over and took his hand, placing it on the left side of her chest. Immediately he felt her warmth, felt her heart which drummed against her ribcage furiously. 'This is what you do to me,' she whispered, her voice hoarse and deep.

Silently Sam took her hand and placed it over his own thumping heart.

Minutes later, when their heart rates slowed enough to be *almost* normal Sam noticed Laylah's brow crinkling and realised she was looking at his chest, at his only tattoo. A tiny sun and moon, with three stars speckled above his fiercely beating heart.

'Do you mind?' She whispered extending her hand forward.

He shook his head and hands trembling, she traced the sun, the moon and the three little stars.

'Did I ever tell you why I chose astrophysics?'

Laylah shook her head.

'James. I don't know why but he was *always* obsessed by the night. Ever since we were both little, all he wanted to do was become an astronaut and it wasn't a phase like every other kid goes through, he *really* wanted it. He even applied to NASA.'

'What happened?' Laylah whispered, hand now stationary on his chest.

'He didn't get in, he was gutted. But he never lost his passion and in a way, he injected it into me.'

'So he is the moon, you are the sun, and the stars?' Laylah asked.

'Mum, Dad and Charlotte. I got it after he passed, this way I will always carry him, just above my heart.' Sam paused. 'Do you have any tattoos?'

Laylah nodded. 'Just the one.'

She unbuttoned her shirt and Sam's eyes were immediately drawn to her tattoo. A quill.

He lifted his hand, poised just above her flesh, a question.

She nodded.

Sam traced the quill which began on her ribcage at the centre of her breasts and swept onto her left side. On closer inspection, Sam realised that the centre of the quill was actually an intricate combination of letters, he recognised them, the Arabic language. He looked up at her, questioningly.

'We have lost so much in the Syrian revolution,' she whispered. 'Art, libraries, thousands of years of culture gone, vanished,' she paused. 'My parents would kill me if they found out, but I got this tattoo after my grandfather died, *Mamas* dad, he was a poet, a liberal, and a good, good man. I only met him once when I was tiny but everyone says I am a replica of him. I would hope so. *Mama* begged him to leave Syria but he wouldn't. He had a heart attack last year…he couldn't live with the terror, with the damage, with the horror, the loss of all of his culture. In the end, the loss killed him.'

'I am so sorry.' Sam paused. 'What does it say in the middle?'

'*Syria.*' Laylah whispered.

Sam lifted his hand and cupped her face. 'Thank you for showing me.'

Laylah nodded, her cocoa eyes solemn, sad and fierce, she stared up at him for what seemed like an eternity.

Something shifted.

'You are doing it again,' she half whispered, half chuckled and Sam realised that his fingers had been caressing her bare waist, making tiny circles.

He chuckled. 'Now you know how you make me feel all the time.'

She leaned her head into his chest, Sam wrapped his arm around her and just held her.

. . .

Laylah and Sam spent the afternoon exploring the rest of the house before Sam's parents returned with Charlotte, at which stage naturally she insisted on showing them her room. By the time the tour was complete, it was time for dinner. Homemade pizza.

Sam watched Laylah carefully spreading out the dough as Charlottes onslaught of questions continued.

'Hogwarts house?'

'Ravenclaw.' Laylah responded.

'Me too!' Exclaimed Charlotte looking up from her own tomato sauce and cheese pizza, her eyes widening in awe and excitement. 'Favourite flavour of ice-cream?'

Laylah pursued her lips awhile in thought. 'That's a hard one, cookies and cream I think. You?'

'I tried Hockey Pokey the other day, we don't have that back home and it was so yummy!' Charlotte grinned, now adding a solid three layers of cheese to her pizza.

Soon enough the pizzas were ready and they all gathered around the table, swapping slices and stealing food from each other's plates. There was nothing quite like family Sam sighed.

After they had all had at least a pizza to themselves, Sam and Laylah insisted on washing up. Naturally Sam's Mum refused to sit down and relax, hovering and drying a dish here and there when she could.

Once the kitchen was clean, hot drinks made tea for Laylah, coffee for Mum and Dad, hot chocolate for Charlotte and Sam they all returned to the living room where Dad had just finished helping Charlotte with her homework.

'Thank you,' he said gratefully accepting the coffee from Sam before turning to his youngest. 'Charlotte, once you finish this hot chocolate it will be time for bed.'

'But Dad! I went to spend time with Sam and Laylah,' she pouted.

'Don't worry, we will be here tomorrow, we can make pancakes.' Laylah reassured as she took a seat next to Sam. Charlotte's eyes immediately lit up and sure enough when it was time for her to go to bed she did, happily taking her Dad's hand.

Sam's Mum watched them go before turning to Laylah. 'So Sam told me that your parents didn't take your relationship well?'

Sam fervently tried to meet Mums eyes, tried to signal for her to drop the topic, but of course, she completely ignored him. Sam's eyes fell onto Laylah's face in concern, her parents were trying, he knew they were, she knew they were. But still, they made Laylah's life hard, for example, this trip? They had not been too pleased to learn that Sam and Laylah were going away together and had interrogated her on their sleeping arrangements. Even though things were *so* much better than before, conversations like that made Laylah anxious and frustrated. Sam could tell.

'Honestly, they took it as well as I could have hoped.' Laylah sighed. 'I know this is hard for them, they grew up in a different culture, in a different time and none of their children are living the life they imagined. But I guess they have to learn to accept that, to accept that we are adults, that we will make decisions that they don't agree with.' Laylah said her voice laced with sadness.

Sam's Mum placed a gentle hand on Laylah's knee and squeezed it comfortingly. 'They will come around in time. When Sam's father and I met, our parents had similar reactions, I am Protestant, he is Catholic and at that time that was a problem. They said it would never work. But they came around, eventually and we are still going strong, despite all the challenges of life. Despite James passing,' she said and took a deep shaky breathy.

Silently Laylah placed her hand over Sam's Mum's and squeezed it, her face painted with love and compassion.

...

Not long after Sam's Dad returned his parents decided to call it a night and without any hesitation they showed Sam and Laylah to the guest bedroom where fresh towels and sheets had been laid out immaculately.

After they left, Sam turned to Laylah. 'Do you mind? I am happy to sleep on the couch.'

She closed the gap between them and Sam noticed a tiny dusting of flour on her cheek. Her cocoa eyes looked up at him, melting his soul. 'No, stay, I like being near you,' she whispered.

He bent and kissed her forehead. 'I am glad, do you want to shower first?'

Laylah shook her head. 'You go, I will take longer.'

Sam nodded and less than ten minutes later he was comfortably under the covers, book in hand.

A few pages later Laylah walked in, damp hair, skin glowing, he could smell her from across the room. He put his book down as she got in and curled herself onto his chest.

'I think Mum already loves you Laylah.' Sam said stroking her hair.

Laylah turned her head towards him and Sam met those cocoa brown eyes he loved so much. 'I think I already love her too,' she said.

Joy flooded Sam, filling him to his core. Joy that he thought he would never feel after James's death. Leaning down he kissed her, soft and slow at first but then harder, firmer. He felt Laylah tangle her fingers through his hair as she crawled onto his lap, straddling him, one leg on either side. Chest to chest they continued to kiss, Laylah's hands beneath his shirt already.

'Do you want this off?' Sam asked breathlessly.

Laylah nodded, her eyes molten once more. Sam pulled his shirt off and felt something stir within him, something hungry, as Laylah ran her hands over his chest, caressing his skin. Their eyes met and Laylah started to pull off her own shirt. Sam's hand immediately stopped her. 'Are you sure?'

Laylah nodded confidently but Sam knew her well, she was biting her lip, nervous. But then again, so was he.

Laylah pulled her shirt off and sat looking up at him, shyly and boldly all at the same time.

Sam extended his hand out. 'Is this okay?'

Laylah nodded breathlessly and Sam closed the gap, feeling her silken skin in his palm. She pulled him close, their chests met, skin on skin. They kissed once more.

'Where do you want my hands?' He asked. 'Tell me what is okay?'

Laylah looked at him earnestly before she drew him in for another kiss, Sam could tell she was thinking and patiently waited, kissing her back, running his hands down her smooth, muscular back.

Finally Laylah whispered. 'I am scared.'

'Of what?'

'I don't even know,' she sighed.

'Well if you don't like it you can just tell me to stop and we will.'

Laylah bit her lip once more. 'I want to have sex with you, but I don't think I am ready tonight.'

Sam kissed her forehead. 'Laylah you are gorgeous and I want you, but we don't have to do anything you don't want to do. Ever. We can go at whatever pace you need,' he promised. 'I love you.'

Laylah nodded. 'I love you.'

They kissed, slow and sweet, she shook in his arms.

'Are you okay?'

'Better than okay,' Laylah promised and she kissed him tenderly once more.

Time stopped and for a while, it seemed that it was only the two of them. Their arms around each other, lips meeting along with flesh. Desire rippled through both of them as they covered each other in a shower of kisses. Sam realised then that he never wanted to let her go and thank god he didn't have to. They belonged to each other.

Chapter Forty-Nine

Laylah: A Life of Sin, A Life of Love

love   is time. whiling away the hours with you
as the sun kisses the earth goodbye,
and welcomes a sky speckled,
with stars.

          love
is   care.
stroking your forehead in sickness,
holding you in sadness.

          love is
endless(ly) want.
tangling my fingers through your hair,
tender lips on mine,
kisses, soft, like dew.
wanting You even when life is
hard.

          love is a future,

a   life that is pregnant with
            challenges but better with you.

            for you? you are a
dream   and i never went to wake.

After two weekends of consecutive travel, Laylah was so glad to be sipping tea from her favourite mug with her best friend. Today Ariana had chosen a gorgeous mustard turban to sweep her hair out of the way.

'What were his parents like?' Ariana asked curiously.

'Exactly what you would expect, the absolute nicest people in the world.' Laylah smiled.

'That's great, at least one set of parents is on your side.'

A peaceful silence filled the air between them but Laylah's stomach gnawed at her. *'Ariana, how do you have sex?!'* She blurted.

'Wait what?' Ariana chuckled. 'Come on Laylah, I know you have watched your share of romantic comedies and Nicholas Spark novels.'

'Yes...but how do you know when you are ready, and does it hurt? Everyone says it hurts.'

Ariana furrowed her brow and Laylah could tell she was taking her seriously, that's why she loved her best friend.

'It hurt for me, a lot, but that's because I was so nervous, terrified, even though I wanted to have sex,' she admitted pausing for a moment. 'But Ron was...gentle and patient. He would stop if it was too much and we just kept trying until after three or four times, it just clicked.'

Laylah bit her lip, this wasn't making her feel better.

'Laylah, just talk to Sam, tell him that you are nervous, tell him you are worried it will hurt. I am sure he would have been gentle anyway but he definitely will be if he knows. And don't grit your teeth and just bear it. Tell him if something doesn't feel right.' Ariana placated.

'And how do you know when you are ready? I am so scared.' Laylah confessed.

Ariana took her hand. 'When how much you want him is bigger than how scared you are. You will just know,' she promised. 'Wait...is he pressuring you into having sex?' Ariana said, a sudden frown crossing her face.

'Oh not at all.' Laylah squeezed Ariana's hand. 'I initiated, he was so...lovely and patient.'

Ariana smiled again. 'Good. I didn't want to have to knock out a six-foot man.'

Laylah laughed, feeling light for a moment

'How was it?'

'Honestly?' Wonderful.' Laylah smiled. 'I was so nervous, but then I remembered that it was Sam, remembered how much I trust him, how much I love him.'

'That's amazing!' Ariana beamed.

Laylah and grinned before a thought crossed her mind, one that had been lingering at the back of her mind. 'Ariana, I am not practising...but should I feel bad about this? Because I don't, not even slightly and I feel like I *should* be worried. It is a sin after all. A big one,' she confessed.

Ariana shook her head. 'It's natural for you to think that you *should*, that's how we were raised right?' Ariana shrugged. 'But sex is normal, natural, and most of all, it's *your* choice. If this feels right, then don't worry about it.' Ariana reassured her.

. . .

Wednesday night rolled around quickly and Laylah was relaxing, with Ariana, Nikau, Sam and a classic Jackie Chan movie. Rush Hour. A knock roused them.

'I will get it.' Sam said, rising from the couch to open the door.

'You must be Sam?' Laylah heard a voice say and her heart stopped. Yousef.

Laylah rushed to the door immediately, making sure she stood between Sam and Yousuf, 'What are you doing here?' She exclaimed.

'Cannot a big brother drop in on his little sister?' Chuckled Yousuf with humour that didn't quite reach his eyes.

'Of course, but a big brother should probably call his sister and tell her.' Laylah said frustrated.

Yousuf shrugged dismissively and without invitation, he entered the living room. Laylah sighed as she looked at his broad back. In some ways, they were similar people; extroverted, expressive and passionate. But Yousuf was a wild card sometimes and whilst Laylah knew he wouldn't stir up too much trouble, she also knew this wasn't an innocent visit.

Laylah took Sam's hand and squeezed it but he looked unconcerned and thankfully when they walked back to the living room, Nikau and Ariana were already chatting away to Yousuf. Laylah was glad for their presence, at least they could act as a buffer. But her relief didn't last long.

'So Sam, I was thinking maybe you and I could go for a walk? Have a quick chat.' Yousuf said nonchalantly.

'No, I don't think that's a good idea...' Laylah started, but Sam interrupted her.

'Sure,' he said, squeezing her hand reassuringly, again not fazed in the slightest, Laylah, however, was *fazed* enough for both of them combined, she knew her brother.

'Yousuf come to the kitchen with me for a second,' she insisted grabbing her brother and dragging him with her before he had the chance to protest.

'What on earth are you doing?!' She hissed with a deadly stare.

But Yousuf stood his ground. 'I wanted to meet the man that was the reason my sister lost weight and was a ghost for months, I want to meet the man that almost cost you, *Mama* and *Baba*. I want to meet this man and make sure he knows how damn lucky he is so that he won't ever dream of hurting my little sister.'

Laylah sighed in exasperation, in anger. 'This isn't the 1900s, you *don't need* to protect my honour, my relationship with him is my decision and mine alone...also, I am not that little!' She added with a growl.

Yousef raised his brow jokingly.

'Yousef!' She exclaimed.

'I know, I know and don't worry I won't be giving him a hard time, I just want to chat.' Yousuf said completely serious.

'Promise?'

'Promise,' he said.

Laylah sighed but nodded and Yousuf headed back to the living room, Sam was already standing, waiting for him and they both headed off. Thankfully Nikau and Ariana remained; distracting her from the clock and her own whirling thoughts. *Why were they taking so long? What was he saying to Sam? What was Sam saying to him? Were they killing each other?*

Half an hour later a knock on the door and the sound of laughter signalled their return and thankfully there was no bruises in sight. Yousuf didn't stay long and after they arranged to have brunch the following day he hugged her, shook Sam's hand and headed into the night. Emma was waiting for him in the hotel they had booked down the road. Not long after Nikau and Ariana also decided to call it a night and finally Laylah was alone with Sam.

She took both his hands in her own and squeezed them. 'I am so sorry, so, so sorry about that.'

Sam chuckled. 'Why are you sorry, you didn't know he was coming.'

'I know but...Yousuf can be a bit much times.' Laylah explained.

Sam furrowed his brow and spoke slowly. 'Yes, but he is actually a lot like you. He loves you and just wants to protect you. Actually...' Sam started before he led her to the couch and they both sat down. 'Actually, he kind of made me realise how much of a sacrifice this is for you, how much you are defying your parents and I guess how good their reaction is in the grand scheme of things.'

Laylah nodded. 'It isn't easy and I don't expect many people in the Muslim community to accept this, to understand this...but I guess that's the path I have chosen.'

Sam smiled at her with sad eyes. 'I am sorry you had to choose between your community and me.'

Laylah smiled back. 'I would choose you every time.'

...

The next day was beautiful, things were beginning to warm up, a sure sign that summer was just around the corner.

By 10 am Sam, Laylah, Emma and Yousuf were seated at their favourite cafe.

Laylah ordered without even glancing at the menu, blueberry and banana pancakes. Sam chuckled, and Laylah elbowed him with a smirk, especially when Sam ordered the same thing. There was nothing wrong with being predictable. Yousuf and Emma were taking a bit longer.

They were an interesting couple. Yousuf was a fireball, he only did things if *he* wanted to do it and would often do just the opposite if someone tried to tell him what to do. But Yousuf also loved people which made him a great realtor. Emma, on the other hand, was quiet, sweet and calm, she was an artist by profession and also the best thing that had ever happened to Yousuf; she cooled him, soothed him, she just flowed. They also completely differed in appearance. Yousuf was pale with light brown hair, brown eyes, average height and a very well-muscled chest which he constantly showed off. Emma, on the other hand, was small, her Fijian roots meant her skin was chocolate as were her eyes. Her hair was curly and filled with life but it didn't envelope her face, didn't consume it. It simply accentuated it.

'So how did you two meet?' Emma asked once the food and coffee had arrived.

Laylah chuckled and turned to Sam. 'Do you want to do the honours?'

And with a smile, Sam launched into the story of how he had refused Laylah's help once...

...

Once the food was eaten, the coffee drunk, they stood to leave, walking out into a beautiful day. Laylah sighed as she felt the sun kiss her bare shoulders, warming her to her core and for the first time in a long time, everything felt right.

But suddenly her heart stopped. Suddenly her blood froze. Amir was walking towards them. She had, of course, talked to Sam about Amir, explained the situation, but the look on Amir's face worried her, clearly he had seen her and Sam together. Luckily Sam and Yousuf had wandered ahead.

Amir stopped in front of her. 'So *this* is what you chose over me? A white man, an American? They kill our people and you date him?!' He sputtered and nodded his head towards Sam and Yousuf who were still thankfully oblivious.

Laylah took a deep breath. '*Leave* Amir, this has nothing to do with you. I left you before I was with him, not that I owe you anything.'

Amir looked at her, his brown eyes filled with sadness and the anger of damaged pride. A bruised honour.

'Amir, leave.' Laylah said firmly, her hands clasped together to hide how they shook.

'What's going on here?' She heard Yousef say.

'Is everything okay?' Sam's voice chimed.

Hearing their voices filled Laylah with dread, Yousuf would hit him and Sam? She wasn't sure, she had never seen Sam aggravated.

'Amir was just leaving, weren't you Amir?!' Laylah demanded.

Amir's eyes roamed from Laylah to Sam before he shook his head with disgust. Turning to Laylah he hissed in Arabic. 'Your relationship is a sin. Your children will be a sin. Your whole life will be a sin. *Allah* will never accept you.'

Instinctively Laylah turned to Yousuf and grabbed his arm, just catching him in time to hold him back.

'*What did you say to my sister? How dare you?!*' He said in a deadly voice as he struggled to free himself. Thankfully at this stage Sam who had looked confused initially caught on enough to grab his other arm.

'Let him go, Yousuf, I don't want to be accepted by *him* anyway.' Laylah said loud enough for Amir who was now walking away to hear.

Once Yousuf had calmed down he explained to Sam what Amir had said. Laylah sat on a nearby bench, frozen, she didn't know why she was so surprised, since the day she and Sam had gotten back together she had heard murmurings. Muslim acquaintances that used to stop and say hello walked past, eyes down, some of her parent's friend's had distanced themselves and she had even run into Shahid who had the audacity to pull out the Quran and lecture her on the verses. Of course, not everyone in the Muslim community had reacted this way, but most of them, even the congratulatory, curious ones, even they were surprised. The communities response infuriated Laylah, it was so sexist, her brother certainly had not received this response. True people gossiped, but no one felt obligated to tell him that his life was to be a sin, that his children would be lost.

Laylah could handle it, all the stares and gossip but somehow it happening in the light of day, outside, with Sam present, she didn't know if she could handle that. Laylah looked up at him now as he spoke to Yousuf and her heart squeezed, she could never forgive herself if he was hurt.

Not long after, Yousuf and Emma had to leave, they had a long drive back home, Emma hugged her reassuringly before Yousuf enveloped her, threatening to rip anyone's throat out who dared insult his sister. Laylah chuckled but deep down she was so afraid and she wasn't even sure why.

...

The next day was wet, the sky heaved, the air was thick with humidity and the rain was relentless. When Laylah was younger she hated this weather, had always felt trapped. Until she realised how much the trees needed the rain. She loved the trees, so how could she possibly hate the rain? In Dunedin, it was certainly true that there was no such thing as poor weather, just poor outfit choices.

That morning, Laylah had decided to take Sam to another one of her favourite trails, five minutes from the city they were surrounded by trees, by nature. Laylah loved this place, a place where you could be surrounded by the earth, where you could forget yourself and become lost in something so much bigger than any of us. This earth.

They walked the trail and thankfully the ancient limbs of the trees provided some cover from the weeping sky. Birds twittered, the rain plopped and their feet made reassuring sounds, sinking into the soft earth below. But despite the calm of their surroundings Laylah felt her gut clench, something was wrong with Sam, he was acting...off. He had been since yesterday. That morning he had greeted her with a loose hug, his face making it clear that he was a million miles away and he was silent through most of breakfast. Laylah had thought that perhaps he was just tired, he was not a morning person after all and things had been hectic lately. But even in the calm of the forest Sam was still silent, still lost in thought and only looked at her when she reached for his hand. This was cold for Sam, who was usually filled to the brim with affection, a hand on the waist, a kiss on the forehead, tangled fingers. But worst of all were his eyes.

Sky blue turned to ice.

'What do you want to do after this?' She asked. But Sam didn't even look at her and shrugged.

Laylah's heart fluttered, she couldn't take it anymore. 'Sam, what's wrong?'

Sam continued to walk as if he hadn't even heard her and her heart sunk.

'Sam!' She called stopping in the middle of the trail, he turned to face her and she pulled her hood away from her face. Almost immediately she began to get wet, patches of her hair turning a deep chestnut, she started shaking, her face was now drenched – with tears, with rain, with her anguish. But she barely noticed. 'I am losing my mind, talk to me,' she demanded.

'Laylah, come on, put your hood back up, let's get going, you will get sick,' he said and hurriedly walked back to her, his eyes still a million miles away.

'No,' Laylah stood her ground. 'What did I do? What happened? You promised you would talk to me, you promised,' and suddenly the exhaustion of the last few weeks crashed down on her and she started to sob gasping for air.

Immediately Sam knelt down in front of her on the soft, wet earth, and pulled his hood back. It took mere seconds for his hair to dampen, but he didn't seem to care as he tried to wrap his arms around her.

'No,' she said again and pushed him away. 'What is wrong?'

Sam looked at her, his eyes had melted, had softened but there was something still there. A residue of ice. Sam hesitated. 'Will your family ever accept me?'

'What kind of question is that?' She exclaimed.

'Please, just answer me,' he said and biting his lip he looked down.

'My parents are trying, you know they are, and they will eventually. But my extended family, I don't know...maybe, not. Probably not.'

Sam stood abruptly, visibly shaking. His cinnamon hair matted against his face and his nose dripped. 'They want me to convert don't they? You want me to convert?' He said, no longer able to hide the anger in his voice.

Now Laylah knew, now she knew what the ice was. 'What?' She exclaimed, incredulous.

'Just admit it, admit it, I am not...I am not good enough...I never will be,' his voice broke, and the anger fell away.

Replaced by hurt. Replaced by frustration. Replaced by insecurity. Pain painted all over his face Sam turned and walked away.

Laylah ran after him and grabbed his hand. 'Samson Hart, don't you dare walk away from me,' she said and struggled to stop him but it was hopeless. Desperate Laylah did the first thing that came to her mind and wrapped her arms around his waist as he walked. Not expecting her weight, Sam stumbled and they almost toppled over.

'*What on earth are you doing*?!' He demanded once he had finally straightened.

'I am not letting you go.'

In one sweeping motion, she swung herself, so that she was facing him and stared directly into his eyes only to find a tear-streaked face filled with sadness and fear.

And sky blue? They were puddles.

Sam extended his hand out to her and tentatively Laylah took it. He led her to the nearest tree so they could sit beneath its large branches which thankfully provided some shelter from the heaving sky, although at this stage it didn't matter. Both of them were drenched.

Laylah sat on Sam's lap, facing him. She cupped his face in her hands and fiercely stared into eyes that were clouded in confusion. Sam looked down, still trembling. Gently she tipped his chin so he would meet her eyes before she kissed him, slowly at first, trying to infuse every ounce of her love into that one kiss. Trying to explain what with words alone she could not.

Moments passed, an eternity and Sam did not move. Did not kiss her back. Laylah pulled away and a sob escaped.

Sam's thumb grazed her cheeks and he looked almost surprised when he caught her tears. His eyes met hers and it was almost as if a switch had flicked in his brain. Sam pulled her to him, his lips enveloping hers, his tongue fierce. Frantic. One of his hands tangled itself in her wet hair whilst the other grasped the back of her shirt and pulled her closer like he was drowning. He was drowning and she was the last bit of fresh air on this earth.

Laylah kissed him back just as fiercely, held him tightly and it was as if they were desperately trying to tell each other something, desperately trying to make each other understand in this dance of their bodies what their minds couldn't say. What they didn't know how to say.

Laylah pulled her head back after what could have been forever and gently wiped his cheeks. 'Tell me,' she whispered once their breathing had slowed a little.

Sam tucked a loose strand of hair from her face. 'I, I...after your mum's questions the other week and what happened with Amir yesterday I couldn't help thinking that maybe your parent's will never like me, maybe they will never accept me and our children. Maybe your community never will. They probably think we are going to hell...' Sam paused.

Laylah opened her mouth to object but Sam hurriedly continued. 'Maybe it would be better for me to convert...maybe then I would be good enough for you. Lord, at least then I would be making your life easier. Then you wouldn't have to fight so hard all the time,' he finished sadly.

'Sam, I love you.'

'But...' He began.

'Sam,' this time she interrupted him. 'I chose you, as you are, I fell for *you*. Not some version of you that just wants to keep the peace. Your faith...it's one of my favourite parts of you, it's one of the biggest reasons I fell in love with you at the start,' she paused. 'Well, that and your height.'

Faces still wet, they both chuckled. Sam sniffed.

'I am serious though. I chose *you*, I love *you* and anyone who doesn't accept that, anyone that doesn't like that, well they can come talk to me.'

'Laylah...' Sam hesitated. 'Ariana told me about the comments, the stares, you are okay aren't you? You don't think our life is a sin, that we are a sin?'

Laylah shook her head and gently unclasped one of her hands from his, stroking his slightly stubbly chin she looked into those eyes.

Sky blue.

'Not at all, how could this love be a sin?' She said and leaning in to brush her lips against his she whispered. 'I love you and love isn't a sin.'

'Are you sure?'

'I have never been so sure of anything in my life,' she replied.

Sam's face was incredulous. He gently cupped her face in his hands, kissed her forehead, both of her closed lids, her nose and finally their lips met once more. Soft as a feather at first, tentative, almost fearful. And then with all the intensity, all the love, all the fire of before. Except this time it was slow, they took their time. After all, they had all the time in the world.

Two Years Later: February

Chapter Fifty

Nehad: Tough Like an Almond Shell

My dear brothers and sisters;

Today marks a week until my daughter marries a non-Muslim. My daughter was always stubborn, her head hard, like an almond, but this...she was right about this. When she was a child, during darss, she would ask, Mama:

Why do boys get more inheritance than girls?

Why do I have to cover my arms?

Why can men marry four-woman?

Then my dear brothers and sisters when I had no answers for her except, hush, this is the way it is, this is how it's always been done. We don't need to know all of the answers. We shouldn't ask too many questions.

But when my adult daughter told me she loved a non-Muslim, this is how it's always been done, was not a good enough reason to say no.

My husband and I ran from Syria, from politicians but also from men with swords and guns who claimed to uphold gods will. We ran so our children could have choices, could have safety, could have a life. We rain so we could live in a world where we could wrong and my dear community we were.

That man was the best thing to happen to our daughter. And in the words of the great Rumi:

'You have to keep breaking your heart until it opens.'

My dear community, our hearts are so open.

Nehad stood and clicked send to the editor of the community newspaper. It was time for Laylah's final dress fitting.

Chapter Fifty-One

Ariana: I Always Will Be

                perhaps it makes sense
                how much i care for you,
                for i have always loved the
stars.

                my gaze travelling up
                as something so much bigger
                than i can ever be calls to me.
                it has always called to me.
are   you not enchanted too?

                when we first met i did not recognise you,
                did not see how you glow. but once i did,
                a connection was
born.

                for you see, that's what stars do
                they do not consume the sky,
                in obnoxiousness,
                but exude quiet strength,
                perhaps that is why we wish

upon   them?

              i know you have crumbled,
              i know you have hurt,
              yet you still have the capacity
              to guide those who
collapse   under the weight of life,
              in the darkest of nights.

'Give your head one last shake for me Hun.' Ariana said, a dozen bobby pins lodged in her mouth.

Laylah obliged, her ruby hair glistening.

Ariana nodded, finally satisfied. 'Okay, you can dance all night long if you want, that should hold.'

Ariana felt Laylah's hand take her own. 'Thank you so much,' she whispered.

Ariana shrugged. 'You are beautiful, it wasn't hard,' she said, squeezing Laylah's hand and leaning forward to kiss her cheek.

Ariana's phone vibrated from the table across the room and she quickly strode over to check the text. 'The car is outside, are you ready?'

Laylah nodded and took a deep shaky breath before taking Ariana's hand once more. Together they walked out of their flat, their home for almost six years, to the car that awaited. The driver was standing ready with the door open. Ariana let Laylah in first, carefully arranging her ivory dress before she slipped in after her.

The car started and they were on their way. Laylah had immediately taken Ariana's hand and as soon as she turned to her Ariana realised that the calm that had surrounded her best friend during these past few months, through all the stress of planning had dissipated. Laylah's olive skin had paled so much that despite her tan she looked ill. She muttered her vows under her breath rocking back and forth ever so slightly as her foot tapped the car floor insistently.

'Laylah, are you okay?' Ariana asked gently.

Laylah took a deep shaky breath and nodded. 'Just nervous,' she reassured Ariana, squeezing her hand even tighter.

The car finally arrived at the venue, the beautiful garden that Sam and Laylah had chosen. Once the car was parked Laylah turned to Ariana, panic now evident in her cinnamon eyes.

'Be brave Laylah, be brave.' Ariana whispered pulling her into an embrace and holding her for a moment that seemed to last forever. Laylah whimpered and squeezed Ariana.

'We have to go don't we?' Laylah said eventually.

Ariana chuckled. 'I think we do. He is waiting for you.'

'Okay but first I have something for you.' Laylah paused before she pulled out a folded piece of paper and handed it to Ariana. 'You have been there for me since day one, seen me at my best, seen me at my worst. I would not be here today if not for you. Last night I wrote this for you.'

With slightly shaky hands Ariana opened the piece of paper that had a poem inscribed, a poem about a star.

'Thank you for being my star.' Laylah whispered, her eyes glowing with moisture.

'Oh Laylah, you are going to ruin my makeup!' Ariana said, her eyes equally wet as she pulled in not her friend, but her sister into an embrace once more.

Eventually, they parted, they couldn't leave Sam waiting forever. Ariana got out of the car first before she carefully helped Laylah. Together they walked to where the ceremony was being held and ever so slowly the murmur of voices rose. They turned one last corner and found themselves facing two rows of chairs, filled with Laylah and Sam's family and friends. Silence swept over the crowd momentarily when they spotted Laylah before they all erupted into conversation, with, if possible, even more, vigour.

Ariana was struck by how beautiful this spot was, Laylah had told her that this was where she and Sam had their first conversation on that fateful night and since then it was where they went to talk, it was *their* place. But symbolism aside it was objectively beautiful, the chairs, wooden and simple shone in the morning sun, at the end of the aisle was an arch, built by both Laylah and Sam's fathers. Jasmines in full bloom climbed it, filling the air with a scent that was simultaneously subtle, yet heady. The entire thing was simple, simple, yet beautiful. Exactly Laylah's style.

Laylah and Ariana met Ayat and Dina on one side of the guests. All the bridesmaids had chosen the colour of their own colour dresses, Ariana was in a striking midnight blue, Ayat a startling mustard, Dina a deep purple. All of them had styled their hair so it fell in waves.

Glancing over, Ariana was relieved to see that Sam, Nikau and Alice were already waiting on the other, all of them in grey. Ariana gave Laylah one last tight hug before she walked to the front of the line.

The music started and a hush fell over the crowd, that was her cue. Ariana faced Nikau and walked towards him. They met at the centre where she took his arm before they walked down the aisle together. Ariana glanced at the Priest and the Imam who waited for them, this truly was the joining of two faiths. At the end of the aisle, Nikau and Ariana separated, each moving to their respective ends. Soon they were followed by Ayat and Alice, then Dina and Charlotte.

Finally, it was Laylah and Sam's turn, even from a distance, Ariana could see that Laylah's hand shook as she took Sam's arm. They stared at each other and for a moment it was like they were the only two people in the world. Sam bent down to whisper something in Laylah's ear and a smile broke over her face, all signs of nervousness melting away. Slowly, they walked down the aisle together.

Ariana admitted that Sam scrubbed up pretty well in his grey blazer and neatly side-swept hair but her eyes were drawn to Laylah at that moment. Ariana had lived with her for years, yet she stole her breath away. Just like the decorations, everything about Laylah was simple yet beautiful, she was flawless, her makeup, minimal. Winged black eyeliner, lips a deep red, eyelashes like wings and her fiery hair knotted into an elegant French twist with a few strands framing her olive skin. But truly? It was all about the dress. Ahh, the dress, one of the few things that in its white colour was traditional. It had long, lace sleeves, a high neckline and plunged to a tasteful v at the back. It hugged her waist perfectly before draping down to her feet. Best of all? It was made by Dee, Alice's partner of completely recycled fabric. Laylah finished the look with small, block heels, that still left Sam towering over her but when Ariana had pointed this out Laylah has simply shrugged, she needed to be able to dance she explained.

Finally, Laylah and Sam arrived at the altar, both of their hands trembling ever so slightly. The Priest and Imam stepped forward and asked Laylah and Sam to say the vows that they had prepared for each other. Sam began:

'Laylah, our journey together has not been the easiest, but I would not give it up for the world. From the moment I met you and you carried my suitcase up those flights of steps I knew you were special. That suitcase, it was almost as big as you and probably weighed about the same, but you were stubborn, stubborn and kind which is what you have been every day since. Laylah I love you and I promise to love you every day for the rest of my life. I promise to kiss you every day, even if that means developing terrible neck and back pain. I promise to support your dreams and to always believe

that you do more than even you think you are capable of. Because you can. But also? I promise to wipe away your tears when you are sick or sad, buy you blueberries and make you dinner just because. I promise to strive every day not to be the perfect husband, but the best husband, the best partner I can be. Laylah, you are my best friend and I am so lucky to have you in my life.'

Ariana fought to contain her tears although looking at the glistening faces of the audience she could see that not everyone was winning their battle and neither were Laylah or Sam. Sam's eyes were visibly wet and Laylah? Her tears streamed without restraint. Luckily her eyeliner was waterproof.

'Laylah?' The Imam asked.

'Well, that is a difficult act to follow.' Laylah said and laughter rippled through the crowd.

Laylah took a deep, shaky breath before she began but her nerves were not the slightest bit evident in her strong, clear voice.

'Sam, I cannot believe how lucky I am to have met you, how lucky I am to have such a kind soul in my life. Every day I wake up and I honestly cannot quite believe it. I promise to love you, to fight for you, to choose you, every day till my last breath and after because Sam? You have my soul. I promise to make you pancakes at least once a week, to read our children Harry Potter with you and to kiss you every day, even if I have to climb onto the sofa. I promise to always think of you when I look at the night sky and to stop and watch every sunset that I can in your arms. I know life won't be easy, it *won't be perfect, it never is, but I know that with you by my side things will always be okay.'*

No one's face was dry now. The Priest and the Imam then blessed the marriage before they kissed, him bending down and her on her tiptoes.

Laylah and Sam walked back down the aisle to the sound of everyone cheering, hand in hand, their faces filled with joy, a joy that was infectious to all those around them as not only did two people meet but two cultures, two faiths and two families. Two worlds.

. . .

The reception was one of the best nights of Ariana's life, she did not sit still and neither did Laylah or Sam. Food, dancing and laughter filled the air. Ariana didn't know what the highlight was, Charlotte and Dina's choreographed dance, the gigantic chocolate cake, Laylah and Sam's first dance or when Laylah and Sam released a single floating lantern into the sky. That was all close Ariana admitted to herself, but truly? The best part of the night would have to be the end when in a moment of calm Ariana finally managed to get some time alone with her best friend.

'Are you okay?' She asked.

Laylah glanced at Sam who had not given up and was dancing alternately with Dina and Charlotte. Joy flooded her face.

'Yes, I think I always will be,' she said and squeezed Ariana's hand.

Glossary

- *Marhaba:* Hello or Hi
- *Jilbab*: Loose, long dress
- *Hijab*: Headscarf
- *Salam*: Hello or Peace
- *Alhamdulillah*: Thank god
- *Zina*: Adultery/Sex outside of marriage
- *Mabrook*: Congratulations
- *Darss:* Class

Yasmeen Musa was born in Jordan and has lived in New Zealand since she was five. Yasmeen is an optometrist by day, she enjoys reading, being active and spending time with loved ones. Yasmeen lives in New Zealand with her partner Matt and her golden retriever Theodore, aka Teddy.

Lightning Source UK Ltd.
Milton Keynes UK
UKHW021902090222
398445UK00010B/2377